D0620126

The Big Laugh

THE
BIG LAUGH

A NOVEL by

John O'Hara

THE ECCO PRESS

THE ECCO PRESS
100 West Broad Street
Hopewell, New Jersey 08525

Published simultaneously in Canada by
Penguin Books Canada Ltd., Ontario
Printed in the United States of America

Reprinted by arrangement with Random House, Inc.

Library of Congress Cataloging-in-Publication Data
O'Hara, John, 1905–1970.
    The big laugh ; a novel / by John O'Hara.—1st
Ecco pbk. ed.
      p.   cm.
    ISBN 0-88001-575-6
    I. Title.
    PS3529.H29B54   1997
    813'.52—dc21   97-17230

Designed by Tere LoPrete

9 8 7 6 5 4 3 2 1

FIRST ECCO EDITION 1997

TO

David Lewelyn Wark Griffith
(1874-1948)

Rudolph Alphonso Guglielmi di Valentino
d'Antonguiela
(1895-1926)

Greta Louisa Gustafsson
(1905-   )

Roscoe Arbuckle
(1887-1933)

The Big Laugh

People know when you are trying to be something that you are not.

This law protects some good people who are in danger of turning bad; it also makes it impossible for a lot of bad people to become good.

By the time a man is forty his people—his family, friends, acquaintances, enemies, and even total strangers who have some reason to be aware of his existence—have decided what kind of man he is. Their judgment may be wrong, but it is their judgment and it is usually final, because people in a group lack the patience to reconsider the evidence they have on one man. (The man himself, when he is being part of a group, makes the same kind of absolute, final judgments of other men as individuals.)

It is therefore unreasonable for any man to expect or to hope for a second mass human judgment that will improve his standing. By the same token, although a man may fall from grace, he will continue to enjoy the good will of those who had earlier convinced themselves that he was a good man. People who have made up their minds about a man do not like to have their opinions changed, to reverse their judgments on account of some new evidence or new arguments, and the man who tries to compel them to change their minds is at least wasting his time, and he may be asking for trouble.

This is a story about a man who tried to be something he was not; who wasted his time, and asked for and got a lot of trouble. As it happens, he was a rascal to begin with, and in a rare surge of perspicacity the people recognized him as such from the start. During his middle period he did nearly everything he could to behave himself, but he only confused the people and while confusing the people he also confused himself, with results that were predictable because they had been predicted. This is a story, by the way, that will comfort those who believe that no man is all bad; in the man's middle period he behaved very well indeed. However, it is not a story that offers much to those who believe in the permanence of regeneration. Reasonable people among those who believe that no man is all bad will be content with this man's middle period, and may feel that the score comes out even, so many points on the side of good, the same number of points on the other side. The people who want regeneration to be permanent are fanatics for the happy

4

ending, dissatisfied with themselves and with everyone else, unrealistic men and women, anti-Christs, who were entertained by the miracles but learned nothing from Calvary. They are always the angriest, too, when regeneration does not take.

Hubert Ward is the name of the man who is the principal character in this story, the public name. His full name, which not many people knew, was Richard Hubert Ward, but when he decided to go on the stage he dropped the Richard in favor of the slightly more exotic, romantic-sounding Hubert. Hubie Ward went on the stage because there was almost nothing else for him to do. He had no money, his education had not gone beyond three and a half years at three preparatory schools, he had no salable talents, and his relatives were already so fed up with him that the only one, a maternal uncle, who could be persuaded to offer any help, consented to use his influence to get Richard Hubert Ward a job with a construction firm in South America. It sounded like an interesting proposition to Richard, who was then twenty years old; the pay was good, and South America, full of señoritas and adventure, seemed a glamorous part of the world. But by the luckiest chance Richard fell into conversation with an engineer who had recently returned from the construction project, and Richard learned that the company was finding it impossible to hire men. Malaria and *siflis* were common, and there was constant danger from panthers, anacondas, and truculent Indians armed with poison-tipped darts and blowguns. No North American had renewed his two-year contract, the engineer said, a bit of information that particularly interested Richard, whose uncle had been insisting that he sign on for four years. Richard never spoke to that uncle again.

Down to his last few dollars, without a high school diploma or the equivalent, with no special training or aptitudes, Richard in the late Nineteen-Twenties for the first time in his life was seriously worried about himself. His first thought was that he might get a job in a boys' summer camp; he was a good swimmer and a fair diver; he had never won any prizes at tennis but he was sure he could beat most twelve-year-olds; he could pick up wood-craft out of a book. But the word book reminded him of his scholastic record, and he well knew that neither of his three schools would recommend him as counsellor at a camp for young boys. He then turned to his assets. He had twenty-six dollars in cash, three suits and a dinner jacket, two pairs of shoes and a pair of evening pumps; a wrist watch and a gold pocket watch and chain; a gold cigarette case that he had taken from a woman he met in a speakeasy. The gold watch and cigarette case could be pawned, but after they were gone the cash situation would be critical. He had pawned his raccoon coat and his overcoat for the summer, and now that he was a city dweller he would never redeem the coonskin. He of course owned no securities or other valuables, and for reasons to be touched upon later in the narrative he had to rule out all prospects of inheriting money or property.

He next considered what he had to offer in the way of intangible assets. He was a handsome young man of slightly more than medium height, with even teeth and a clear complexion, and even if he had been willing to do so he could not deny that girls and women of all ages— although not all girls and not all women—regarded him as attractive. Many members of the opposite sex (each thinking she was being original) had commented on his blue eyes: "They're very deceptive," the women would say. "So innocent at first, like a choir boy's. But now you look more like a choir boy gone wrong." They often spoke of his roguish eyes, sly eyes, devilish eyes, eyes like Wallace Reid's. He knew his appearance to be an asset, and so were his manners, his taste in clothes, his conversational line. He danced rather well, played the piano just well enough to read sheet music, played bridge well enough to sit in with his contemporaries, and he had a very good memory for names and faces. When he went to a restaurant the headwaiter usually treated him with that special amused respect that is reserved for young men who look as though they might some day be rich. But Richard Hubert Ward was not given to the kind of self-deception that would cause him to overestimate the cash convertibility of his intangible assets. For the first time in his life he was completely on his own, and he was momentarily terrified. He did not blame himself for his present condition, but his predicament was so serious that he postponed the pleasure of blaming others. This, he realized, was a time to put his brain to work—and if he had had one thing drummed into him throughout prep school and the earlier years it was the fact that he had a good brain.

At the moment he was living in an apartment in East

Tenth Street, but he would have to get out in two weeks, when the regular occupant returned. Phil Sturtevant, a writer for *Time*, had lent him the apartment while Sturtevant, a very junior writer, was on a late spring vacation. He had known Sturtevant at Andover, the first of Richard Hubert Ward's three prep schools, and Sturtevant may have been surprised to be reminded that they had been such close friends, close enough so that Sturtevant found himself lending his apartment to a younger schoolmate whom he had almost forgotten but who remembered him with such enthusiasm. Their reunion took place at Dan Moriarty's speakeasy; Richard Hubert Ward went home with Sturtevant that same night, stayed on a few days, and offered to pay half a month's rent for three weeks' occupancy. Sturtevant did not mind taking Ward's post-dated cheque.

Richard Hubert Ward had not remembered to include the cheque among his liabilities, and he was not too confident that Sturtevant would accept his explanation. He therefore had to be out of the apartment before Sturtevant's return, and it seemed advisable to be out of New York City. It was Ward's first bad cheque—indeed, his first cheque of any kind—and he had drawn on a non-existent account in the New Jersey bank where his mother kept her small account. In her present frame of mind his mother not only would not cover the cheque; she might well tell the bank to go ahead and prosecute. Richard Hubert Ward conceded that he had done an impulsive, stupid thing, but having done it for such a piddling sum as $37.50, he repeated it at a speakeasy for a hundred in

8

order to finance a party in Sturtevant's apartment. The idea of the party was an initial part of his new campaign to use his brains: he would have some people in, give them drinks, and one or two of them would surely lend him money or show him a way to make some. Richard Hubert Ward had always believed in his luck, and with luck and brains he might come across something that would enable him to give Sturtevant cash in return for the cheque.

He decided to invite five young women and five men; the men from the financial district, the girls from Greenwich Village. He ordered the liquor from Sturtevant's bootlegger and the canapes from Sturtevant's delicatessen man, fully intending to pay on delivery, but the bootlegger and the delivery boy assumed that Sturtevant was to be charged, and Ward did not correct them. At six-fifteen of a warm June day the guests began to arrive, and at half-past six the party was in progress.

The young men were all a few years older than Richard Hubert Ward and none of them knew him very well, but in inviting the men he had said over the telephone, "Having some girls in. Actresses and models. So I can't ask you to bring your wife." The implication was plain enough, the inference was correctly drawn. The girls came because they were asked; a party required no other explanation. Some of the girls knew each other and so did some of the men, but none of the girls had met any of the men until the evening of the party. Before nine o'clock, however, one of the girls and one of the young men had retired to the bedroom, and another couple seemed to be well on their way. The men had taken off their coats and vests, the girls had taken off their shoes and one had removed her girdle. "Thizz a hell of a good party," said one young man to the host, but the host did not think so. His plans were not working out. The young man who had retired to the bedroom suddenly appeared, embarrassment or disgust on his face, and left the apartment without saying goodnight to anyone. His father was a vice-president of the Bankers Trust, and Richard Hubert Ward had particularly counted on doing some business with the young man. The girl appeared a few minutes later and calmly helped herself to a rye and ginger ale. "Who was that Eagle Scout?" she asked her host. "He wanted to know if I'd ever had a Wassermann, the son of a bitch. *I* didn't ask *him*. Dick, I think you have some very unattractive friends. I mean I really do."

"Yes, but rich, Audrey," said Richard Hubert Ward.

At a few minutes past ten o'clock, as though a gong had struck, the party collapsed. The second eager couple were still in the bedroom, but all the others simultaneously decided to leave, and did so together without inviting the host to join them. Apparently they assumed that Audrey and Richard wanted to be together, an assumption that was only half right. In any event, Audrey and Richard were now alone in the livingroom.

"Oh, I'll be so glad to get out of New York," said Audrey.

"You going somewhere?"

"I sure am. Didn't you read in the papers? I got my

name in the papers. I have a job in a summer stock company on the Cape. The East Sandwich Players."

"Does it pay well?"

"Does it *pay* well? Pays nothing. But we get room and board and a chance to act in some very good plays. The best kind of experience for somebody just starting out. I'll have different parts in four, maybe five plays this summer. Some of the company have been on Broadway. But the great advantage in addition to the experience, the managers go from one company to another, looking for new actresses."

"Where do you live?"

"On the Cape? In a boarding-house in Buzzards Bay or Woods Hole, they aren't sure. Come up and see me. You've never seen me in a play. I'm good."

"I didn't know you'd ever been in a play."

"Last season, I had a walk-on in *Just for the Three of Us*. Terrible play, but at least I can say I was on Broadway. Twelve performances, not counting two weeks out of town. Oh, I'm an actress, and I'm good. *You* could act, Dick."

"What makes you say that?"

"Oh—I don't know. You wouldn't like it if I told you."

"Go on, tell me."

"Well, I don't see you as anything else. I thought you were like one of these Wall Street fellows, till tonight. But when I saw you with them I knew you were different. And you never reminded me of a writer, or an artist. You must be something, so maybe you're an actor."

"Nuts."

"All right, I'll tell you. I think you're such a big phony that you ought to be an actor."

"Oh, you do, do you?"

"You have the same kind of phoniness about you that actors have."

"When did you come to that conclusion?"

"I always thought so, but especially tonight. Playing up to those stockbrokers, and you didn't know what you were talking about. They saw through you, too, but they were getting your free liquor."

"And you were in there humping like a donkey with a guy you never saw before."

"Well, I'll never see him again, you can be sure of that."

"I don't care whether you see him or not."

"Bad enough asking me if I ever had a Wassermann, but do you know what he did? Take a look at this." She reached in her purse and held up some banknotes. "Eighty-one dollars. He gave me all the money in his pocket. Eighty-one dollars. He didn't even count it. I'm no whore. But I'm going to keep it just the same."

"Profitable evening."

"I'm glad you think so. I went with him because I liked him, the son of a bitch, and all he thought was I was a whore. Well, if that's what he thinks I'll keep his money. God, if my parents ever thought I took money for going to bed with a man, they'd positively die." She laughed.

"What's so funny?"

"Maybe I ought to give you half, it's your apartment. But try and get it."

"Call him up next week, I'll bet you could get some more."

"You know, I'll bet I could, too. Oh, he'll want to see me again. You should have heard him when I got undressed. 'Apples of ivory.' He must have a very frigid wife he's married to, that boy."

"Well, wouldn't that be better than going to the Cape and working for nothing?"

"Certainly would not."

"If you liked him once you could like him again, and his father's one of the richest men in Wall Street."

"You suggesting that I become his mistress?"

"No, but why don't you? It isn't as if you were in love with somebody else. Unless you're in love with me."

"You? Anybody that would fall in love with you would have to have bats in their belfry."

"Says you. I had plenty of girls in love with me, and not only girls. The last school I went to, I was kicked out on account of the school dentist's wife, and she was thirty-five or -six years old. They're getting a divorce on account of me—partly. I've had plenty of women in love with me."

"Then all I can say is God help them."

"You were pretty close to it."

"No. I had fun with you, but that's a different story than being in love with you. I nearly always have fun with you, Dick, except when you take yourself too seriously. Will you come up and see me this summer?"

13

"Maybe I will, I'm not sure."

"Come up and hang around for a while, maybe they'd give you a job painting scenery, selling tickets. You could have fun, and you're not doing anything better. I can't figure you out, whether your parents have money or what. But I'll bet you'd have a good time if you came up. There are two other girls besides myself in the company, and one of them you'd like. The other one's too serious, but this one you'd like. Julie. Her father teaches at Yale."

"I don't know. There're plenty of girls around New York, especially in the summer."

The conversation was interrupted by the appearance of the couple from the bedroom, their arms around each other's waist, and both somewhat groggy.

"He's plastered to the hat," said the girl.

"Lashed to the mast and plastered to the hat," said the man. "You waiting to use the bridal suite? I can guarantee it's comfortable."

"Audrey knows. She tested it," said the girl.

"And now you've tested it, so you know too," said Audrey.

"Everybody go home?" said the man. "The hell time is it?"

"Looks like fi' minutes of four," said the girl.

"*Five* minutes of *four?*" said the man. "God, I won't get three hours' sleep."

"You had some sleep," said the girl. "Anyway, I don't think that *is* five minutes of four. It's more like twenty after eleven."

"Well, that's better. Then we can make a night of it."

14

"Starting with you take me out and get me some dinner," said the girl.

"Too hot to eat," said the man. "But I'll take you out and buy you a bucketful of stingers. How would you like that?"

"I'll have a stinger but I want something to eat, too. Are you coming with us, Dick? Audrey?"

"No thanks. But before you go, tell your boy friend to button his fly," said Audrey.

"My fly open? So it is. I wonder how that happened? Come on, Jezebel."

They left, and as they closed the door Audrey stuck out her tongue.

"Is that at him or at her?" said Richard.

"Him. I hate those bond salesmen. They make everything dirty," she said. "Well, Dick, you coming up to the Cape?"

"I'll let you know. Write down on a piece of paper where I can reach you."

"The East Sandwich Players, that's all you have to remember. And no kidding, you could have some fun. I can't guarantee you a job, but if you just hang around a while they'll give you something to do."

The bad cheques were a good enough reason for getting out of New York, but Richard Hubert Ward was influenced less by fear of the law than by a new, irresistible appeal to his vanity. He had never thought of it before, but Audrey had made him suspect that the stage was where he belonged. All his years in suburban New Jersey and prep schools and in his brief career in the

15

night life of New York he had felt some pull toward an
occupation that no one in his family or among his friends
had been identified with. No one had ever suggested the
stage; he had never gone out for dramatics at school. But
someone who had been on the real stage—Audrey—had
put it to him so simply that he immediately recognized
the thing he wanted to do. It was so much the thing he
wanted to do that he was convinced there was nothing
else for him to do. He was without any awe of it, of getting up before a lot of people, of memorizing lines; without fear of awkwardness in moving about or not moving
about. He had never read a modern play, he had never
seen a play-without-music by his own choice. The great
names of the theater meant nothing to him except as cele-
brities in the night life and in the tabloids. And yet he
already had the feeling that he had found where he belonged.

And he was right.

He remained in Sturtevant's apartment until the day
before Sturtevant was to return, and then, without notify-
ing Audrey, he took the train to Buzzards Bay, found a
room, and bummed rides to East Sandwich and had a
look at the barn that called itself a theater. He was wearing white ducks and scuffed saddle-straps and no one
noticed him particularly. He entered the barn theater
by the front door and seated himself in a rear row of camp
chairs. It was rather dark where he was sitting, and on the
small stage a group of men and women were obviously
rehearsing a play. A man in a crumpled linen suit and yellow foulard bow tie was addressing one of the women.

". . . And the whole point of it, Mary, the whole point is this is no accidental shooting. You really want to kill the son of a bitch. He's thrown you over for your kid sister, so you have two reasons for hating the bastard. He's given you the air, and now he's going to run away with your sister, that you happen to be very fond of. Shall we try it again, or is there something eating you?"

"No, the only thing is, I'll have a real gun in my hand, won't I?"

"We're getting you one from the hardware store," said the director.

"Well, when Paul sees the gun, shouldn't he be afraid?"

"No. He thinks you're bluffing. He's been sleeping with you for three years, remember, and you've threatened him before. First act, second scene."

"But not with a gun," insisted the actress Mary.

"He still thinks you're bluffing," said the director.

"I don't think I ought to let him see the gun," said Mary.

"Well, the author thinks you should, and I agree with the author, so let's do it the way it was written."

"Only a suggestion," said Mary.

"Yeah, I know. All right, places please, everybody in this scene. Paul, take it from your line, 'I never thought of her that way.' "

" 'I never thought of her that way, that's your suspicious mind,' " said Paul.

"Audrey! Where the hell are you? You're supposed to be onstage with the tray so you can overhear that line.

You testify later that you heard him accuse her of having a suspicious mind. You have to be there right on cue."

"I'm sorry," said Audrey. "I was waiting for Mary's line."

"No, no, no, no, no. Paul's line. Your cue was Mary's previous line."

"Oh, of course," said Audrey.

They tried the scene once again, and Richard Hubert Ward found that he was mouthing all their lines, knew precisely where each actor should be, and—happy discovery—was completely and perfectly at home. In spite of knowing nothing about the preceding events in the play, knowing only what he could learn from this one brief scene, he understood the play, which was not difficult, and, moreover, he was sure he could improve upon it and on the director's presentation of it.

As Richard Hubert Ward was making these discoveries the director chanced to turn to speak to a young man who was seated behind him, and in so doing noticed the stranger. "You back there, who are you?"

"Me? Just a visitor," said Richard Hubert Ward.

"Well get the hell out," said the director.

"I'm not bothering anybody," said Richard.

"You're bothering me."

"No wonder," said Richard.

"What do you mean, no wonder?" said the director. "Who are you, anyway?"

"Try and find out," said Richard. He got up and left the theater, angry and disappointed that he had so quickly botched his entrance into the only career that

18

had ever interested him. He made a guess that the director was a third-rater, professionally on a level with the masters at the worst of the prep schools he had attended; tacky, voluble, overauthoritative, mean, and afraid of their own mediocrity. Richard hid in the apple orchard until he saw the actors coming out of the barn, and when he was satisfied that the director was not with them he caught up with Audrey and some others.

"Dick! Was that you Ruskin was giving hell to? When did you get here? Where you staying?" She cut off her questions to introduce him to a very tall, very thin young man, a pretty girl, and a middle-aged woman, none of whom he had seen before. They acknowledged the introductions and promptly left.

"Not exactly the friendliest people I ever met," he said.

"Ruskin has everybody scared. They're all afraid they'll be sent home before they get in the first play," said Audrey.

"But you're not scared."

"Well—no."

"Oh, that's how it is? Who the hell is this Ruskin? He must be King Shit around here."

"Shows how much you know. He's a very successful Broadway director. Directed some of the most famous hits on Broadway."

"Then what's he doing in a dump like this?"

"This isn't a dump. A lot of famous playwrights try out their new plays here because Martin Ruskin really knows the theater. And he's the owner here."

"You seem to've changed your mind about the place. You didn't make it sound so important the last time I saw you."

"I didn't change my mind one bit," she said. "Where you staying, or are you staying?"

"I got a room. Where are you staying? With Ruskin?"

"No, but what if I was?"

"Listen, you got me to come up here."

"What if I did? You didn't have to pick a fight with the manager and director the first time you show up . . . I have to leave you."

"You don't want Ruskin to see me talking to you."

"I certainly don't."

"You're as afraid of him as the others."

"I'm not afraid of him. I like him. And he likes me."

"Well, then that's that."

"You could have saved yourself the trip if you'd have bothered to write me a note. Coming here without any advance notice."

"Was that girl you just introduced me to, was that the one you said I'd like?"

"No. You wouldn't like any of the girls here."

"Hell's bells, I like any girl as long as she's pretty and can be laid. But you want me to get out of here, is that the idea?"

"Yes, before you spoil everything for me."

"I'm not going to spoil anything for you, but you got me up here and now I think I'll stick around a while."

"Please go away. I'll meet you late tonight if you'll

20

promise to go away tomorrow. I'll pay your fare back to New York."

"My fare?"

"No use trying to fool me, Dick. I found out some more about you. That boy that gave me the eighty-one dollars? I saw him again and he told me all about you."

"He doesn't know all about me."

"He knows enough. Have you got an uncle that's some kind of a builder?"

"What if I have?"

Audrey nodded. "Your own uncle told Jack not to have anything to do with you. Your own uncle."

"Well, if Jack Dunbar's going around spreading stories about me I'm glad I know one about him. I better go back to New York tomorrow, to protect my reputation. I can't have Jack Dunbar going around—"

"I shouldn't have told you that."

"Listen, *thanks* for telling me."

"No, now wait a minute, Dick. You don't want to ruin things for everybody."

"Don't I? When the vice-president of the Bankers Trust Company's son is spreading stories about me? He was supposed to be a friend of mine. If he wasn't, why did he come to my party? I have plenty of witnesses that he was there. And what did he give you eighty bucks for?"

"There's Ruskin. See me tonight. I'm staying at Mrs. Amos Pierce's, West Falmouth. Okay?"

"What time?"

"One o'clock. I'll meet you on the front porch at one."

She ran from him, and he watched her get in a green Packard roadster with Ruskin. As they passed the spot where he was standing she let her hand fall outside the door of the car and waved it.

She was in Mrs. Pierce's porch swing when he arrived a few minutes before one. "I don't know what I came here for," he said.

"Yes you do," she said. She put her arms around his neck and kissed him.

"Oh, cut it out, Audrey. I didn't come here for that, and you're faking anyway. Wasn't Ruskin enough for you?"

"Then what *did* you come here for?"

"I told you I don't know, but not to have you faking hot pants. I want to finish that conversation this afternoon. Why shouldn't I go back to New York? That sanctimonious son of a bitch, I'm going to make him pay for what he said about me."

"You mean money?"

"Well, why not money? He drank my liquor and that cost *me* money. Yes, money."

"You mean you'd commit blackmail? You'll end up in jail, the first thing you know."

"Don't be so sure. And what if I did? My uncle'd like that if it got in the papers. I'd like to fix him too. I always did hate that son of a bitch."

"You're only twenty years of age, Dick. That'd be a

terrible thing to live down. That'd be a black mark for the rest of your life."

"What do you care if I have a black mark the rest of my life? Protecting Jack Dunbar."

"I didn't say I was in love with you, ever, but I like you enough so I wouldn't want to see you disgrace yourself for life. Honestly I do. It isn't only protecting Jack Dunbar. I like you better than I like Jack. Honestly. He shouldn't have told me those things about you."

"What did he tell you?"

"Oh—things your uncle told him. I didn't believe half of them, or else how did you get into other schools? Your uncle said he got you in three schools and you were kicked out of all of them."

"I was shipped home from two. The first one they asked me to withdraw. Did he say what I was kicked out for?"

"Morals."

"Is that all he said?"

"That's all Jack told me. Morals. I knew what one was because you told me. The doctor's wife."

"Dentist's wife. The doctor's wife was a fat old cluck, I wouldn't have touched her with a ten-foot pole."

"Dick?"

"What?"

"Put your arms around me. I don't want to fight with you. We don't have to do anything. Just put your arms around me."

She took one of his arms and drew it around her waist. "That's better," she said. "Dick?"

"What?"

"Are you a fairy?"

"The hell I am. You know better than that. Why did you ask me that?"

"Isn't that what they kicked you out of one of the schools for?"

"God damn it, he did tell you more, didn't he?"

"He said it was immorality with another boy."

"He ought to get the story straight if he's going to tell it around. It was one boy that was a fairy and they caught him with me and two other boys, but he was the fairy, not us. They were just waiting to catch him, but we were all sent home. They could have sent the whole school home, practically. Cuban boy. We hated him. We used to send for Ricco instead of a girl. We all made jokes about him all the time, but there were only three of us sent home. Us and Ricco. It's a wonder they didn't get wise to him before that. Maybe they didn't want to because his family were so rich."

"What else did you do?"

"At school?"

"No, I mean besides school."

"Did my uncle tell Dunbar about other stuff?"

"Oh, he gave your life history."

"Was there an automobile accident mixed up in it?"

"Yes."

"Then I guess he told him about that. When I was fourteen I swiped my uncle's car. He had a Wills Ste. Claire, and I took it one day while he was playing golf. I killed somebody."

24

"You killed somebody? How?"

"I drove over to South Orange to a girl's house to take her for a ride, but she wasn't in. So I was on my way back, and I could have made it in plenty of time so my uncle wouldn't have known I'd taken the car. But an old woman crossing the street in East Orange . . . There was a trolley car stopped and she walked in front of it and right in front of my uncle's car. I smacked her, she went up in the air and down on the street. I kept on going, but somebody took the license number and I was arrested that night. It was the old woman's fault, but I didn't have a license and I didn't stop. They sued my uncle and he had to pay them around five thousand dollars, even if it was the old woman's fault. Five thousand dollars. He won that much when Dempsey beat Willard, but you'd think it was his last penny. And the kids at home—I was practically ostracized. Never allowed to have a car, and I wasn't allowed to apply for a license till last year. What else do you want to know? There's plenty more, once I get wound up."

"Yes. What do you live on? Where do you get money?"

"What money?"

"Well, you have to have *some* money. To pay your rent. To eat with. To come up here cost you *some* money."

"The man with the three balls."

"What?"

"I hocked some things, but now I haven't much left to hock. I was hoping I could get a job as an actor."

"I told you they don't pay us anything. Why don't you try to get a job as a waiter or a bellboy, at one of the hotels? That would tide you over for the summer."

"I wouldn't know how to be a waiter, and I wouldn't like it. I might as well try to be an actor. I know I'd like that."

"Yes, but what are you going to live on?"

"They feed you at your theater, don't they?"

"Room and board, but Ruskin isn't going to give you a job, and he has the say."

"I don't know. I had experience with men like Ruskin. Teachers. I could always get around them."

"Not Ruskin. He's a very smart Jew, too smart for you, Dick."

"If he's really smart, he'll give me a job."

"Why should he?" she said. "He doesn't even like you."

"I know, but I have something, and if he's smart he'll see it. That is, if he's smart. And if he's not smart, I can outsmart him. I'll bet you he gives me a job."

"You're the most conceited bastard I ever heard."

"I hope Ruskin thinks so. I'm counting on it. I had a lot of experience with men like Ruskin."

"You don't know the first thing about him."

"You're wrong there. He doesn't know anything about me, but I know a lot about him. I watched him for two hours yesterday afternoon, and he reminded me of two teachers I used to have. This time tomorrow I'll have a job with Ruskin."

"Not a chance. Not a prayer."

After a while he left her, and in the morning, toward

26

noon, he went to the theater and sat in Ruskin's car. When Ruskin appeared and saw him in the car Richard Hubert Ward spoke first. "Do you remember me?"

"You're the fresh punk from yesterday. What the hell do you think you're doing in my car? Get out, make yourself scarce."

"How about taking me to lunch and we can talk it over."

"Talk what over?"

"Listen, Ruskin, I didn't come all the way from New York for nothing."

"You did as far as I'm concerned. Get outa my car."

"Make me get out—and make a horse's ass of yourself trying. In front of everybody. A lot of people are watching us, Ruskin. You don't want to look like a horse's ass in front of them."

Ruskin recognized simple truths. He got in the car, barely controlling his rage, and put the car in motion. "I'd like to know what you think you're doing? Who are you, anyway?"

"I don't want to talk to you till you calm down. Do you want me to drive?"

"No. *Yes.* I'll move over and you take the wheel."

"Oh, come on, Ruskin. You want me to get out and you'll drive away? Come *on,* Ruskin."

"Well, I won't get out. You'd steal my car. I think you're a crazy man."

"You're not the first one that said that. But I'm harmless."

"What the hell do you want? Speak your piece and stop bothering me."

"Let's ride around a while till you calm down."

"I'm stopping right now," said Ruskin. He switched off the engine and put the key in his pocket.

"Suit yourself. Want a cigarette?"

"I have my own cigarettes. Just tell me what this is all about?"

"It's a frame-up," said Richard Hubert Ward.

"A frame-up? What are you talking about?"

"If a cop came along now, I'm twenty years old, and you're a lot older than that. If I wanted to tell the cop a nasty story, you could get in a lot of trouble. You shouldn't have stopped the car on a country road. You should have done what I asked you—take me to lunch. But there goes a car with two people in it. What do they think a man your age is parked with a young guy like me for? Here comes another car. I advise you to get going, Ruskin. We'll go somewhere and have lunch."

"You wouldn't get anywhere with that. That's one thing I haven't got a reputation for. Quite the opposite, in fact. So you've outsmarted yourself."

"Have I? A lot of people saw me waiting in your car, and then saw me driving away with you at the wheel. What is your reputation for? Girls? They'd say you were covering up. And maybe you are, Ruskin. That's what I think."

"God, I never met a son of a bitch like you. I swear to Christ you're the worst son of a bitch I ever met in my whole life. You're what crawls out from under stones. What do you want? Money?"

"How much would you give me?"

"Not a God damn cent. I'd go to prison before I paid you any money."

"No you wouldn't."

"There you're wrong. I would. Before I gave you money I'd go to prison. Try me. But I got an idea you don't want money. You want something else besides money. What is it?"

"I want a job in your theater."

"Well, you not only don't get it, but I'll fix it so you never get a job in any theater, anywhere."

"Is that final?"

"You bet it's final."

"Without knowing what I'm going to do next?"

"I don't care what you do. Just get out of my car. And never show your face around here again."

"All right. I'll get out of your car." Richard Hubert Ward peacefully turned the door-handle and stepped down to the roadside. "Go ahead, Ruskin. I'm not going to do anything to you. You can go. Don't be afraid."

"Afraid? Afraid of what?"

"Oh, well, that's another story." Ward smiled. "Go on, Ruskin. What are you waiting for? I haven't got a gun on me. I'm harmless."

Ruskin put the car in gear and moved the car forward a few yards, then stopped.

"Keep going," said Ward, over the noise of the engine.

Ruskin again put the car in gear and now he continued shifting into third speed, which took him out of sight of Ward. Ward sat on a fence and lit a cigarette.

In less than five minutes Ruskin returned. "Get in," he said.

Ward casually tossed his cigarette in the ditch and lazily got in the car. "You changed your mind," he said.

"What's your name?" said Ruskin.

"You giving me a job?"

"I'm giving you nothing."

"Then I'm not giving you my name."

"Why do you want a job in my theater? You're not an actor."

"No information till you say you'll give me a job."

"You took a big chance. The police around here know me. I've been coming here every summer."

"You're taking a big chance right now, Ruskin."

"How am I? I don't happen to think so."

"You thought it all over, and you decided you were safe."

"Correct."

"But you had to think it over first, didn't you? Why did you come back?"

"Frankly, to get another look at the worst son of a bitch I ever met. To see if you were for real."

"I'm for real. And now I'm sore. I wasn't sore before. But now I am, and you look out."

"You're a real specimen, all right."

"So are you, Ruskin, or you wouldn't be here. Just a little bit afraid. And why are you afraid? Because I guessed you right, didn't I?"

"No."

"Yes I did, and you know I did. And *I* know it now. I was only guessing before, but not any more. Do I get the job?"

"What job? What could you do? You're not an actor."

"I'll *be* an actor."

"There's nothing for you."

"There's plenty for me. I don't mind working at the other stuff. But I won't take the job unless you guarantee I get on the stage sometime."

"You won't *take* the job? I haven't *offered* you a job."

"Cut the shit. We're past that."

"Do you know there's no pay to it?"

"To me there is. Room and board, and I want ten bucks a week spending money."

"And what do I get out of it?"

"Nothing."

"I don't get it. If I were what you think I am, I'd want something out of it. But if I'm not what you think I am, why should I give you a job?"

"Because I'm me, Ruskin, and you know I've got something. I know what you are. You're double-gaited. I detected that watching you yesterday. Showing Mary how to act. But me, I'm an actor. I'm going to be a big actor, and you're the first one to know it except me."

"I don't think you'll ever be an actor, if you live to be a hundred. But a stage personality—I'll give you that much. Are you hungry?"

"Yes, I am."

"Well, we'll turn around again and I'll buy you some lunch. What's your name?"

"My name? Hubert Ward."

"The hell it is. Hubert?"

"Well, it's Richard Hubert, but I decided Hubert was better than Richard."

"All right, Hubert. Room and board."

"And ten bucks a week."

"No. No money. I'll give you a job because maybe you do have something, but the money would be blackmail and I won't pay it."

"All right."

"The worst son of a bitch I ever met in my whole life. But what the hell? In this business. What about your people? Where do you come from and all that?"

"I have no people."

"They kick you out?"

"Yes."

"But they were what they call nice people? Conservative suburbanites? And you're the black sheep of the family. What did you do?"

"Don't ask too damn many questions. I don't want to be reminded of them."

"How did you know about me? Oh, sure—Audrey. Yeah, you're true to type, all right. But the personalities make the money while a lot of good actors are starving. Hubert Ward. The goniff. The schlemiel. The schmuck. Who's your favorite actor, Hubert?"

"I don't know. Al Jolson, I guess."

"Yep. You wouldn't even say George Arliss." Ruskin

shook his head, and looked at the specimen at his right.

If Martin Ruskin had been a little more evil than he was or a better man than he was, his interest in this new Hubert Ward might have become more intense, either on the side of corruption or of regeneration. But Ruskin was a reasonably competent hack director, a failure as a writer but an experienced and knowledgeable hand at getting the most out of the second-rate plays that came his way. He made a good living out of the theater, with at least one new play a season and not infrequently he had had two plays running concurrently. He had on several occasions got himself credited as co-author of plays he directed, and this maneuver was of considerable financial benefit to him over the years through stock company and amateur productions far removed from Broadway. He had got into the theater as a press agent—more accurately as a boy-of-all-work for an established press agent. He was then nineteen years old and living with his family in The Bronx. His father was dead, and he and his mother were being supported by an older brother, George, who was on the road for a yard-goods firm and doing well. George wanted Martin to go to college and study law—which was what George had wanted to do—but Martin's best marks in high school had been in English and his only prizes had been for declaiming Spartacus and the other classic oratorical exercises. George thought Martin would make a good trial lawyer; Martin thought Martin would make a good actor, in parts that did not demand a personable leading man. He was not a comely youth, and he knew it. Through family connections he got the office boy job in the press agent's office, and almost immediately he abandoned the idea of becoming an actor and during his spare time he read and wrote plays, and more or less in line of duty he spent as much time as possible watching rehearsals. His presence was tolerated, and he was quick to learn, and at twenty-one he produced his first play.

It was a just barely legal theft of *Clarence,* written by a young man recently out of the Baker English 47 Workshop at Harvard. The young man was the same age as Martin, but because he had seen Martin behind a desk in a Broadway manager's office he assumed that Martin was someone of some importance. Martin had grown a moustache to make himself look older, and Ralph Harding was exactly what he had been looking for: someone with a play and some money. Martin knew that the play, *Dickie Takes a Walk,* had been rejected and was waiting for the convenience of the playreader to send it back to the author. Martin saved her the trouble. On Ralph Harding's next visit to the office Martin jumped up and greeted the anxious playwright. "Mr. Harding, I been hoping you'd come in today. I want to have a talk with you," he said. He took Harding's arm and steered him out of the office to a Childs restaurant. They ordered pancakes and coffee, and Martin made his first speech as a producer.

Without ever stating his own position in the office of the producing firm he told Harding he believed in the play, that it was not the kind of play that should be put on by a big firm. It needed personal attention. He believed it could be put on for ten or at the most fifteen thousand dollars, and he thought enough of the play to make it his initial venture as a producer. If Harding could raise ten thousand, he would raise the rest. He meant every word he said, he said, and all he asked of Harding was that he keep the transaction a secret until he resigned his job with the producing firm. A good comedy was a real moneymaker—look at *Lightnin'*. And he had hopes that this would be the beginning of a real, lasting partnership.

The play was put on, ran just under three weeks, and Martin Ruskin came out about two thousand dollars ahead. The notices were not entirely bad, and Martin, in addition to the quiet profit in cash, had acquired a new friend. He and Ralph Harding had been through a blood bath together. Ralph at Martin's urging decided to retire to Dark Harbor, Maine, to get to work on his new play, a serious drama something like *Troilus and Cressida* but not really Troilus and Cressida. It would be up-to-date— "modren," Martin then pronounced it—and it would give Ralph the opportunity to express himself about women. Ralph did not like women, and Martin had not had any success with them either. Ralph had had what might be called some success with men, and Martin was surprised but not shocked to discover that Ralph had become very fond of him in that way. On the closing night of *Dickie Takes a Walk* Ralph abandoned all restraint and made love to his new friend. Later he begged Martin to forgive him, promised it would never happen again, and went off to Dark Harbor to write his drama. Martin did not mind. He was only confused by what he considered a kind of compliment. In any event he was now really in the theater; he had had his name in the programs as producer,

he had made a nice piece of change, and he had been se-
duced by a playwright who was also a society boy. The
next move was to get a woman, and that turned out to be
as easy as opening his office door in the morning.

The play brokers now began to send him the works of
the new and the passé and the firmly second- and third-
rate authors. He was well aware that the brokers offered
him only junk that had been rejected elsewhere, but so
long as he did not stand to lose his own money he was
willing to produce plays that would, if nothing else, get
his name more firmly established. He in turn began to
make it a condition of producing plays that he could function as co-author on plays he thought had some possibilities. Here he struck a snag; the brokers demanded a
commission, which he refused to pay. For a time the brokers sent him no plays, but he won out against them because it was better for them to take ten percent of their
clients' royalties than no percent of nothing from their
clients' unproduced plays. In a very short time he was
well hated on Broadway, and thus he advanced to a second phase of his theatrical career: he was known as Martin Ruskin, that son of a bitch, although he was only
twenty-five years old. (In interviews he added five years
to his age, and he affected older men's dress and was care-
less about shaving his beard. There were those who believed he was lying when he said he was only thirty.)

He lived at a Broadway hotel, two blocks away from
his office. The women who went to his room came away
with stories that contributed to his legend, some true,
some at least half true. At twenty he had never had

a woman; at twenty-five he had a surfeit of them, of those wanting jobs, and then of those who were in part wanting jobs but were also investigating the legend. He wanted no woman for very long, but out of perversity a few women convinced themselves that they were in love with him. The extreme exhibitionists among them outranked him on Broadway; there were two great beauties and one excellent actress who would not for a moment consider appearing in one of his plays, but who made public fools of themselves over him. They had paid no attention to him while the legend was being created, and they recovered quickly when he failed to achieve any form of first-rate prominence. Martin had become a small name at twenty-one, a promising newcomer at twenty-three, and at twenty-five he was forever, irrevocably marked as deficient in superior talent and great good luck.

He began to suspect his standing when he announced a play to open on a night in October and the Theatre Guild subsequently announced a play to open on the same night. He knew immediately that he would not get reviews from the first-string critics, and he thereupon changed his date. It was not so much that he was being honest with himself as that he was having honesty forced upon him by the gesture of the Theatre Guild. The Guild people obviously had seen his earlier announcement and in effect had assigned his play to the second-string critics. They were professionals at the Guild, and theirs was a professional judgment. "Due to scenic difficulties, the opening of the new Martin Ruskin . . ." was his face-saving statement to the press. It deceived almost no one, and he became an

37

ideal man to operate a summer theater. There he could bully authors, direct when he wanted to, make a little money, live cheaply, sleep with whomever he chose, and make like a king. In his way he loved the theater, but above all he loved his summer theater.

The Martin Ruskin East Sandwich Playhouse, personal supervision of Martin Ruskin, was in its third consecutive summer when Hubert Ward joined the East Sandwich Players. The enterprise was therefore a going concern, not subject to the difficulties and exigencies of a summer theater that was just starting out. It had its patrons and patronesses, its mailing list, its comfortable arrangements with the tradespeople and the summer hotels in the neighborhood, and mutually beneficial understandings with various organizations that would buy tickets in quantity. Martin Ruskin lived in a saltbox that he rented furnished, and ate most of his meals at the Paul Revere Inn, where he had a due-bill. He got his gas and oil free, along with similar perquisites that were exchanged for curtain advertising. The first summer had been the hard one, but he had convinced the natives that his Playhouse was an attraction and that his Players were well behaved or at least kept their misbehavior in the company. The Yankees took to Martin, up to a point, and in his second and third summers his principal problem was in finding maid-bits and small walk-ons for stagestruck daughters and nieces. Martin was not summer-people; like the Yankees he was out to make a dollar off the summer people, and this fact enhanced his relations with the natives. They were out to make a small dollar off him, but they found him pretty sharp, pronounced shap.

Because the Playhouse was on its way to becoming an institution, Martin Ruskin could permit himself the luxury of devoting most of his time to the plays and players, with the non-creative details taken care of by Sylvia Stone, who was his New York secretary in the winter. Sylvia was even shapper than Ruskin, a stout, jolly woman who could laugh a merchant into lending her some stage props that he knew would never be returned. It was up to Sylvia to find a bed for Hubert Ward to sleep in.

"I don't understand you taking on this Ward Hubert," she said to Martin Ruskin. "What's he got to offer?"

"I don't understand it either."

"You got reasons for everything, Marty. This is Sylvia you're talking to."

"Maybe he's a kind of another version of me. I don't mean with the looks."

"No, I don't see any resemblance in any manner, shape or form. Physically, I'm speaking."

"There isn't any. But he put me in mind of Richard Barthelmess. He has no resemblance to him, either, but they're both clean-cut, you know what I mean?"

"The all-American boy."

"The all-American goy, did you say? Anyway, Syl, I'm putting him on."

"As what?"

"The bottom of the ladder. One of the Martin Ruskin apprentices."

"I'll give him the toilets to clean."

"Suit yourself. But I don't want him to quit."

"Then I won't give him the toilets."

"No, I don't think you better. You don't like him?"

"Such a stuck-up! He irritates me beyond words. He sat on my desk and informed me he wanted a room by himself, not with anybody, and I told him that was impossible. Impossible. And then he said did he have to eat with the others and I told him if he wanted to eat he did. The next thing was he tried to put the touch on me for twenty dollars, so that was so ridiculous I humored him. I said when would I get it back, and he gave me some bushwah about a letter from his guardian. He said he had a guardian."

"You didn't let him have any money."

"That you can be positive I didn't. Lending money to actors is the quick way to the poorhouse, I know from experience. Then he asked me did I have a car, and with my car sitting outside the office I couldn't say I didn't. Why? He said he wanted to make sure who had cars in the company, in case he wanted the loan of one. He said your car was too conspicuous. For what, I said. Was he planning to hold up the bank? No, he said, not hold up any bank. Oh, in five minutes' time he tried everything, and ended up walking away with my pack of cigarettes I had lying on my desk. We had one like him the first summer."

"No, we never had one like him. This one is going places, Syl. Don't you honestly think so?"

She paused to reflect. "It goes against the grain, but I guess I have to admit it. Personal magnetism is one word for it. It's too bad it has to be wasted on people like that."

40

"If you were an agent would you sign him?"

"Think I would," she said.

"Then be an agent. He wouldn't know the difference. You can get a copy of one of those contracts. Sign him."

"Marty, I wouldn't want him around me that much. He's the kind of a man that I'd be a mess before I was through humiliating myself. Women like me have to steer clear of that type man or suffer the consequences. One man like that could take all the fun out of life, and for what? A cheap thrill, only not so cheap. What would I be if I wasn't good-natured, Marty?"

"You're afraid of this fellow?"

"I don't have the looks to get another man in a hurry. Yes, I'd be afraid of him if I gave in. I wish he never came here. That's my personal reaction, you understand. As far as the Playhouse is concerned, you think you made a discovery so that's okay by me, Marty. You're thinking of tying him up some way?"

"If my hunch is correct. I don't say he'll ever be an actor. That I doubt. But I'll see if he can learn the basic elements, and maybe I'll find a play that he can play himself. That's as good as money in the bank."

"As long as that's what you can tell yourself, Marty."

"That—and some day I'll be able to say I discovered him."

"He'll deny it. Just don't you get injured."

"Me?"

"Marty, there's some topics it isn't my place to discuss, but give me credit for having two eyes. I know you five years, Marty."

"Yeah. Well, find him a bed, and don't lend him any money."

"It won't be my bed, and it won't be my money, that you can be certain."

"By the way, his name is Hubert Ward. You had it ass backwards."

"So?"

Never again would Hubert Ward work so hard for so little return, never again would five or six years' difference in ages carry any weight, and not again for many years would any man—or woman—be obeyed by him as Martin Ruskin was obeyed that summer. This was brought about by a combination of circumstances: Ruskin, busy with rehearsals of the plays on his schedule, had no time to waste on Hubert Ward and in his preoccupation he accidentally gave the appearance of aloofness; Sylvia Stone, in self-protection, learned to despise the newcomer and gave him the heaviest and least interesting chores; and Hubert Ward, once he had been made a member of the company, began to discover that there was more to acting than memorizing lines and speaking them aloud. And there were two other circumstances that made him want to remain at the Playhouse: he was broke, and through Audrey he learned that Phil Sturtevant had put the rent cheque in the hands of a lawyer. Hubert guessed that no one would look for him at a summer theater, and the Playhouse seemed a safe place until after Labor Day.

Hubert Ward was given two small acting parts: in one he played a collegiate type, complete with ukulele; in the other he played a chauffeur, in ill-fitting livery and oversize puttees. As the chauffeur he had only to say: "The limousine is waiting, Madam," but as the college boy he had several wisecracking lines. He made the most of them. He very nearly made too much of them, and antagonized the aging matinee idol who was the visiting star of the play. "Martin, those are throw-away lines," said the star. "But our friend here isn't reading them that way."

"Don't worry about it, Phil. When we have an audience they won't be listening to anybody else but you," said Ruskin.

But the opening-night audience laughed at the lines and spoiled the star's entrance. The lines were therefore toned down in succeeding performances. Nevertheless Hubert Ward continued to be noticed by the audience. The star had once offended Hildegarde Finney, a woman in her early forties who was a permanent member of the Players, and she taught Hubert his first lesson in scene-stealing. "When Phil comes on, you're sitting on the porch step, right? Well, when he crosses, you start tying your shoe. But don't let him catch you at it."

Martin Ruskin caught on immediately, and after that night's performance he summoned Hubert to his office. "Who gave you that business of tying your shoe in the first act? You didn't think that up yourself."

"My shoelace was untied and I was afraid I'd trip making my exit."

"Twenty-four-carat horseshit. I know who tipped you off—Finney. Well, tomorrow night, no business with the shoelace, see? I don't pay a star big money to have funny tricks played on him. The people come to see Philip W.

Carstairs, that's what they pay their good money for. You
got that clear?"

"All right. But if he's that big a star why was he so
worried about my four lines?"

"You'll find out. You'll be worse than he is if you ever
get anywhere. And I'll tell you something for your own
good. Philip W. Carstairs could have made a real horse's
ass out of you if he'd wanted to. You just weren't worth
the trouble."

"How could he? I want to know these things."

"All right. Last night, when your funny lines were still
in the play. He could have come on and before he makes
his opening speech he could have stopped dead in front
of you and stared at you and then slowly, slowly walked
away from you, still staring at you. The people would have
laughed at you the way he intended them to, and you'd
have had to make your exit with your tail between your
legs and no exit line. He could have destroyed you. Don't
fuck around with old-timers like Philip W. Carstairs, if
you know what's good for you. He could do more with his
left eyebrow than you'll ever be able to do with both
hands and both feet and lines written by George Bernard
Shaw. The rest of the time he's here you do yourself
a favor. Just study the way he walks, onstage. Every step
is thought out. Every step. Watch the way that man puts
his left hand in his coat pocket when somebody else starts
a speech. Then just as the speech is ending he starts taking his hand out of the pocket. You think that's accidental?
Listen, fellow, I don't only pay him to come here and draw
the crowd. I study him like going to school, every re-

44

hearsal, every performance. And you think you can crab a scene for him. Huh! Are you screwing Hildegarde? Or is she just getting even with Phil?"

"Her? I'm not that hard up."

"You're missing something, but I guess you never laid a real woman."

"That's all you know. I was kicked out of school for laying a woman thirty-five. She got divorced on account of me, partly."

"Save it for some other time. While you're here, I got something else I want to talk to you. Lay off the town girls. I got a big investment here, a lot of good will with the natives. Now don't give me any of your lies, I don't have the time to listen. Just lay off, or out you go. George Shackleton happens to be one of the Selectmen, and one word from him and we don't come back here next summer. If you want to get laid, Audrey or Hildegarde, but Shackleton's daughter is out of bounds for you."

"She's waiting outside."

"Why do you think I'm warning you?"

"What'll I tell her?"

"Tell her anything. Tell her you have a clap. Or I'll tell her."

"I never had a clap."

"Then you don't want me to tell everybody you have. You wouldn't even get Hildegarde if I passed that around. I don't care how you get out of it, but you get out of it."

"I didn't go after her, she came after me."

"Aren't you used to that by this time? I'll get you out of this tonight."

"How?"

"I'll tell the kid her old man's getting wise."

"All right. She's afraid of her old man."

"So am I. Did you ever see him? Built like Zybysko. If he ever got a hold of you he could break your spine. You stay away from these Yankee girls, and the Portuguese, too. *Their* fathers carry fishing knives, or you'll end up married to one of them."

"I don't want any trouble with them."

Ruskin went out and came back a few minutes later. "As soon as I mentioned her old man she ran."

"Thank you," said Hubert Ward.

Ruskin was astonished. "You getting polite?"

"Oh, not only for getting rid of her."

"What else?"

"I don't know how to say it. You know, working here, acting. This is the first time in my life I ever had a good time. I guess I ought to apologize for the way I acted that day in the car."

"Well, for Christ's sake."

"I'm not a bad fellow, Mr. Ruskin. I didn't mean to be, or want to be. I just always got into scrapes all my life, and people looked down on me. My father committed suicide when I was a kid."

"Over what?"

"I'm not sure. Something about money."

"Are you kidding me?"

"No, it's true. He shot himself."

"I don't mean about your old man. But this politeness and all, all of a sudden."

"See? People always get suspicious of me. There's something about me. Every time I went to a new school some older boy or some teacher'd start giving me hell before I ever did anything. Before I had a chance to. A fellow pushed me in the lake with all my clothes on the second day I was at one school. He said he just didn't like my looks."

"You could of drowned."

"No, I'm a good swimmer. It wasn't that. It was having somebody hate me that never saw me before."

"Yeah, I can understand that. I had that experience more than once, myself. On account of my religion."

"Well, I don't know about that, but the last couple of days I suddenly realized I began to feel like a new human being. I never knew any actors before. They're funny people, all right, but I like them just the same. I don't know why."

"You feel at home with them?"

"I guess that's it. Not exactly, but sort of. Yes, I guess so. I'm getting to be more at home with them. They all gossip about each other and they're always complaining about something, but I guess that's it. I never felt at home with people before, and I do with them. They're kinder than most people. Two or three of them were sore as hell because Mr. Carstairs took away my lines, and nothing like that ever happened to me before, people sticking up for me. It was always just the opposite."

"You're a funny kid, all right," said Ruskin.

"Kid? I'm almost twenty-one."

"When is your twenty-first birthday?"

47

"The end of August. The thirtieth. Why?"

"You'll be twenty-one then, huh?"

"Yep. All the fellows I grew up with, when they were twenty-one their families gave them a car, or a trip to Europe. I won't even get a postcard from my sister. They don't know where I am, and I don't want them to know. Some day the bastards will wish—oh, well, what the hell."

Ruskin reached in his pocket. "Here, take this. I know you're on your ass. Consider it a birthday present, your twenty-first birthday."

"Ten bucks? Thanks, but I wasn't giving you a hard-luck story, Mr. Ruskin. Are you sure you want me to have this?"

"Sure I'm sure."

"Well, thank you very much. I'll take it if you really mean it."

"It'll keep you from stealing butts from Sylvia Stone. Now I got a lot of work to do. Rehearsals at ten-thirty."

"Goodnight, Mr. Ruskin. And thanks." Hubert Ward, a happy young man, went out.

"The poor son of a bitch," muttered Martin Ruskin. "*I* should be so poor."

It was the first and last happy summer in the life of Hubert Ward. The Playhouse and the work there were like a boarding school where the tasks were tasks, but of the kind he liked to do; and the recreation was of a more mature character than at any boarding school but there was a simple enjoyment of it because he convinced himself that he had earned it. At the Playhouse, instead of the algebra and plane geometry that he was pretty good at,

48

he took tickets, lined up the camp chairs, drove the old Ford station wagon—and rehearsed his small roles. For recreation there were Audrey and Hildegarde and the unsuccessful pursuit of Julie. And always there was a feeling of safety, of security; he had enough to eat, a place to sleep, and he tried not to think too much of the summer's end and the serious problems that awaited his return to New York. He did not quite expect that the police would be at Grand Central when he got off the train, but he was worried about Sturtevant's lawyer and that bad cheque, and only somewhat less worried about the bad cheque to the speakeasy owner. Sturtevant's lawyer signified the police; speakeasy owners sometimes had people beaten up. Late in August Hubert Ward in a moment of desperation thought of writing a cheque for $200 and cashing it on the Cape. Then he thought of writing four $50 cheques, which would be much easier to cash. Then he thought of simply stealing the box-office receipts on the Labor Day weekend. And then he discarded all these plans because none of them made any sense. His future was in show business, as he had begun to call it, and his immediate future depended entirely on Martin Ruskin.

Hubert put his brains to work on the problem of Martin Ruskin—and he was a problem. He was sure that Ruskin was attracted to him, and that if he gave him the opportunity, Ruskin would confirm his suspicions of him.

During the few times when they were alone together Hubert saw a different Ruskin from the public one. Ruskin was not a Ricco, the Cuban boy at St. Bartholomew's. Ricco was indiscriminate, promiscuous; Ruskin

49

was *attracted* to him, more the way girls were attracted to him. But the problem of Ruskin was that he could not be compelled to give him money. He had always believed that Ruskin had spoken the truth when he said he would rather go to prison than pay him money. And in his two months with show people Hubert had learned that the blackmail value of an accusation of homosexuality was considerably less in show business than in a boarding school, where there were frightened teachers and students. Philip W. Carstairs, for example, was known to have a boy friend in New York and had been whisked off to Provincetown by two men and two women at the end of his Playhouse engagement. Even Audrey, the least knowledgeable of the Players, referred to Carstairs as an old queen, and she was neither shocked nor repelled. A great artist, she also called him. Hubert Ward therefore concluded that if he was to get any money out of Martin Ruskin it would have to be voluntarily on Ruskin's part. And Martin Ruskin appeared to be the only man in the world at the moment who would be good for two hundred dollars, the absolute minimum with which to return to New York.

Hubert's twenty-first birthday passed with no notice taken by anyone. He had not mentioned the occasion to anyone else in the company, and they were all busy with their own plans. It was the last week for the Playhouse, and the actors and actresses were full of talk about casting the new plays on Broadway. Hildegarde and Julie already had jobs for later in the fall season, and the others had somehow found out which new plays would have parts they could apply for. "What are *you* going to do?" said Audrey.

"I wish I knew," said Hubert Ward.

"Are you going to look for a job?"

"I wouldn't know how. How *do* you?"

"The best way is to find out what parts are in the new plays. Then you show up every day at the managers' offices."

"And then what?"

She shrugged her shoulders. "Then what, yes? I personally go to St. Malachy's and light a candle. Not that I'm a Catholic, but it's supposed to be good luck."

"Where do you find out about the new plays?"

"Well, the Algonquin, when I can afford it. That's where you got a chance of being introduced to an author. Or if you just want to hear the latest news, the English Tea Room is where I go. And at night, Tony's. Or Tony's in the afternoon, too. That's a speakeasy on Forty-ninth Street. I know a girl friend of mine that went there one afternoon. It's better to sit in the kitchen. And this man was fried and he picked her up, and who should he turn out to be but Harold Kingston Schobel, the playwright? She's living with him. Of course that doesn't happen all the time."

"What does a man do? Actors? What do they do?"

"I don't know. The best way is to be a chorus boy."

"That lets me out."

"Yeah. Well, I guess it's the English Tea Room for you, Dick. I mean Hubert. Ruskin doesn't want you?"

"For what?"

"For *what? The Jumping Jack!* Didn't he say anything to you about it? You should have asked him."

"The play I was in? The son of a bitch. I could play that part. I was all right, wasn't I? Wasn't I, Audrey?"

"I thought so. You looked the part, and you never went up. Not that it was Hamlet. But some people with only one line can blow it. You should have asked him. Maybe he thinks you don't want the part."

He left her hurriedly and went to Ruskin's office, having no idea what he was going to say, but actuated by desperation. Ruskin and Sylvia Stone were doing some paperwork together.

"Mr. Ruskin? May I see you a minute please?"

"You're seeing me. Wuddia want?"

"Can I talk to you?"

"He means without me," said Sylvia.

"Can it wait?" said Ruskin.

"That's all right, Marty," said Sylvia. "I can come back." She picked up the larger of two piles of bills and went out.

"You're all het up about something. Sit down, Hubert. Take a cigarette and marshal your thoughts."

"No thanks. I don't feel like a cigarette. Mr. Ruskin, I did good work this summer, didn't I?"

"Yes, I guess so."

"I mean I worked hard. I did everything she told me—Sylvia. And I was often here till two o'clock in the morning hanging scenery. The next morning out with the station wagon, putting those cards in store windows. And I saved you a lot of money on that station wagon. I cleaned the valves with a screwdriver one Monday when everybody else was taking a day off. And painted and varnished it. Not to mention I waxed the Playhouse floor, and a lot of other things I did that you probably never heard about."

"Sylvia gave you credit. You mean you want to come back next summer?"

"Jesus Christ! Mr. Ruskin. Do you know how much money I have? Beginning Monday I have no place to sleep and no money to last me out the week."

"Well, you knew that's the way it was going to be. I didn't give you any different impression. You were just the same as everybody else. Only three members of my company get paid, everybody knows that."

"But I worked hard, Mr. Ruskin. And now I've got nothing to show for it. I can hitchhike back to New York, but I have nothing when I get there."

"Leading up to a touch, Hubert, you're wasting your time."

"Listen, I could have ruined it for you with the Shackleton kid. She kept trying to get me to go out with her. I could go out with her tonight if I wanted to. I did everything you asked me to do, and Sylvia. And you're not even putting me in *The Jumping Jack*."

"Oh, that's what you want. No, I have somebody else in mind for that. Somebody that can understudy the brother. You couldn't go on and play the brother."

"Christ Almighty, I *am* the brother. Those are the kind of people I grew up with, and they don't talk that horse-shit way you have them talking. Have you ever been in a country club in your life? If you have, you didn't listen to young people talking."

"You want to rewrite the dialog, too?"

"Somebody ought to. The part I played was just wisecracks, but the brother's serious. Yes, I could play the brother, much better than anybody *you* ever knew. If you ask me, you never knew anybody that came from that kind of a family. Except me."

"The man that wrote the play is a graduate of Princeton."

"Well, I didn't graduate from prep school but I could do better than that."

"All right, do it. Write a play, and if it's better than *Jumping Jack* I'll buy it."

"You're a mean son of a bitch. You know I can't write. But if I could I'd write something true to life instead of that slop." He stopped. "Aw, what the hell. You're all phonies. Every one of you. And you, you're the worst because you don't even recognize a phony play. If it was about the Civil War, you could tell it was phony. But it's about now, 1928, and you don't know how phony it is. I said too much, but I feel better." He reached in his pocket and took out some keys, which he tossed on the desk. "The station wagon. So long."

Sylvia Stone slowly re-entered the office after Hubert Ward left. She resumed her place at the desk and put the stack of bills in front of her. She adjusted her glasses and picked up the top bill from the stack. "Lester D. Meadows, Hyannis. To repairing roof, thirty-eight seventy-five,"

she said. "That was where a couple limbs were blown off during that storm."

"Quit putting on the act," said Martin Ruskin. "You heard the kid shooting off."

"That's not my department, Marty."

"He's right about *Jumping Jack*."

"So? When you go take in a show you pay two-twenty to hear people talk true to life? That I can get for a nickel on the Jerome Avenue Line. That I can get from my various relatives and their in-laws. Who knows from country club conversation? Me, forking over two-twenty? I make the trip downtown to take in a play, I prefer leaving all that behind me for one evening."

"I don't know, Syl. He put it into words what I've been thinking. I couldn't put my finger on it, but this play never got across to me. Reading it, yes. Seeing it performed, hearing the lines, no. My own dialog, too. If the son of a bitch could write I'd give him a couple hundred." He slapped the top of the desk. "I'm gonna put him in the play."

"Marty, don't do it."

"Mind your own business, Sylvia Steinbrink. I follow my hunches."

"Such hunches you should be reserving for the opposite sex."

"Listen, fuck you and your nasty innuendoes. All summer you been hinting, hinting, hinting. Hinting what was none of your business even if it was true, which it isn't."

"If the shoe fits," said Sylvia.

Martin Ruskin got up and went to the door and

55

called to Hubert Ward, who was halfway down the lane to the main road. "Hubert! Hubert Ward!"

Hubert turned around and came back, looking down at the ground so that Ruskin would not see his tears.

"Step in my office, I want to talk to you," said Ruskin.

Sylvia was already out of the office and Ruskin told Hubert Ward to take a seat. "If *Jumping Jack* is such a terrible play why do you want to work in it? Tell me that."

"I didn't say it was a terrible play. I only said you had the people talking all wrong, especially the brother."

"Give me an example, for instance."

Hubert Ward thought a moment. "I don't remember the exact words, but where he's talking to his sister. They're talking about their mother."

"You're speaking of the first act where they're talking about their mother, or the second act?"

"I was thinking about the first act."

"Phyllis sitting on the piano stool. Ronnie is swinging the golf stick."

"Yes, and even that's wrong, Mr. Ruskin. They're supposed to have just come home from the club. He wouldn't bring his golf clubs home with him, Mr. Ruskin. He'd leave them in his locker or in the pro shop."

"Business. Not important. What I'm interested, why do you think his speech is phony?"

"I'm trying to remember exactly what he says."

"Here's a script. Show me," said Ruskin.

Hubert leafed through the playscript. "Here it is. 'Ronnie: Unfortunately Mother is dining out this evening with Mr. and Mrs. Van Lear. Therefore we must postpone our discussion with her until tomorrow morning. However, you may rest assured that I shall devote no small part of this evening to a preparation of my remarks to her.' "

"What's wrong with it? They're supposed to be educated people. Rich, upper-class society."

"I never heard *anybody* talk like that."

"You consider yourself an authority on upper-class society people?"

"The kind of people these are supposed to be, yes. Maybe not an authority, but even my uncle wouldn't talk that way, let alone Ronnie, a young fellow around my age."

"What *would* he say, according to you?"

"Well—I'm not a writer, but I know this is all wrong."

"Make a stab at it."

Hubert Ward studied the lines. "Well, something like this: 'Mother's going to the Van Lears' tonight, but I'll give her an earful tomorrow.' Something like that."

"*He's* going to give his *mother* an *earful?*"

Hubert Ward put down the playscript. "Oh, I don't know. Anyway, why should I rack my brains over your script?"

"What if I let you play Ronnie?"

"Ronnie? Not the college boy? I'd give my left nut to play that part," said Hubert Ward.

"You don't have to give anything. I'm giving you. I decided to take a chance on you. Seventy-five dollars a week, that's all it's worth."

"You mean it, on your word of honor?"

"As a gentleman." Ruskin pronounced the word as though there were no *t* in it. "This is your first big break, Hubert, and I'm taking a big chance on you. You know of course, I can let you go if you don't make good in rehearsals. You know that."

"Listen, Mr. Ruskin, if I'm not any good I'll tell you so myself."

"What I was thinking, though," said Ruskin. "It's a small part, but important, and in places where the lines don't sound right to you, you could screw things up. So I tell you what I'm gonna do. You wait and drive back to the city with me Tuesday and I'll get you a room in a hotel and you make suggestions how I can make the lines easier to say. I don't want the audience missing plot points because you're going up in your lines."

"I haven't got any money. Three dollars and some change."

"I know a place on Forty-third Street. Get a room there for six dollars a week. A lot of actors live there. And two dollars a day ought to carry you for meals and miscellaneous. That's fourteen—that's twenty a week I'll advance you and I can take it out of your pay after we open."

"I really don't know how to thank you. This is the greatest thing that ever happened to me, Mr. Ruskin. And five minutes ago I was seriously thinking about committing suicide. Really I was."

"Well, Hubert, don't do anything like that till after the play closes, huh?" Ruskin grinned.

The play opened in late October and with the help of the cut-rate ticket agencies ran until just after New

Year's Day. It reminded one critic of Noel Coward's *The Vortex* and another of Sidney Howard's *The Silver Cord*. Percy Hammond said it was unpretentious, and George Jean Nathan said it was delicatessen, but all the reviewers welcomed back Hildegarde Finney as the mother and Alexander Woollcott thought a newcomer called Hubert Ward had possibilities if he would overcome a rather slavish admiration of Glenn Hunter. "Who is Glenn Hunter?" Hubert Ward asked Hildegarde.

"You'll get there," said Hildegarde Finney. "Anybody that knows as little as you do, and has your luck."

When the play had been running two weeks Hubert was having a drink in Tony's with Audrey and some young people from other shows. It was a Saturday night, the place was crowded. In the kitchen people were standing, and others were wandering through the front rooms, hoping to be invited to join a table. Hubert Ward became aware that one wanderer had stopped at his table, and he almost knew before he looked up at the man's face that it would be Phil Sturtevant.

"Hello, Dick," said Sturtevant.

"Hello, Phil. I didn't know you ever came here."

"Once in a while. Congratulations."

"Thanks."

"Something I want to talk to you about."

"I know. But you don't want to talk about it now, do you?"

"As good a time as any. Oh, hello, Audrey."

"Hello, Phil."

59

"Isn't anybody going to ask me to sit down?" said Sturtevant.

"You can sit down if you can find a chair," said Audrey.

"I don't see any chairs," said Hubert Ward. "Phil, how about if you come around to the theater Monday night, and I'll have that for you."

"That'll be a good idea, Dick. You won't forget."

"I didn't forget. I just didn't have it."

"No, you certainly didn't. Well, I'll be around Monday night. What's a good time?"

"Eleven o'clock. You going to bring your lawyer?"

"What do you know about my lawyer?" said Sturtevant.

"I know all about your lawyer. Getting a lawyer for a lousy thirty-seven fifty, or whatever I owed you." Hubert addressed his companions. "Big-hearted Otis, here. Sicked his lawyer on me for a lousy thirty-seven fifty." Hubert's friends stared at Sturtevant coldly, the thin bespectacled Shylock in the Brooks Brothers suit, the enemy of the arts, the intruder on a Saturday night at Tony's. It was the hostility of the girls that finally drove him away. "He writes for *Time*," said Hubert.

"Oh, that thing," said one of the girls.

"His father owns a flour mill out West," said Hubert.

"He looks it," said the girl. "All that *Time* crowd. They push their way in everywhere and nobody ever knows who they are. They all have an inferiority complex, because they don't sign their articles and nobody knows who they are. That one's a perfect example."

"As it must to all men, death came fortnight ago," said one of the young men.

"To newsstand-buyer Glubglub," said the girl.

"A sharp rebuke to *Time*'s Medicine editor," said the young man. "God!"

"What can he do to you, Hubert?" said Audrey.

"I guess he could have me arrested. I don't know. I'll ask Ruskin's lawyer."

Sturtevant did nothing. He did not even appear on the Monday night. But he continued to visit Tony's and to stare across the room at Hubert Ward. The two young men did not speak to each other. With the confidence of his first success Hubert Ward began to think of himself as a member of a profession. He was hardly even the most minor of minor actors, and yet he was conscious of some pedestrians' second looks at him when they saw him on the streets of the East Side, and in the theatrical district men and women whom he guessed to be actors and actresses showed definite signs of recognizing him. He wore a Harris tweed jacket and grey flannel slacks and carried a Malacca stick, and he took longer steps in walking in the foot traffic. He had been mentioned with the other actors by nearly all the critics, and singled out for personal mention by two, but this limited publicity in the press was not an accurate measure of the extent of his acquaintance with the public. He had made his debut in a season when interest in the Broadway legitimate theater was nearly at its all-time high, and anyone who had a job in a Broadway show was certain at least to be recognized by everyone who had any connection with or fondness for the theater. One play, even so unremarkable a play as *The Jumping Jack*, had made the difference for Hubert Ward between being and not being show people. It had likewise made the difference to show people themselves. Hubert Ward was *working*. Whatever he had done or not done before, no matter how he had got his job, he was working, and to all those actors and actresses who were not working, he was legitimate, a professional. He would walk past the lay-offs in front of the Palace Theater, men who had played in hundreds of vaudeville houses and—some of them—who were paid a thousand dollars a week, and they knew who he was, the young juvenile in that thing of Marty Ruskin's. Among his out-of-work contemporaries there was inevitably some envy, but they also felt a curious pride in his small success because he was their age and their representative on the current playbill.

Martin Ruskin was at the theater every night, and he always stayed to watch the curtain calls from out front. It was a small cast—nine actors in all—and the curtain calls had been rehearsed so that the players of the smaller parts walked rapidly from the wings and took their places in a row which ultimately included the entire company. There would be a company bow, then the smaller-part actors would move aside to give the center of the stage to the featured players. The biggest hand was always for Hildegarde Finney, but she had been a star in several previous plays. Unmistakably, night after night, the next biggest hand was for Hubert Ward.

"You see? You see?" Ruskin said to Sylvia Stone.

"Listen, I won't give you an argument. You were right. I can't explain it."

"Don't you wish you'd of signed him up when I told you?"

"Nope."

"Well, I'll never get him again for any seventy-five dollars. He has two offers already."

"He tell you that?"

"No, he didn't tell me that. He didn't tell me anything, and I don't have him under contract."

"Plenty of other actors, Marty."

"Seventy-fi'-dollar actors, yes. And wait till this kid gets the right play. Jesus!"

"Which he will have to rewrite the dialog?"

"Don't remind me. He's a bad boy, Syl, but he's got the thing they call class, and you can't get that out of a jar of Outdoor Number 7. You can't smear it on, and you can't rub it off."

"And that's why you got this crush on him, because he has class. Yeah? You better get married and start raising a family."

"That's your solution to my problem, eh, Syl? That'll take care of it, eh, Syl? For how long? And in the meanwhile, what do I do tonight?"

"You get drunk and go to bed with one of your whores."

"That's right. Well, it's better than getting married to some poor unsuspecting dame. The whore I can give a couple dollars and send her home. A wife stays. What did we do tonight?"

63

"A little under nine hundred."

"Not good enough. I guess the notice goes up next week. Goodnight, Syl. See you tomorrow."

"Goodnight, Marty. Don't hang around, huh?"

"Oh, I avoid him."

"You'll get over it when the show closes, you won't have to stand here every night."

"If it was that easy."

On the closing night of *The Jumping Jack* Martin Ruskin gave a party for the company and about a hundred invited guests from the Broadway world. He rented a suite in one of the Fifth Avenue hotels because he wanted the party to have class, and since many of the guests were going on to the Mayfair Dance at the Ritz, most of those present were in evening dress. Marty's personal guest for the evening was Tessie Gibson, an agreeable beauty from the George White show who found it almost impossible to pronounce *r*, and who compounded the defect by her habit of saying, "Right," to nearly every remark addressed to her. "Wite," she would say, nodding slowly. Her high, full breasts were so firm that they barely moved when she walked, and Marty asked her if they were made of cement.

"Wite. Cement," she said, smiling, and looking down at them. "Cement." She was wearing a vivid red dress cut low. "Most people like 'em that way, Motty."

"Oh, I like them, Tess. I'm not complaining. I just wondered, if I gave them a little push would they give?"

"Twy it and see, why don't you?"

He pressed his hand against her. "Yeah, they give."

64

"Cu-yossity satisfied now, Motty?"

"Partly."

"Wite. It's bettah if it's only pahtly," she said.

Martin Ruskin looked at her. "You know, the funny thing is I understand you. Maybe that's a sign I'm a little coo-coo too."

"Wite."

All who were coming—the guests and the crashers—had arrived by one o'clock, and at two there was a good-sized exodus of the Mayfair Dance crowd, leaving the *Jumping Jack* company, the less chic, and the crashers. The character of the party changed at that point from a polite gathering of professional people to a drunken brawl. The three-piece orchestra—piano, trumpet, and accordion—played show tunes, and there was a good deal of singing, solo and group. There was some dancing in the foyer, but in the rooms the carpet discouraged it. Some of the men and women were in groups of four or five, and the others were pairing off in the interests of seduction. At about half-past two the first fight took place; the actor husband of an actress punched the writer of drama news for one of the morning papers, and Marty Ruskin told all three to get the hell out, which they did, together. A few minutes later an ingénue from a drawing-room comedy grasped the hand of a man who played the priest in a prison play and led him to a coat closet in the foyer, only to discover that it was already in use by a recently married leading woman and a musical comedy conductor. (The leading woman's husband was in Baltimore with a play.) Two chorus girls were busy decorating a middle-aged actor who was passed out on a divan. They put a lily in each of his hands and a rose above each ear, and stuck a white carnation in his fly. At 3:10 A.M. Sandra De Moe, the showgirl, emerged from the bathroom clad in a bath towel in front and a bath towel in back, which she held in place with her hands. She paraded through the two rooms and returned to the bathroom unmolested, but when she returned to the party in her evening dress a young man whose father owned a chain of theaters in Philadelphia bit her on the neck. He was thereupon beaten into insensibility by Sandra's younger brother, a tackle on the N.Y.U. football team. The beating and kicking took a little time, and when it was over many of the guests went home. The theater magnate's son was carried out of the suite and placed on the floor in front of the elevators. He had a nasty reputation anyway.

The musicians departed at four o'clock, and now the suite was occupied by the bartender, a waiter, a waiter captain, and half a dozen people including the host, Tessie Gibson, an advertising salesman from *Variety*, a detective from the Broadway Squad, the two chorus girls who had been decorating the drunk, and Hubert Ward, who for one of the few times in his life had had a little too much to drink. He and the host were the only persons present who were not sober. Martin Ruskin took a roll of banknotes from his pocket and peeled off three or four and handed them to the detective. "Thanks for taking care of Sonny Boy, Jim," said Ruskin.

"Any time, Marty. Son of a bitch comes over from Philly and always causes trouble, without fail. One of these nights he'll get it. I only hope I'm some place else. His old man's a friend of Walker." The detective nodded to one of the chorines, the *Variety* salesman nodded to the other, and the four departed.

"Well, wuddia say? The Clamhouse?" said Ruskin.

"No, I don't like Hahlem," said Tessie. "I don't want to be stuck up theh with you two passed out. Too fah f'm home foh me."

"Well, Dave's? A speak? It's too early for Reuben's."

"Let's take a couple bottles of that stuff and go to my place," said Hubert Ward.

"Wheh's you' place, Hubie?"

"Sheridan Square."

"That's the Village! Wite. Let's go theh, Motty."

"All right, what the hell. Hey, waiter. Gimme, oh, two bottles of the Scotch and two of the rye. And here, this is for you. Captain. For you. Barkeep, take this." He gave them money, and he and Tess and Hubert Ward left the suite.

"I'd like to see what kind of a joint you live in, too," said Martin Ruskin. "You got it alone, or with somebody?"

"The money you paid me, naturally I have a duplex penthouse."

"Make a deal with me and you *will* have a duplex penthouse," said Ruskin.

"I can get one now without making a deal with you," said Hubert Ward.

"Well, let's not talk money tonight," said Ruskin. "Let's forget about money."

"Wite, at least foh the pwesent, Motty," said Tess. "Foh the pwesent."

Hubert Ward's apartment, sublet month to month and costing him more than a week's pay every month, was a large room, a bath and kitchen, with windows on three sides. It was furnished and decorated in restrained modern style and obviously not cheaply. "A woman that writes books," Hubert Ward explained. "Some magazine sent her to Europe to write an article, and I got it because I was known. She saw me in the play."

"I think it's ve'y snappy," said Tess. "Look. Just a hand. And look at this. A little gazelle, isn't it? Isn't that a gazelle? And all ivowy. A lot of books. I *like* books. What's this? This man, he looks dead."

"He is dead. That's a death mask," said Ruskin.

"Oh, the pooh fella. What do you mean, Motty? They put a mask on him when he died? Is that some weligion?"

"You want me to explain it, Tess?"

"I guess you bettah not. I might not like it. I have to see a man about a little puppy. I'll be wite back."

Ruskin prepared Scotch highballs for himself and Hubert. "This is better than going to the Clamhouse. I saw enough people for one night. Here's wishing you luck, Hubert."

"Thanks, Marty. You too."

"Oh, with me it isn't so much a question of luck. I make a dollar. I make a lousy dollar and I probably always will. I don't try for anything big. I'd like to have something big some day, but I know I won't. My chance I had, and I blew it. I don't know how I blew it, but I did. The biggest thing happened to me recently was you. You, Hubie. You're going places and doing things."

"Maybe. I hope so."

Tess appeared. "Fascinating in theh. She has a pictsha of two dikes and a young gi'l. Theh not doing anything yet, but all you have to do is look at it to wealize, one of the dikes is going to get the gi'l. The one ovah the bathtub, Hubie?"

"Yeah."

"Who are you rooting for, Tess?"

"Oh, I don't know, Motty. Go on in and take a look. And the man with his thing bwoken off. A pictsha of a man with his thing bwoken off. Ooh, I bet that hu't. Only I think it's a pictsha of a statue and the thing got bwoken off, maybe when they dug it up. One of those statues. The one ovah the washstand, Hubie."

"I know."

"The woman you wented this fwom, what kind of books does she wite?"

"I don't know. I never read any."

"You stop to think, all the pictshas show nudes. And ovah theh, that statue, the two necking and theh ready foh it. They got no clothes on."

"That's a good start. When they take off their clothes they mean business," said Ruskin. "That statue was made by the man you asked about."

"That old man?"

"He wasn't always old, Tess. How about if you take off your clothes, Tess?"

"You want me to? Wight away?"

"Sure. All of us will."

"I didn't know it was gonna be that, Motty."

"Do you have any objections?"

"Hubie's as su'pwised as I am."

"I'll bet if you start taking off your clothes Hubie'll take his off too."

"How ah we going to awange this? You just want to watch, Motty? I don't like two at a time."

"But I heard you did, Tess."

"Oh, that's why you invited me. I wond'ed why you invited me to you' pahty when you only met me once befo'. I thought I was just foh you. Ahn't you twicky? I think you want to make a pass at Hubie, is that it?"

"Well what else?"

"Wight. Now I unde'stand it."

She stood up and got out of her evening dress and panties, all she was wearing, and ran her hands down over her lovely body, in which she took a nearly impersonal pride. "I don't think Hubie gets it yet," she said.

"I get it all right," said Hubert Ward. He took off his clothes and let them fall on the floor, and now Ruskin stripped.

"Motty, I think I like Hubie bettah. You haven't got any muscles, and Hubie has nice shouldahs." She held out her arms and she and Hubert embraced, standing up. Suddenly, as though a switch had been turned, she wanted Hubie immediately. Her good-natured quality was all gone and she backed on to the bed, taking Hubie with her. "Don't let him touch you," she said.

"I won't, I won't," said Hubert Ward.

"Go away, you di'ty faiwy," she said to Ruskin. She kicked at Ruskin, then lay back on the bed and embraced Hubie. "Do it to me, don't let him touch you," she said. When he was inside her she laughed. "We fooled him, we fooled him, we fooled him," she said.

"You lousy dirty bastards! You pigs! You lousy filthy pigs," said Ruskin, and he stood almost directly above them and watched and listened to their rising and falling passion and their contentment with each other that followed.

"Look at him. He didn't like that," she said. She had her arm around her new lover's neck. "I stole you away fwom him, and now he doesn't want you any moah."

"You horrible bitch!" screamed Ruskin, and he came at her with fists like hammers. She covered her breasts with one arm and her face with the other, and Hubert Ward fought him off. It was easy, since Ruskin's attack was concentrated on the girl and he did not defend himself against Hubert Ward. Hubert Ward got a stranglehold on Ruskin and pulled him away from the girl, and Ruskin now began to weep. His arms fell to his sides and there was no fight in him. Hubert released him, and he put his clothes on. The girl sat up in the bed.

"That wasn't twue about me, Motty. Only once, and I didn't like it. You shouldn't believe all you heah."

"Don't speak to me, you whore."

"I'm not that eithah, Motty. Not weally."

"She's a whore, I tell you," said Ruskin.

"You better shut up or I'll give you a punch in the nose."

"A haw's bettah than a faiwy, Motty. And I nevah hea'd you wuh a faiwy till tonight you admitted it. Did you know he was, Hubie?"

"I knew it the first time I saw him," said Hubert Ward.

"Did you evah go with him? I don't ca', but did you?"

"Hundreds of times," said Ruskin. "He's been my sweetie since last summer."

"You lying son of a bitch," said Hubert. He punched Ruskin in the mouth.

"I had him any time I wanted him, and so did anybody else. This is the easiest piece of trade on Broadway."

"Hit him again, Hubie. Don't let him say that about you."

"Go ahead hit me, but that won't take away from the truth." Ruskin was now dressed, although he had not tied his tie. He put his hand to his mouth, looked at the blood on his hand. "There was a lot of talk about you and I, Hubie. Now I'm going to tell them it was true. You'll never live that down."

"Huh. Who cares, even if it was true?"

"Your people. Those respectable people you came from."

"Get out of my apartment."

"You kiss him goodnight for me, Tessie." Ruskin brandished an ivory statuette of a praying nun. "Stay away, Hubie. I'm going." He tossed the statuette in a chair and quickly got outside the apartment.

"Now we got nobody to distu'b us, dahling, and we

got all Sunday and all day tomowwow. I like you, Hubie.
I honestly do. Honestly."

Franklin Hubert was not one of the visionary sort of
engineers. He had his degree from Stevens Tech, he had
worked in the field, he had served his country well in the
102d Division, and he came home from France and the
Army of Occupation at Coblentz with the impatient de-
termination to make money. All his experience and observation had shown him that the real money in his profession went to the men who stayed close to the home office.
The men in the field, even the superintendents of the biggest projects, were lucky to make fifteen thousand a year,
and at forty Franklin Hubert had not yet been given a
major project. The firm kept its 1917 promise and took him
back at ten thousand, but he knew that if he got sent out
to the Philippines or the Sudan or Wyoming he would
never again have the chance to get out of the ten-
thousand-dollar class. He could not marry and have a family—it was already getting a little late for that—and he
would be running risks of bad health and accidents. At
fifty he would be brought home, given a dinner and a silver tray, and retired at half pay, with no family of his own
and probably some physical handicap that would make it
impossible to play golf.

He therefore took a negative stand when the firm
assigned him to a pipe-line job in Arizona. "But that's the
kind of job we thought you'd like," said Ike Neidlinger,
the engineering vice-president of the firm. "It's not very
tough. Not very different from army engineering, and

you'll be able to finish it up in about eighteen months."

"That's a year and a half, Ike, and I'd be forty-two. Why don't you let one of the younger fellows have a crack at it?"

"They're dying to, but what did you have in mind? Pretty soon we're going to want something for our ten thousand a year."

"That's only fair, and I can earn it. Put me in the business end."

"Which end of the business end? Accounting?"

"No. New business."

"You want to be a salesman? That's what it amounts to."

"I'm young enough to get around, and at the same time old enough to represent the firm. I came out of the army a lieutenant-colonel, and that's a pretty respectable rank, Ike. Most men my age stopped at major."

"I thought your promotion was for bravery."

"Well, it was, but no matter how I got it, I was a lieutenant-colonel."

"Generally speaking, this firm never made a practice of going after new business. *It* came to *us*."

"I know. But are you pleased with that policy? You personally? Ike, we could double our business without doubling our overhead."

"You've thought about this, I can see. Of course our overhead has never been a problem. It's fairly constant from year to year."

"All right, all the more reason why we should go after the new business that's coming up, all over the world."

"We're not J. G. White."

"But in ten years, we could be."

"Darn you, Frank, you know darn well this appeals to me. It's what I was advocating before the war, and now you've got me stirred up all over again. All right, let's just keep this under our hats for the present, and I'll go to work on the other partners."

In engineering circles the news that Stieglitz & Overton were bidding against much larger firms was taken to mean that Ike Neidlinger was at last getting his way and prevailing over the ultra-conservative policy of D. D. Overton. This interpretation was prematurely accurate: Darius Draper Overton had a stroke and died at a directors' meeting, and Ike Neidlinger was elected president of Stieglitz & Overton. His debt of inspiration to Franklin Hubert was discharged by Hubert's election to the board of directors, and Franklin Hubert at forty-one was likewise and finally on his way.

But his enjoyment of his new status was almost immediately marred by troubles that afflicted him only because they concerned his favorite sister. Kitty Ward was his only sister, but she was very dear to him and he always referred to her as his favorite. Her husband, Sanford Ward, a trust officer in a Newark bank, was caught in an unimaginative theft of $100,000 worth of securities with which he had met some margin calls. He did not deny the accusation, he did not give any thought to the various ways in which whole or partial restitution could be made and the matter hushed up. He simply reached in his desk drawer and took out a Savage automatic and fired it in his right temple. He had always been a weakling, Franklin Hubert had opposed the marriage, and the manner of the suicide was as messy as the man's failure to realize that the bank was more vitally concerned with hushing up the theft than with his penitent splashing of his brains. Ward's bond covered the loss, and the bonding company could have been placated by contributions by relatives and Princeton friends. But Sandy Ward had never in life given much thought to anyone but himself, and in like manner he died.

Franklin Hubert could hardly bear to see his sister. She had always known he had never altered his original opinion of her husband: a snob who traded on two family names and all their distinctions and connections; a mandolin player, a cotillion leader, who he was sure sat down to pee. It was a mystery to Hubert why Sandy married Kitty as well as why Kitty married Sandy. The Huberts were Somerset County farming stock, who had never hunted the fox on horseback and had moved to Newark only one generation ago. And Kitty was not a great beauty at any time in her life. But Sandy's mother liked Kitty, and at parties and dances Sandy found that he was always going back to the Hubert girl after dancing with prettier and richer girls, who failed to appreciate the honor of his attentions. As for Kitty, she loved him from the start, and she never attempted to explain that to her brother. They had a daughter, a second daughter who died aged three weeks, and a son, Richard Hubert Ward, named at Sandy's suggestion for the Richard Hubert who had given his life at the Battle of Monmouth. Great-great-great-

great-uncle Richard Hubert, whose portrait, painted circa 1840, hung in the Hubertville, New Jersey, Borough Hall.

Kitty Ward had anticipated her brother's discomfiture, and when Franklin Hubert kissed her she said, "You don't have to say anything, Frank. But I'm glad you came so soon. If I'd listened to you—but then I wouldn't have the children. The children and you. I'll be all right. Just hold me for a little minute, and then we'll talk about other things."

Franklin Hubert fell into the habit of Sunday dinner with his sister and her children, and very soon he was becoming a stereotyped uncle—with the difference that Richard Ward made it unlikely that a stereotyped relationship could exist there. Franklin Hubert liked women, and he found that the prospect of settling down with one woman became less inviting now that he could easily do so. Too easily; women wanted to marry him, women his own age and a little younger, who were attracted to him and apprehensive of lonely years ahead. Franklin Hubert became, in a still current phrase, an artful dodger and, in another current phrase, a confirmed bachelor, who got from his sister and her children all the family life he really wanted. The girl was no problem: she was informally engaged to a young man at Lehigh, a predictably solid citizen whose father had a real estate business in East Orange. But Richard Ward, in his uncle's private opinion, was a little prick. The day of his father's funeral he pulled out a pack of Omars and offered his uncle a cigarette. "Your mother doesn't approve of that, does she?" said Franklin Hubert.

"No, but she knows I smoke," said Richard Ward.

"Then cut it out."

"Who's gonna make me?"

"You're going to be a great help, I can see that," said Franklin Hubert.

"I don't see what smoking has to do with it. My father didn't smoke, but look what he did. Stole, and left Mother penniless."

"Your mother isn't penniless. She isn't rich, but she isn't penniless."

"Papa didn't leave her any money."

"She'll have a little from his insurance, so don't go around saying your mother is penniless."

"Oh, then I can go to Andover?"

"I doubt it. But you can go to high school."

"High school? With a bunch of niggers and Italians? I like *that!*"

"Your mother hasn't got enough money to send you away to a place like Andover."

"Well, you have, haven't you? I heard you won five thousand dollars on Jack Dempsey beating that Frenchman."

"The sum was five hundred dollars."

"Papa said you won five thousand. I guess he was a liar about that, too. He was always bragging about everything, just so it was somebody in our family. Even about you."

"What do you mean, *even* about me?"

"Well, you didn't like him and he didn't like you, but you were Mother's brother. You would have thought our family were the richest and better than anybody else. I got sick of listening to it. All you had to do was compare our old Dodge with anybody's Pierce-Arrow. Now I guess we won't even have the Dodge. Have to take the trolley if we want to go anywhere. I'm thinking of running away. I won't go to high school with a lot of niggers and Italians. I won't *do* it."

"What you need is—"

"Oh, shut up. Hang a piece of crepe on your nose, your brains are dead."

Franklin Hubert provided the money for Andover and paid for his niece's wedding. Kitty Ward protested that every time he accumulated a bit of money to spend on himself, some urgent need occurred in her own little brood. Franklin Hubert had had the same thought, but reassured her with the observation that blood was thicker than water. He could not bring himself to add that it was also thicker than whiskey, which Kitty had taken to in the quiet of her lonely house. He pretended not to notice. She was alone most of the time, and the reports she got from Andover were not items she saved to show with pride when Frank would come for Sunday dinner.

The hit-and-run accident was so outrageous and yet so much in character for Richard Ward that his uncle, even in the fury of his indignation, could convince himself that Richard himself must feel revulsion. But Richard told Hubert's niece that old women were always saying that when they go they wanted to go quickly, and this particular old woman probably never knew what hit her. Richard's sister Hope, now Mrs. Albert W. Pierce, Jr., and the mother of twin daughters, stared at her brother. All the conventionalism that had been drilled into her willing soul, and that she had acquired in her marriage and motherhood and suburbanism, made her impervious to the shock that her brother's brutality might have conveyed. She was seven years older than Richard, had been able to ascribe earlier misbehavior to another conventionality—that of the nasty younger brother—but in the happiness and security of her orderly life she had no room for such a creature. "I just don't know him," she told her husband. "Is that possible? He sat there and told me these things, and it was like an actor playing a part. Just as if he didn't believe what he was saying any more than I did. But he did believe it. And I never want to see him again. I *never* want him to come anywhere near the twins. Or me. Or you. I don't hate him. I just—nothing." Until he was twenty years old Richard Ward's home was never more than ten miles from his sister's, but she never invited him to visit her, and saw him only twice, quite by accident. She seemed so preoccupied that he abandoned her to her dull husband and he-forgot-how-many children.

To Franklin Hubert it seemed as though his sister had an inexhaustible store of patience for her son, that every new piece of wrongdoing by Richard found her ready with forgiveness and excuses. But perversely she was becoming more and more impatient with those who sought to help or console her for Richard's misdeeds, and when Richard at last killed a human being, Kitty Ward behaved as though her brother and her friends were persecuting her. She conceded readily enough that Richard had done a horrible thing, and she refused to listen to him and his perfunctory self-justification; but she lashed out at Franklin Hubert, cruelly and recklessly—and drunkenly. "What did you expect? You hated his father, you tried to stop me from marrying him. And you never liked the child, never. Nothing I did was right. Marrying Sandy, or the way I was raising Richard. You've always interfered."

"For God's *sake*, Kitty—"

"Don't deny it. You always sneered at Sandy, and you said terrible things about Richard. Terrible things. Why don't you leave us alone? Stop interfering with our lives."

Franklin Hubert was not a subtle man. He believed in friendship, in love of mother and country, of a man for a woman; he believed in fighting for what he thought was right and in helping those who needed help; in fair contests with husband-hunting women, in honest business dealings, and in taking defeat without grumbling. The war had taught him that bravery and cowardice appeared sometimes in unexpected places, that a quiet sissy could act more courageously than a Dartmouth he-man—a judgment that had been confusing to him when Sanford Ward had shown no courage at all. Nearly everything that Franklin Hubert believed in in his twenties lasted him all his life, and his sister's turning on him now wounded him because she had been brought up to believe the same things. The wound hurt enough to make him wonder why she had inflicted it, and he was conscientiously dissatisfied with the quick explanation that she was over-wrought and quite possibly going through change of life.

With so little equipment for analyzing Kitty's behavior—no more than brotherly love and a sense of decency—he put his unsubtle mind to work. It took him days, then weeks, but he found his answer: Kitty was defending herself. She was defending what she knew to have been an unwise choice of husband, and an unlucky motherhood of a son. Franklin Hubert was convinced of the accuracy of his diagnosis, and he never again attempted such an analysis of a human condition; but he was thereafter guided by this analysis in his relationship with Kitty in matters concerning her son. It helped a great deal.

It helped, for instance, when Richard was sent home from Andover and from St. Bartholomew's, an undistinguished "church school," and from Chichester's, a catch-all institution near New Haven that contained youths who were cramming for the College Boards and other youths who had no chance whatever of getting into college. It was as dubious a distinction to be enrolled at Chichester's as to be fired from it. There was a youth at Chichester's who graduated at twenty-one because a condition of his grandfather's will was that he must be accepted at Yale to qualify for a two-million-dollar legacy. But most of the boys had no ambition beyond athletics and nights at the Pre Cat—Pre Catelan—a Thirty-ninth Street cabaret. Richard Hubert Ward did not excel in sports, and by the time he reached Chichester's the Pre Cat had closed forever. Still, he did achieve expulsion from Chichester's, which in the world of Eastern prep schools and universities was like Phi Beta Kappa at Harvard; "The same thing, only different."

Franklin Hubert met each new crisis with a calm that was born of his analysis of Kitty Ward's reactions to her son's troubles. He developed a method of conducting these interviews with Kitty. "I'll ask around and write some letters, and we'll see where we can get him in. We'll get him in somewhere, don't worry," he would say.

"The expense—I wish I could make him understand," she would say.

"Important thing is to find a school that will take him. Never mind about the expense."

"It's just not fair, Frank."

"Well, I have none of my own, and blood is thicker than water."

No mention was made of Sandy Ward's rich relatives. They had never considered Sandy as close as Sandy had considered them, and they had never indicated that they felt any obligations toward Sandy's widow and children. Kitty had never heard from any of them, and her brother was privately convinced that the scandal had given them a good excuse for keeping their distance.

"If I thought it would do any good to have you talk to him," she would say.

He would give her the reply she hoped for: "No, Kitty, that wouldn't do any good. He knows everything I'm likely to say, and it would only mean unpleasantness all around."

Nothing, therefore, was said, since Kitty likewise wanted to avoid unpleasantness. In the summers that followed the Andover and St. Bartholomew's expulsions she told Richard to look for a job, but he said in all truth that he did not know how to look for a job. For a week or two he skimmed lightly over the Help Wanted advertisements at breakfast, but after breakfast, or before he was quite finished, someone would call for him to play tennis or go on a picnic. When she made good her threat to cut his allowance he charged golf balls to his uncle's club account and sold them as lost balls—Silver King balls for a quarter apiece, a seventy-five-cent saving to the purchasers—until Franklin Hubert put a stop to that. Richard charged, and immediately pawned, two new suits from Bamberger's in Newark. There was nothing very ingenious about his methods of obtaining cash, but he ignored none of the obvious ways.

Then, a week after he was sent home from Chichester's, the long-postponed serious talk with his mother took place, and the only preparation she had made for it was to allow her anger to rise and to take a few extra drinks. "Take your leg off the arm of that chair," she began.

"If you're going to bawl me out at least I want to be comfortable."

"You're going to be very uncomfortable when I get through with you," she said.

"All right. Get it over with. I was kicked out of school."

"Three schools, and every time it gets worse. The

second time it was such a nasty thing that I couldn't even talk to you about it."

"But you can talk about this time, which is even worse? I don't follow your logic, Mother."

"I can talk about this because it's something normal. The other thing wasn't even normal."

"What do you want me to do? Promise I won't see her again, the dentist's wife? All right, I promise. Is that all? Now can I go?"

"Sit down in that chair and wait till I tell you you can leave."

"I don't see what there is to talk about. I was caught with a woman and got kicked out for it. You don't hear me denying it, do you? I don't know what else there is to say. I'm not going to try and fill you up with a lot of lies, because it wouldn't be any use. The only thing is you don't expect me to take my solemn oath that I'll never have anything more to do with women. That wouldn't be logical. If you want me to be normal, that's normal. But Judas priest! That wasn't the first time I ever had anything to do with a woman. Or anyway a girl."

"What kind of girls have you been seeing behind my back?"

"You'd be surprised. One just got married not so long ago and you went to her wedding."

"The only wedding I've been to—" Kitty Ward was remembering, and she remembered a girl, twentyish, in a beaded Juliet cap, a veil, a smooth silken bodice. The girl was handing a tiny bouquet of stephanotis with brief streamers dangling from it to her maid of honor. She was turning, this girl, with a confident, frank smile to the young man in a cutaway. And then a little later the girl, with the same smile, was coming down the aisle on the arm of her husband, and she had a special smile and a special "Mrs. Ward" that she made with her lips.

"I don't believe you! I don't *believe* you!" said Kitty Ward.

"You don't have to if you don't want to," said her son.

"You're a filthy liar. The only woman that was nice to me."

"Who? Judy Boswick?"

"Her mother, you unspeakable horror."

"I had nothing to do with her mother."

"You spoiled that wonderful smile, that lovely girl," said Kitty Ward. She was not speaking to her son, regardless of the pronoun. "I know you're lying."

"Well, there's no proof that I am or that I'm not. I'm sure Judy wouldn't admit it, now."

For the first time in more than ten years Kitty Ward slapped her son. "Get out of this house. Get out, and never come back. Take your things and go away. Away, away, away." He attempted to stare her down, to frighten her with a silent threat of violence, but she was unafraid. And he was afraid. He turned, left the room, and she could hear him in his room, opening drawers, slamming doors. Then his footsteps on the stairs, and on the front porch. She stood at the window and watched him while he stood at the curb. A taxi arrived and he got in, never looking back, and the taxi drove away.

She remained standing at the window. Across the street the rich new Armenian family were putting luggage and parcels in their Cadillac touring car. Next door the painters were busy at the MacBrides'. Two nurses slowly pushing prams were conversing in front of the Mac-Brides'. To the left of the MacBrides', at the Boswicks', good kind Amy Boswick was filling the bird-bath with water from a sprinkling-can. There had been a dry spell.

Franklin Hubert could not find out what finally had turned his sister against her son, but he did not inquire very deeply. He could imagine that it was something so awful that it shamed her to speak of it, but whatever it was, sending Richard away had been an act of firmness. She had made a decision and acted upon it; and decision and act had made her hold up her head again. He was pleased to see that she was going out again, taking an interest, having friends in for bridge, even planning a Garden Club trip with Amy Boswick, who had been so wonderful during the Sandy ordeal and the time Richard had his automobile accident. It just went to show that a person can stand only so much and then you have to begin looking out for yourself. Either that or call it curtains.

There were some unfavorable opinions of Ralph Harding's third play, *Yours for the Asking*. Percy Hammond said it was "less than a masterpiece" and George Jean Nathan called it delicatessen. But for Hubert Ward in the demanding role of Christopher there were only de-

grees of praise. Kelcey Allen said that Mr. Ward reminded him of Glenn Hunter, and Alexander Woollcott
said that Hubert Ward must now be considered among
the precious few young actors in the tradition of Alfred
Lunt; sprites who could do serious drama as well as comedy without confusing the audience as to their intent.
Gilbert W. Gabriel did not like to think what Mr. Hard-
ing's play would be without the newcomer Hubert Ward.
One of the Broadway gossip writers said: "Recommended
to diversion-seekers: Hubert Ward as the mamma's boy
(Oedipus Complex, to you) in 'Yours for the Asking.'"
And for weeks after the first night Ward Morehouse reported Hubert Ward lunching at the Algonquin or the
Hunting Room of the Astor, or simply *at* Frankie &
Johnny's or *in* the after-theater crowd at Tony's. *The New
Yorker* ran a piece about Hubert Ward in its Talk of the
Town department, in which Mr. Ward related some of
his non-theatrical activities; he had been a deckhand on
freighters, surveyor in South America, life guard at Rock-
away Beach, art student in Paris. He had never intended
to be an actor but had thought of becoming a playwright
and after making a few suggestions to Martin Ruskin, the
producer had persuaded him to accept a part in *The
Jumping Jack*. He was born, he told the *New Yorker* interviewer, in Denver, Colorado, son of a retired army officer. He attended Exeter for three years, then left school
to go to sea. He was of course pleased by the critical ac-
claim, but was not sure he wanted to stay in the theater.
He had refused all offers from Hollywood, and would
continue to refuse them. "I want to get out and see more

of the world," he said. The interviewer commented on Hubert Ward's apartment in Sheridan Square. "I read a lot," Mr. Ward told the interviewer. "I'm a great admirer of Rodin, and if I had more money I'd collect ivory." *The New Yorker* concluded that Mr. Ward would soon be able to fill his apartment with ivory.

A few nights after the interview appeared Hubert Ward was in Tony's and the *New Yorker* man came in. "Ward, you're a phony son of a bitch," said the reporter. "We got twenty-five letters about you. You're from Montclair, or some place over that way. And all the rest you gave me was crap, sheer crap."

"You fell for it."

"I fell for it, but I just wanted to tell you, you're a phony son of a bitch."

"What are you going to do? Sue me?"

"No, I think I'll tweak your nose."

"See this bottle of club soda? You touch my nose and I'll break this over your skull."

A waiter spoke up. "Now, now, now, now, now. Gentlemens, gentlemens. Not in here. He's drunk, Mr. Ward."

"He's not that drunk. Throw him out."

"Well, I don't throw him out, but come on now, Mr. Parrish. Don't make any more trouble now. *Mister* Parrish, behave you'self."

"Crap. All crap."

"My dear fellow, I heartily agree with you. Most heartily." The newcomer was a short man with a deep voice and an English accent to go with his tweeds and the Malacca stick that hung by a thong from his wrist. "Do me the honor of joining me, Parrish old boy."

"You don't think I ought to tweak this phony's nose."

"Under the circumstances, no."

"Hey, Ward. What did Rodin ever write?" said Parrish.

"Quite," said the man with the accent. "Now come with me, Parrish."

But most of Hubert Ward's encounters with press and public were conducted without friction. There had been no interviews after *The Jumping Jack,* but people who had met him during that period now claimed old acquaintance. He had some letters from people who remembered him from Denver, who had known his father, Colonel Ward; who remembered him at Exeter when his name was Johnny Trapnell; who had known him in Paris when he was living with an English girl called Joyce Paternoster. In spite of the fact that he was not yet and contractually could not be the star of *Yours for the Asking,* it was his picture that got in the papers and not Elizabeth Vandermeer's. That old trouper could have played tricks on him, but the cleverest trick she played was to be graciously cooperative onstage and generous in her statements to the press about this boy, this find. Before the play had finished its run it belonged to her again: the critics and the feature writers were calling attention to the quiet strength of her acting. An anonymous writer on *Vanity Fair* declared that the veteran actress (upper right) gave one of the most satisfying performances in the current theater, which had been overlooked in the enthusiasm for young Hubert Ward (lower right).

Her best performance, as is frequently the case, was in her dressing room, where she played the kindly professional to Hubert's tyro. She intimidated him by being graciously cooperative where he had been warned to expect trouble, and after every performance he would knock on her door, have a cigarette with her, and ask how he had been that night. "You were good," she would say. "I have no suggestions. Just don't think too much about the play when you should be relaxing. Long runs are not an unmixed blessing when you're young," and he would go out gratefully, full of respect for an elderly woman who had an old Rolls-Royce town car waiting to take her home to her little house on Sutton Place. She had never offered to give him a lift, never invited him to her house, and of course he had never heard her describe him as a male ingénue. Only her husband had heard her say, "Master Ward is a little shitheel who'd better get in the movies before the people get wise to him."

On the closing night of the play Hubert Ward invited her to his party in the back room at Tony's. "Thank you, my dear, but opening night or closing night, I always go straight home." She went straight home—to her own party, which was attended by her friends the Lunts, Woollcott, Katharine Cornell and Guthrie McClintic, Noel Coward, Beatrice Lillie, Alice Duer Miller, Philip Barry, Ina Claire, Jack Gilbert, Marc Connelly, Deems Taylor, the Damrosches, Jascha Heifetz, Condé Nast, Carmel Snow, William Lyon Phelps, Charles Hanson Towne, Walter

Prichard Eaton, Sidney Howard, Elisabeth Marbury, Gerald and Sara Murphy, Neysa McMein and John Baragwanath, and the Edgar Scotts from Philadelphia. "Not a one of them will ask me what it was like to have Master Ward sitting on my lap for a hundred and thirty-two performances," she told her husband.

"All I can say is they'd better not," he replied.

"Oh, I wouldn't forget that I'm a lady," she said. "Although I'm not going to let Condé get away with calling me a veteran. *Veteran?*"

Two days after her party and Hubert Ward's he was, as they said, poured on the Twentieth Century Limited. He had a contract with Paramount, and even before he arrived in Pasadena he was becoming accustomed to the designation: "Hubert Ward, New York stage actor." It took him two or three weeks to realize that the designation was not intended as a compliment. In Hollywood it was only an identification, so that he would not be confused with writers, directors, cameramen, associate supervisors, hair-doers, film cutters, second-unit men, press agents and other such personnel. "Hubert Ward, New York stage actor" he would remain until the studio took up his first option.

"*You* tell *me* what he's got. I wish you would please do me that favor. When I look at him I don't see a Wally Reid, a Charley Ray. I don't see no Dick Barthelmess. Those boys come across to me like typical American boys, typical, and don't bother me with gossip stories. I know all them gossip stories and I don't care. Just as long as

the public has a different opinion. But you know what I
see when I look at this young fellow? I see a young fellow
that if I look at him quick, I'd hire him to pose for Arrow
collars. I see stills with him in them and I think to myself,
a dime-a-dozen pretty boy and why does New York go
to all this expense, railroad fares and all, not to mention
putting him on salary as soon as he closes in some Broadway play. Why do they do that when I can send a man to
Catalina some Sunday and he'll bring back twelve gross
of these dime-a-dozeners? But then I take a look at this
young fellow in the rushes. This morning, ten o'clock, I
walked over and took a look at the rushes. With all the
takes there was about eighteen and a half minutes of film.
But I didn't get out of the projection room till a quartera
twelve noon. You know why? Because I had them running take after take, over and over again. For what? Because I seen another Charley Ray? Another Dick Barthelmess? A Wally Reid? Like hell. I wish I did. This fellow
looks like one of your typical American boy types—till
you get him before a motion-picture camera. Then you
know what happens? Evil. E, v, i, 1, evil. Bill Powell.
Stroheim. Who else have we got that you always want to
see him suffer? Well, you get the idea. He's gonna rape a
sweet little innocent girl like Lillian Gish. Mae Marsh.
Not your Louis Wolheim heavy. An officer. That's it! An
officer! This young fellow is an officer, and maybe he
knocks up Mae Marsh or anyway he foists his attentions
on her, but is he gonna get it in the end? You want to see
him in agony, he's gonna get it, the dirty son of a bitch.

And now we got sound, you can *hear* him begging for mercy.

"Why is this? I'll tell you why. Because the average person, they're gonna take a look at this young fellow and they're gonna trust him, because they think right away, a clean-cut typical American boy. But the first thing you know, they're gonna get the same feeling I got. I don't trust him. He's what I call shifty-eyed. He can't look you straight in the face because he's a shifty-eyed fellow. That's the feeling I get, and that's the feeling the American audience are gonna get. Therefore I decided it's too late to make any changes in this picture. I won't hold up production on this one. But I want you to find a story or get a couple of our contract writers—not the highest priced, but not the cheapest—and put them to work on a story. I tell you the kind of a story I want. What's his name again? Ward? Herbert? Hubert Ward. Hubert Ward is a young fellow comes to this typical American town. He meets say Mary Brian. Pretty, innocent, good respectable family and maybe George Bancroft for her father. Or maybe we put it down South and let Miriam Hopkins play the daughter. Anyway, Herbert Ward comes to town and starts monkeying around with Mary Brian. She gets knocked up and Herbert deserts her in her condition. How we're ever gonna get this by the Hays Office I don't know, but we can skirt around as much as we can. What I want is to see this young fellow get his just deserts. I want to see George Bancroft give him a good beating. Kick the living shit out of the son of a bitch. Maybe Mary's really in love with Phil Holmes, her child-

94

hood sweetheart. I don't know. I just thought of this idea during lunch, but I'm convinced. If we can make the American audience hate this young fellow enough, he could turn into an American Stroheim. A clean-cut heavy. That would be revolutionary, and the foreign market would eat it up. They're always complaining about our stories, we'll give them something sophisticated, and at the same time hold on to our American audience. That's what I want to do with Herbert Ward, and the first thing we do is take up his option before some other son of a bitch can get hold of him and make him another Dick Barthelmess. Once this young fellow gets the hero build-up they'd be crazy to try to turn him into a heavy, but we have him and we can make him anything we like."

Hiram J. Zimmermann was delighted to discover that Hubert Ward did not have to be sold the idea of playing a heavy; he *wanted* to play a heavy. It gave him a better chance to act, and he readily agreed with Hiram J. Zimmermann that the public soon tired of dime-a-dozen typical American boy types. He was not always going to confine his acting to Hollywood, and when he returned to the New York stage he did not want Eugene O'Neill and authors like that to think of him as a Hollywood pretty boy. The screenplay by Martha Kensington, Joseph Hutchinson MacDuffie, and Ted Fenstermacher, with additional dialogue by J. Frank Youngblood and Sara Jaffe Winston, based on an original story by Martha Kensington and Joseph Hutchinson MacDuffie, was rumored to be an entirely new departure for Hollywood, as realistic as any-

95

thing Theodore Dreiser had written, and was likely to end Hollywood's dependence on plays and novels as the bases for scenarios. For that reason the industry momentarily suspended the usual advance judgment of the picture, and the opening at Graumann's Egyptian attracted writers as well as the usual executives and stars, in a kind of remote defiance of Fourth Avenue, the Algonquin, Broadway, Sardi's, and all the rest of those New York book-and-theater snobs. After the Hollywood opening—that same night, immediately after—there was a meeting of executives at which it was decided to spend an additional $60,000 on advertising and publicity, but the realistic fact was that Dreiser and O'Neill had nothing to worry about. The picture opened on a Friday morning at the New York Paramount, and on the following Tuesday the house was half empty in spite of Waring's Pennsylvanians and George Dewey Washington for the stage presentation. The picture had cost about $400,000 and did not lose money—few pictures did—but Hiram J. Zimmermann was not given Nancy Carroll for his next picture, and with that strong hint thrown at him he settled his contract and moved to another studio. The only considerable gainer from the picture was Hubert Ward.

Hiram J. Zimmermann: "Where I made my mistake, who the hell can predict what women are going to like, I ask you? Women. You ask the average man in the audience how he feels about Hubert Ward and the answer you get is they don't like him and they don't dislike him. Whereas the women will come right out and tell you they don't like him, but that don't stop them from wanting to pay fifty-fi' cents to see him in a picture. Here you got a genuine paradox where they can dislike an actor, and I was right on that. But they don't want him done away with. The women that go for this young fellow, which is about fifty percent of your audience, not all, they don't trust him, they know he's a wrong bozo, but they don't want him done away with. It's the hooker in every woman, with very few exceptions. If they could sneak him in through the kitchen door, they would. And that's where this young fellow is gonna make his play. He'll never be big like Jack Gilbert was big with Garbo. If I had Garbo I'd never team her up with Hubert Ward, that'd be a waste of Garbo. Garbo you want real old-fashioned romantic love stories, and the women wouldn't want Garbo to end up with this young fellow. They wouldn't be pulling for him and her to end up together. I know plenty of women that would shoot you if you said they were queer, but you get them started on Garbo and I think some of them are queer without knowing it. And they don't want a fellow like Hubert Ward anywhere near Garbo. But he'll draw. You know what he is? He's perfect supporting. I'd always put him in with two big stars and I bet you'd find out that the women went to see *him*. Maybe they wouldn't admit it, but he's the one they'd go to see in preference to the big stars. He'll be working till he's sixty-five years of age, the son of a bitch. Nothing's gonna stop him. But he'll never be able to carry a picture by himself. Never."

It would not have been an auspicious debut for most actors. Indeed careers had begun and ended for other

New York actors and actresses with only one such box-office disappointment. But *Starstruck,* Hiram J. Zimmermann's last picture at Paramount and Hubert Ward's second picture anywhere, had been produced in an atmosphere of Art. Zimmermann had seen to it that the industry was told over and over again that this was going to be a *different* picture, that the industry *had* to be proud of it. The highbrow critics—Sherwood, Cohen, Watts, and Lorentz—were tipped off to expect a *different,* an *artistic* picture, from Hollywood this time. The boy-meets-girl, boy-loses-girl, boy-gets-girl formula was to be abandoned. Willy Gropertz, the terrific German director, was to be given a free hand, and the critics were privately advised to look for Gropertz touches in certain love scenes that were being sneaked past the Hays Office. The industry and the critics dutifully commented on Zimmermann's courage and Gropertz's naughty subtleties; there was a great deal of in-the-know writing which had to remain obscure to the lay reader because Gropertz employed several phallic symbols, the slightest mention of which was impossible in family publications. (One seemingly innocent scene had the girl shyly caressing a pillar on her front porch as Hubert Ward spoke the seductive words of J. Frank Youngblood and Sara Jaffe Winston.) For these and other reasons the picture *was* different. Willy Gropertz went back to Germany, and Hiram J. Zimmermann moved out to Universal, but *Starstruck* became one of those pathetically numerous films by which unartistic people hoped to buy artistic recognition. Gropertz was especially bitter because five months after he told the

ship news reporters that he was convinced that Hollywood was sincerely interested in Art, he was homeward
bound and telling the same ship news reporters that Hollywood shtunk. In Hollywood, he said, an artist could not
breet, which confused the reporters until they realized
he was saying *breathe*, not *breed*.

Nevertheless *Starstruck* was significantly helpful to
the career of Hubert Ward. His first important picture
had been an Art job, instead of a horse opera, a prison
epic, a campus cutups film, or a Cecil B. DeMille specta-
cle. He moved right into Hollywood Society, a curious
combination of the powerful, the able, the glamorous,
and, among the males, the wearers of the Brooks Brothers
shirt. The actor or writer who continued to get his shirts
by mail from Brooks after beginning to make movie
money was somehow considered to be well connected
socially back East, and in some cases he was. But Hubert
Ward's connections with Eastern Society were remote. He
had an uncle who belonged to the University Club, but
he was not on speaking terms with Franklin Hubert. His
mother belonged to a suburban New Jersey country club.
His brother-in-law belonged to the Essex Troop. But those
relatives of his late father, who might have been considered Good People by a New York society editor, were frost-
ily indifferent to his existence. Hollywood Society, however, took him up without any investigation of their own
claims for him. They appeared to like what he was not:
he was not unemployed, he was not from Los Angeles, he
was not a Latin or a Jew (the older Jews in Hollywood
Society rebuffed younger Jews, even their own children,

99

who were old enough to go to parties), he was not a booze artist, he stayed out of the gambling that he could not afford; he was not actorish; he was not pugnacious; he would be miscast in a gangster part. On the positive side he was making pretty good money, he was of the theater, he had been given good notices in an Art picture, he was not confused by an oyster fork, he stood up when ladies entered the room, he danced reasonably well, he could read sheet music, he seemed ready to please, he was clean and dressed Eastern. Nearly all these new friends had themselves come to California in fairly recent years, but back East they had seldom known the type of young man they considered Hubert Ward to be, and they were eager to forget the hoofers and sharpies and pitchmen and shipping clerks and prizefighters and truck drivers and stool-pigeons and seminarians and rabbinical students and epileptics who were the young men they had known in their various pasts. This Hubert Ward seemed affable, but he was not liable to antagonize people with a sense of humor or to make them uncomfortable with a lot of serious intellectual stuff. He won many friends with his disarmingly candid answer to a question about what it was like to work with Willy Gropertz. "I wouldn't have missed it for the world," he said. "But sometime I'd like to see the picture with him and have him explain to me what I was doing half the time."

In this company he was careful never to be contemptuous or patronizing of the industry. He revealed a genuine curiosity about the camera and the art of cutting, and when someone commented that he was learning the argot quickly he said, truthfully enough, that some day he wanted to direct pictures, but only after he had learned a lot more than he knew now. In this company he could not have made a more generally flattering statement, and they returned the courtesy by saying that he had a lot of good acting to do before the public would let him turn to directing.

He became a fixture in this group: he went to their Thursday and Sunday dinner parties, their Sunday luncheons, their beach and tennis parties. On his second Christmas in Hollywood he was astonished by the number and costliness of the presents they gave him, for which he was unprepared, having already sent out his English coach-at-the-inn cards to people who sent him gold-clipped billfolds, gold cufflinks, gold cigarette lighters, gold pencils, invariably from Brock's; and scarves, dressing-gowns, and other haberdashery, invariably from Pesterre's. He wrote a note of thanks for each of these gifts, and so unaccustomed were the donors to any such gesture that they apologized for the insignificance of the gifts. Among themselves they remarked that Hubie Ward was a real gentleman; you could always tell; he had class.

But he was not altogether happy with his status in the group: he noticed that when the men were having their cigars after dinner he was not expected to enter the conversation unless asked a specific question. The men were apt to be friendlier with him when women were present than in an all-male gathering. In due course he figured out the reason: he was the only man who was not an important executive, top director, or top-billing star.

He was a junior officer in a senior officers' mess, as surely as though they all wore insignia of rank. He was making good money, he was appearing in high-budget pictures, but his name was not yet appearing on top of the titles of the pictures. He was now twenty-three years old, young for this group but not too young for top billing. He was getting to be known all over the world—he actually had a Japanese fan club, which sent him Japanese fans. He had a comfortable suite in an apartment hotel on North Rossmore; a Lincoln convertible coupe; and nearly $70,-000 cash in two banks. But he was not yet being taken seriously by the important industry figures whose houses he went to for dinner. It was annoying because he did not know what to do about it. His contract had another year to run, and the billing terms were stated in it. The studio could change the billing voluntarily, but he could not demand a change.

He had a talk with his agent, Jack Golsen, who shook his head. "Sooner or later you want to stir up a hornets' nest, and with actors it's always the billing. Here you got a contract that at the present moment you're in the fifteen-hundred-a-week phase. No layoffs. You get paid whether you work or you're off nuzzling up to some broad at Malibu. You got fifteen years ahead of you before you're forty years of age, and you don't look to me like you're the type that puts on the blubber. You got straight yearly options for two more years, so why stir up a hornets' nest, Hubie? Two years from now, granted we renegotiate, and you bet your sweet ass we do renegotiate. But leave sleeping dogs, Hubie. Go away and don't bother me, will you like a good fellow?"

"No. I made five pictures since *Starstruck* without any change in billing. Do you know I got a fan club in—"

"Aw, now don't give *me* that *fan* club. Or the studio either. The studio organized the fan club."

"In Tokyo, Japan?"

"In Tokyo, Japan. In Manchester, England. In Pratt Falls, New York. In Pottsville, Pottstown, and Chambersburg. Get wise to yourself, Hubie. A live-wire exhibitor can organize a fan club for John Wilkes Booth, if he wants to take the trouble, so don't give me fan clubs. Why do you want better billing? Who put that fig up your ass?"

"Nobody did. I think I'm entitled to it."

"Listen, Hubie, believe me, things are going nice between you and the studio. You stir up a hornets' nest and you be surprised how uncomfortable they can make it for you. They put you in nothing but high-budget pictures with the biggest stars in the world, but there's nothing in the contract that says they can't put you in low-budgets with some dying swan. One big credit after another and two years from now I can talk to them. I can talk about a lot of things, billing amongst them. Money. Billing. Time off between pictures and et cetera."

"Selection of stories?"

"No. Don't get that in your noggin, either. I'd rather you get somebody else to handle you before I'll try to get you selection of stories. You know who has that? Nobody. No studio will stand for that, not from a contract player. So if that's what you're leading up to, Hubie, forget it. I'll tell you here and now, I won't fight that battle for you or anybody else, because when I go to renegotiate I want to have a chance of winning. I'm in business, too, you know. I think what you need is a good piece of tail, something new that's maybe hard to get. Maybe you ought to get married, I don't know. Redecorate your apartment. I got my sister-in-law that will do it cheap. Redecorate, I mean. The other you wouldn't be interested. Maybe you ought to take a trip. New York, you never been back there since you come to Hollywood. The Islands. A trip on the *Lurline*. You ever been to Tia Juana? Buy yourself a new car. Spend some money for a change. A high colonic. You ever had a high colonic? Take up golf. What you need is something different, Hubie. You're chafing at the bit, through sheer boredom. I know two Chinese broads that would give you an entire new perspective. You want me to fix you up with them? I give them a call about once or twice a year when I want to be real relaxed."

"Mary and Nancy Lee? I know them."

"Well, then all my other suggestions, but don't bother me with billing till two years hence. Show you what a good fellow I am, I'll take you to lunch. Levy's okay?"

If star billing had been the real cause of his discontent he would have fought for it—and stood a good chance of winning. But billing was not his trouble, nor even the after-dinner behavior of the Hollywood powers. He did not particularly want to choose his own stories; he knew without Jack Golsen's telling him that he had no chance of gaining that concession, and he was at least honest enough to admit to himself that acting was no more than a reasonably easy, satisfactory way of earning a pleasant living. Motion picture acting was the easiest, most satisfactory way of earning an extremely pleasant living, not to be compared with acting on the stage. In pictures the hours were longer, but he was not required to learn 120 pages of dialog, and if he made a mistake it could be corrected, and it was corrected. Between pictures there was loafing in the California sun; swimming, tennis, and even a half-hearted attempt to play polo; and the variety of acquiescent women who came to the North Rossmore apartment should have staved off boredom. Nevertheless boredom had begun to set in, and the list of suggestions Jack Golsen had made to offset it was rather like the cures Hubert Ward had considered for himself, differing somewhat in detail but similar in character.

He went down to Malibu for the weekend of his twenty-fifth birthday, telling no one that it was his birthday because he wanted no fuss and because it emphasized the difference in age between him and the powerful. By his early standards he was rich, and by any standards he was famous, but by the standards of the powerful he was young and not very rich. And he was as bored as anyone of any age.

On this weekend he was the house guest of Charles and Mildred Simmons (né Simon). Charley Simmons at forty-two was one of the six or seven most powerful executives in the industry and he had made it on his own, to the extent that he was not related to any of the industry

families. He had got into the business through his ability
as a junior partner in a New York law firm, pushed and
fought his way past the illiterates in several studios, and
now was vice-president in charge of production at U. S.
Films, Incorporated, which was in the business of making films rather than the business of supplying films for a
theater chain. His wife had been his secretary during his
lawyer days. They had a son at Lawrenceville and two
daughters, who were attending a Catholic day school in
Los Angeles. It was said of Mildred Simmons that she was
half of Charley's brains, which was a complimentary ex-
aggeration based on the actual fact that he discussed—
"thought out loud"—every business move with her, as at
one time he had discussed law cases with her. She sat in
on the high-stakes poker games with the men, won fairly
consistently, lost infrequently and in small amounts. She
was a statuesque Jewess, a good two inches taller than her
husband, strikingly homely as to face, but proud of her
figure and extravagant in clothing it. There was not a
man in the group who had not at some time sounded her
out on an experiment in adultery; some of them had been
drunk, some had been completely sober, but she had had
more propositions than many of the famous beauties who
came to her house, and when Hubert Ward as a newcomer
to the group proceeded on the mistaken notion that he
had seen possibilities that others had overlooked, she put
him forever in his place. "Little boy, maybe I'll send for
you some time I want you to scrub my back," she said.
"Only don't count on it." But Hubert Ward had not made
a mistake in inviting her to his apartment. She had be-

come so accustomed to drunken and sober invitations to fornicate that she questioned the virility of any man who failed to proposition her. "I personally know he's a fag," she would say, if a man did not show interest after a reasonable length of time. Other women were afraid of her, since they could not discover any points of vulnerability. She made jokes about her face—"Alongside of me Fanny Brice is Rosamond Pinchot"—and made jokes about other women's figures. They could not gossip about her conduct, and they could not hurt her through Charley, who was above temptation and always left his office door open while conversing with a female star. She was, moreover, a terrible enemy for any woman to have: ruthlessly vindictive, sporadically witty, and as the only female regular in the men's poker games she had their ear and attention at least once a week. She was not the social leader of the group; no woman was; it was basically and essentially a male Society, a fact which always seemed strange to those onlookers who did not know about the comparable male domination of Society in Eastern cities where the men decided who would—and would not—be invited to membership in the cotillions, assemblies, balls, germans, and dancing-classes that separated the ins from the outs. In this Hollywood group the women spent the money and competed in the niceties of the entertainment, but no man or woman was admitted against male opposition. On the other hand, the women were sometimes influential in having an individual dropped, and therein lay Mildred Simmons's power. She could relay—or withhold—female gossip that the men might not otherwise hear, and she could be destructive.

Hubert Ward amused her. Since he had not achieved full comradeship with the men, he spent a great deal of time in conversations with her, and they amused each other. He talked to her as he would have talked to the men, and she listened with lubricious attention to his descriptions of adventures with women. In time he found that this was expected of him, and he did not fail her. The girls and women were not likely to be friends or even acquaintances of Mildred's; she strictly observed the caste system of the industry, which meant that she associated only with wives on her own executive level and the actresses—stars, featured players—who belonged to her group. But this did not prevent her from acquiring a movie fan's knowledge of minor stars and featured actors and bit players. In the projection room in her house in Beverly Hills she saw pictures three or four nights a week, and sometimes she would nudge Hubert Ward and whisper, "Is she the one you took on the boat?" Or "Is he the one that has a girl on Central Avenue?"

They would talk together and laugh together, and the married women in their group, who did not have to guess how he amused her, soon gave up any thought of casual dalliance with Hubert Ward. Among these men and women divorce was infrequent; it was costly not only by reason of the community property laws, but because it could mean radical realignments of interfamily, intra-industry connections. A director's wife was not only the wife of a director; she was the sister of the production head of a studio, and quite possibly the first cousin of the chairman of the finance committee at another studio. Divorce, with a consequent redistribution of voting stock, was as calamitous as death. The women got the jewelry, but the men held on to their shares. Not even Mildred Simmons owned a single share of U. S. Films, Incorporated, nor did she expect to inherit any if Charley dropped dead.

The men in the group had mistresses, and some of the women took lovers. In the group itself there had been some —but very little—adultery, always put to a stop before it reached the phase where it could be discussed openly. It would be known that one Harry had seen a lot of one Joe's wife during a trip to New York, but when Harry and Joe's wife returned to Beverly Hills they were expected to have got that out of their systems. Harry's family and closest friends would see to that—and a year later Harry would be advising one Sidney to watch *his* step. It was not very different from Philadelphia, or the Court of St. James's.

The danger in an affair with a Hubert Ward was that an actor, any actor, was always an associate member of the group, subject to banishment. A woman whose affair with Hubert Ward compelled her husband to divorce her could expect rough treatment. The resources of the studio publicity departments would be directed against her, and she might easily be left with an actor whose box-office appeal was not strong enough to overcome the personal prejudice against him. It was obvious to the women that Hubert Ward told Mildred Simmons all he knew; it was therefore not worth the risk to have an affair with him. As a result he had slept with only one woman in the group: Ruth St. Alban, twice divorced and a full-fledged star, who could not really see much difference between one man and another after the first pint of champagne. She was neither oversexed nor vicious; it was simply that champagne made her complacent and the attentions of a man added to her complacency. She had told Mildred Simmons, among others, that she got very little fun out of sex; Hubert Ward, among others, had told Mildred that Ruth St. Alban sometimes fell asleep before she should have.

With the other women Hubert Ward was polite, agreeable, noticed new dresses and hair-dos, and complimented them on the more obvious expenditures in and about their households. He could tell them little stories about what went on on the set. Nearly all talk in the group had to do with the making of motion pictures, and most of the husbands of these women were concerned with the financial aspects of picture-making, high fiscal policy, so that Hubert Ward's stories provided the lighter touch in a non-stop one-topic conversation.

The only other topic was the behavior of the stock market, and this inevitably was related to picture-making, film distribution, and profits and losses in the theater chains. The caprices of the stock market never quite matched the introduction of sound for conversational interest among the group as a whole, and during the current debate between the optimists and pessimists over the state of the national economy, the men were generally agreed that the motion picture industry could lead the country out of the depression. Charley Simmons dissented from this view, but his colleagues reminded him that he was a lawyer, not a showman, and loud voices were heard after several dinners. Simmons did not believe that ten, or twenty, or fifty smash-hit movies would solve the nation's economic problems and save the capitalistic system, but when his colleagues demanded to know how he would bring back prosperity, he weakly replied that he did not know what had brought about the depression, an answer which restored his friends' self-confidence. "Charley," they said, "you don't know any more about it than anybody, but you always want to be a little different." He thus for the moment escaped being called a traitor to his industry and his country.

But he was disturbed, baffled, and increasingly irritable as a result, and he was not looking forward to the weekend. He saw Hubert Ward's red Lancia coming through the wall gate, and now it was too late to invent an excuse to go away. The weekend had begun.

It was Saturday, luncheon would be served at half-past two, the house guests would come and go as they pleased all afternoon; people would be dropping in from the neighboring beach houses and driving down from Beverly Hills and the Rossmore section. There would be actors and actresses and directors who were kept at the studios on Saturday afternoon. There would be letter-of-introduction visitors from the East, come to look in on a Hollywood revel. The staff would be serving food and drink for the next sixteen hours. It would all be paid for by U. S. Films, Incorporated, but it never failed to offend Charley Simmons's sense of thrift to see so much money spent on the same people, week after week, to no purpose, especially since he had originally bought the Malibu beach house to get away from those people. He realized that it was inconsistent argument to come to Malibu to get away from picture people, a thought that at another time would have amused him, but in his present frame of mind only added to his irritability. The only change at Malibu was more people got drunker there than they did "in town," as Beverly Hills and the old Rossmore section were called in Malibu. Without actually deciding to do so, Charley Simmons picked a cocktail off a passing waiter's tray. It was a concoction of Bacardi, lemon juice, and a dash of Pernod, so pleasant to the taste that although he was usually a slow as well as a moderate drinker, he tossed off two Delmonico glasses in less than fifteen minutes.

"Charley, you with a cocktail?" said Hubert Ward.

"Me with a cocktail. Don't you think I'm entitled, Hubie?"

"Sure. Who better?"

"That's the way I look at it. Have you had one? It's made of Bacardi rum and it has absinthe in it. You know, Pernod. I have a feeling they're probably stronger than they taste, but if it knocks me on my can I won't play polo this afternoon. Aren't you playing polo any more, Hubie?"

"Are you playing polo?"

"Christ, no, I was just kidding. That's for the goyim. Wouldn't I look great on a horse, provided the God damn nag would let me on in the first place. But don't you play any more?"

"I never even got to one goal, so I quit. If Will Rogers

and Johnny Mack Brown want to play, that's all right. Will was a cowboy and Johnny Mack was an all-American football player, but the few times I played I had the shit scared out of me. What if I got a broken nose? I'd be driving a taxi, or working as a dress extra. They wouldn't even hire me for that if I had a broken nose."

Charley Simmons looked at him for a moment. "Hubie, you nonplus me."

"What do you mean by that?"

"I'm nonplused. I've never been able to figure you out."

"There's nothing much to figure out."

"There! That's just what I mean. You don't truthfully give a God damn about acting, do you?"

"About being a Barrymore, no. But——"

"I know. It's a good easy living. But what if you did for instance break your nose? What would you *want* to do?"

"You want to know the truth, I think I'd marry a rich woman."

"You have no ambition to do anything else?"

"Direct pictures, maybe. But the directors are all either ex-cameramen or a few writers. You wouldn't give me a job as a director, would you?"

"Till we had this conversation, no. And tomorrow I probably wouldn't. But today I might. You know, you have more brains than you let on. A picture actor doesn't need much brains, but all the same it's a shame to let your brains go to waste, Hubie. God gives brains to very few people. Take me, for instance. Phi Beta Kappa, C.C.N.Y., and

Columbia Law Review. Practised law a few years, then I got greedy. You know, this money was lying on the ground waiting for me to pick it up. But it's not gonna be as easy as it was. I think we're in for some bad times."

"You mean on account of the stock market."

"On account of what the stock market is an indicator of. Don't ask me what caused it. It's too big a problem for me, it's too big a problem for the trained so-called economists. They don't know either."

"Well, I'm sure I don't."

"I'm sure you don't, too, but as long as you don't break your nose you don't have as much to worry about as I do. You see all this? This house, the cars, the tennis court, swimming pool, all these waiters—hey, don't be in such a hurry, Jeeves—I want one of those Bacardis— thanks—I was saying, all this could evaporate in less than two years. I only make pictures, I don't have a chain of theaters and a big corporation behind me. If I got voted out of my job—and I could be—I doubt if I could get a good job with one of the big studios. I made enemies, and I'm making more every day because they don't like to hear the facts of life. So what would I do with myself? I'm out of touch with the law. I could be as big as Maxie Steuer if I'd stayed in it, or a good safe judgeship, life tenure at twenty-five, thirty thousand a year, not bad. But who the hell wants a flop movie producer? I keep telling Mildred, buy half as many dresses and put the money in bonds. Then she says 'What bonds?' and I don't have an answer. But any bond is better than two dresses at five hundred a crack. Five hundred dollars for a dress, and Western Costume won't give you thirty dollars for it. Mildred says I'm too pessimistic."

"Well, you are, Charley."

"Balls."

"You're the smartest man in the business, you'll always have a good job."

"That doesn't follow. Some of the stupidest schnucks in the business have the best jobs, and they're holding on to them. Why? Because Uncle Moe married Aunt Reba. You know what a shegitz is, Hubie?"

"I found out since I've been here."

"Be one. Then you don't have to worry if you break your nose. Maybe they'll even let you direct. You know, I think I'll go up and lie down a while. These cocktails, and the sun, I'm not used to it." He put his hand on Hubert Ward's shoulder. "You're all right, Hubie. You're not a bad fellow."

"Thanks, Charley. Neither are you."

Charley Simmons laughed. "You son of a bitch, you're pretty fresh, though. Well, what the hell? As I said, in two years maybe I'll be glad to come to your house." Now they were joined by Mildred.

"Where are you going?" she said. "They'll be starting to want lunch in a couple minutes."

"They won't miss me."

"Charley, are you drunk for God's sake?" she said.

"No, but I'm not sober, and that's a fact. I'm farther from sober than I am from drunk, and I'm going upstairs and lie down a while." He left.

"How many did he have?" said Mildred Simmons.

"Two, while he was talking to me, but they weren't the first two, I'm sure of that."

"Why didn't you stop him?"

"Oh, come on, Mildred."

"All of a sudden he gets drunk. What was he talking about?"

"Well, he said all this could, uh, evaporate. The house and pool and tennis court."

"Oh. And losing his job, I guess."

"Yes."

"The damned stock market. Do me a favor, Hubie, and don't go around repeating this. You know how those people are."

"Oh, hell, Mildred, he didn't say anything he hasn't said before."

"I know, but he's saying it too often. He's giving himself a black eye, all this pessimism. The important men don't like to hear Charley Simmons talking that way. It gets back to New York. And now getting plastered, Charley Simmons never gets plastered."

"He's not so bad. He'll sleep it off."

"I wish I thought so. Not just the getting drunk. As a friend of mine, did you ever hear any gossip about Charley?"

"Women? No. Never."

"You said it awful quick."

"I didn't even have to think. I never heard a word. In fact, the opposite. Charley is one man in this business you *never* hear that about. It's the stock market, and losing his job. And the sun and cocktails."

"Well, I don't know. I wouldn't mind so much if he played around a little. It gets offered him on a silver platter every day, and they're weak, men. It may be on his mind without him knowing it."

"You're wrong about that, Mildred. I'm sure of it. I'd have heard rumors by this time, a man as big as Charley. And you know who'd start the rumors?"

"The women."

"Right. If a woman was Charley Simmons's girl friend she'd like people to know about it, in Hollywood."

"That kind of a woman, I wouldn't mind. Or like Ruth St. Alban. But Charley could have had much prettier girls than me, and with money. That's what makes me think if it's a woman, it wouldn't have to be one of these picture stars."

"You're getting yourself all worked up over nothing. Man is worried about business and takes a few cocktails."

"I wouldn't let him get away with it. I get propositioned all the time, and if he thinks I'm just gonna sit and take it, I'm entitled to some fun."

"I never thought I'd try to argue a man's wife out of cheating on him, but I am."

"You tried to argue me into it one time. Maybe I should of given you a different answer."

"You said I could scrub your back. I never thought much of that idea."

"Maybe you'd be surprised how quickly I could turn around."

He said nothing.

"What are you thinking?" she said.

He slowly lit a cigarette, blew out smoke before he spoke. "How soon are you going to start lunch?"

"Five or ten minutes."

"Then after lunch, what?"

"I don't know."

"You shouldn't start something you're not willing to finish, Mildred."

"Did I start something?"

"Yes."

"Yes. I started it with myself, too. After lunch you go on up to your room. I'll be there as soon as I can."

"You wouldn't rather drive into town with me?"

"Here is better. I'll meet you, and then I'll go and change my dress. That's what they'll think I went upstairs for."

"But you're going to change more than your dress, Mildred."

"I know, but now I made up my mind."

His boredom vanished, the memory of it vanished. Their private conversations after so many dinner parties had in the beginning excited him, then had ceased to excite him but had given him a larger understanding of her, which created a curiosity that was active without titillation. For several years now they had conducted an artificial relationship, man-to-man conversations between a man and a suppressed woman, and the inevitability of what was about to happen made the conversations seem like preparation. He waited in his room for her, and when she came in she made straight for the windows and lowered the shades.

"Who'll see us? The sea gulls?" he said.

"Too much light," she said. "Another five minutes and I'd have made a pass at Eric."

"He'd have fainted."

"The worst of it was he was talking dirty all through lunch. As if I needed anybody to remind me. Unhook me."

She made all the first moves, and they were thought out and well timed, none of it as though this was their first adventure together. She did not speak until they had finished, and then she said, "How was I?"

"Wonderful," he said, rather surprised by the question.

"Now you know what you've been missing."

"That wasn't my fault."

"It wasn't anybody's fault." She lay back and looked at the silver-starred ceiling. "You want to know something? Every man in our bunch tried to make me. All except Eric, and he doesn't count. You got what they all wanted, does that flatter you?"

"Sure."

"Well, be more enthusiastic, for God's sake. The next time is your apartment. Charley has to go to New York maybe the week after next. If he got good and drunk maybe I could sneak in tonight—but no. No. Week after next, the whole night. You're quite a man, Hubie."

"What the hell did you expect?"

"Not as good. I feel wonderful, I hate to leave. But in an hour they'd miss us, and we don't want to spoil this. This is a laugh, getting all dressed again just to go down the hall. Hook me, will you?"

119

No one missed them, in any case no one among their intimates would have suspected anything after the years of their tête-à-têtes. His reputation was that of any heterosexual young bachelor in the industry, which assumed as custom the right to have as many women as he wanted, so long as public scandal could be avoided. The men in the power group did not trust him with their wives or mistresses or with important actresses for whom they had publicity plans. But Hubert Ward, though untrusted, was believed to prefer the more obscure actresses and completely unknown younger girls, and to be clever enough to protect his associate membership in the group. He slept for an hour, then returned to wander among the guests at the pool.

There were perhaps ten young children in and about the pool. They were of various ages from five to twelve, the youngest in the shallow end and on up to the oldest who were going off the elevated diving-board. Hubert Ward cared nothing about children, but he could identify all those who were swimming, with one exception: an extremely blonde girl, seven or eight years old, who was a stranger not only to him but obviously to most of the other children. The Simmons daughters, who were ten and twelve and fully aware of their father's standing in the industry, came up to Hubert Ward and said, "Hello, Mr. Ward. Do some dives."

"Hello, Wendy. Hello, Charlene," he said.

"Will you? Will you do some dives?"

"I will if you'll stay out of the way."

"We will. We'll make the other kids stay down at the

shallow end." The Simmons sisters officiously directed the children to the far end of the pool, and Hubert Ward slowly climbed to the higher board. This was one of the things he was good at. The board was not of championship height, but it was high enough to repel most of the guests who swam at the Simmonses' pool. He walked out and tested the springiness of the board, waited until the hum of conversation was noticeably diminished, and began with a swan dive, then performed a satisfactory jackknife, and followed it with a one-and-a-half gainer. Applause followed each dive, but after these and his earlier exertions, climbing the platform ladder was too much for him and he called to the Simmons children, "That's all. Show's over."

He took a high-pile towel off the stack near the platform, and went to an umbrella table where there were cigarettes in a crystal box. A young woman was sitting alone at the table and she held up a lighter to his cigarette. "Congratulations. Those were nice dives," she said.

"Thank you," he said. "I don't think I've met you."

"You haven't. I'm Mrs. Stephens, and of course I know your name."

"Mind if I sit down?"

"Please do. I don't know anybody here, and I haven't spoken a word for two hours."

"How do you happen to be here?"

"That towhead is my daughter. We're staying with the Barleys, and Mr. and Mrs. Simmons very kindly let the Barley children and my youngster come over for a swim."

"Yes, I know the Barley children. I don't know Mr. and Mrs. Barley except to say hello to."

"The twain never does meet, does it? Movie people and non-movie."

"Not very much."

"But at least now I'll be able to go home and say I met one movie star."

"You could have met as many as you wanted to if you'd been staying some place else, but the Barleys—"

"Josephine Barley is my sister."

"Thanks, then I won't say what I was going to say."

"I didn't think you would. This way I miss hearing what you people think of my sister and her friends, but I guess it isn't hard to imagine."

"No, it shouldn't be. Where is home, Mrs. Stephens?"

"Chicago. Outside of Chicago."

"Here we call that 'back East.' "

"Yes, even Josephine does. My sister. I should know, but are you a native son?"

"Lord, no. I'm back-Easter than you are. Where I come from you're out West. Northern New Jersey."

"My husband went to Princeton, but I've never really spent much time in New Jersey."

"What does your husband do?"

"He was in the printing business, but he died a year ago. Died in an aeroplane accident. You may have read about it, a transport plane accident in Michigan. My husband and sixteen others."

"I remember. Tragic. Is that your only child?"

"Yes. She's nearly seven."

"She's a beautiful child. Coloring."

"I suppose she'll get darker. Children as fair as she is usually do. But don't let me keep you, Mr. Ward. You have your friends, and I think those children must be waterlogged by this time."

"Oh, I'm enjoying myself."

"Are you? I am, but I don't think you are. Do you work terribly hard?"

"Not really. Why?"

"You only did three dives, but you seem very tired."

"I'm not tired, Mrs. Stephens. I'm just God damn bored. Not at this moment, but when you leave I will be."

"Bored? At your age? Twenty-five? Twenty-six?"

"Exactly twenty-five. Couldn't be more exactly."

"Then why don't you pack up and go away? Go tiger-hunting in India or something like that. And yet—you'd probably be just as bored there after a while. I know."

"*Oh, there you are!*" The voice was Mildred Simmons's. "They said you were doing some dives. How do you do, I'm Mrs. Simmons, Mrs. Charles Simmons."

"This is Mrs. Stephens, her sister is Mrs. Barley," said Hubert Ward.

The possessive hand that Mildred Simmons placed on Hubert Ward's shoulder . . . "How do you do. It's awfully nice of you to let us use your pool."

"Oh, we don't mind, if it gives them pleasure."

"It certainly does that, but I think they've had enough of it for one day." The possessive hand on Hubert Ward's shoulder.

"Give my regards to your sister, Mrs. Barley. Tell her she shouldn't be such strangers, she and Mr. Barley. They can come over and have a dip any time, tell them."

"Oh, I think they impose enough as it is."

"Christmas they sent us—you see that rubber float? They sent that to Charley and I for Christmas. If you're not doing anything tonight, we're entertaining about thirty or forty couples. You and your husband *bring* Josephine and Dwight."

"Well, thank you. I'll tell them. I have no idea what their plans are, but I know they'll appreciate—"

"Just tell them it's nothing formal. If Dwight has his Tux, but some of the men don't all wear Tux."

The possessive hand gripping Hubert Ward's shoulder. "I'll tell them. Thanks again, and goodbye, Mr. Ward. Mrs. Simmons." She gathered the children and departed.

"Kind of a wish-washy dame," said Mildred Simmons. "How'd you get talking to her?"

"She lit a cigarette for me."

"Oh, I know that type."

"The type that lights cigarettes?"

"That supposed to be sarcastic?"

"No, but I'll bet she's the only one here that guesses where we were an hour ago."

"I wouldn't be surprised. Her type—she's probably like Ruth St. Alban, only Ruth at least gets in the hay. This one just goes around lighting cigarettes. Very symbolic, if you know what I mean. Why would she guess about us? Why do you say that?"

"Your hand on my shoulder."

"Do you object to that, considering where else it was?"

"No, but I saw her give us a quick look."

"What do we have to worry about her and her quick looks? But you're right. Charley'd notice that right away."

"You bet he would, and so would a lot of others. Is he awake yet?"

She half smiled. "He *was* awake, but I guess he went back to sleep again."

"Did you put him to sleep, Mildred?"

"You might say that. He woke up when I went in the room. And he's my husband."

"Was he wonderful?"

"He's always good. The little son of a bitch, I just wonder who he's got. But I'll find out. He wants to know will I go to New York with him, and I'm sure he's covering up."

"Do you know why he asked you to go to New York?"

"*I* figure because he has a girl in L. A."

"No. If you want to know what I think, I think he's getting all worked up and he wants you with him."

"Well, he picked the wrong time, didn't he? We can have a whole week."

"Half a week. I start shooting a week from Thursday."

"Well, okay. Tonight I was thinking, what if I said I was going over to Marion's? We could leave here around twelve o'clock and drive into town. If we're back here at five, they'll still be playing cards, Charley and the others."

"What makes you want to take a chance like that?"

"I don't know. I guess because I never took a chance

before, all the time Charley and I been married. But if he wants to take chances, I'm getting as much fun out of it as he is. You know, we'll be married nineteen years in January. January the eighth. And today it was like when I used to live on 151st Street before we moved. I had an Irish cop that I used to love him up in the super's closet, in the hallway. I was a virgin when I married Charley, but with my shape a lot of boys used to want to love me up, and this Irish cop. Certain weeks he was on duty from four to midnight, and I used to tell my people I was going downstairs to my girl friend, to help her with her homework. When I was nineteen I started going to business and I was with the firm when they took on Charley. After that it was nobody but Charley, but I remembered when I used to meet that cop. We shoulda been caught a thousand times but we never were. Terence McGlatty. A no-good Irish bastard when you stop to realize. And that subway, all the way to 149th Street every night, five nights a week. Boys. Young men. Old men. All colors, shapes and sizes. The summertime was the worst, but the winttatime was bad enough, because I was head over heels in love with Charley Simmons, Mr. S. J. Feinberg's new protégé."

"And you're not now?"

"Who said I'm not? But he came to the conclusion he wanted to have a little fun? All right. *I* have a little fun. With me it'll always be Charley. That I guarantee you. But not revealing my age, but I have a nearly seventeen-year-old son. *You* know. Maybe I ought to be thankful to Charley for starting it. Maybe he's doing me a favor, unbeknownst to him."

Hubert Ward laughed. "You make up your mind about a thing, and nothing can convince you otherwise. But you haven't got a single fact to go on."

"That would stand up in court, no. But a circumstantial case, believe me. And woman's instinct."

"Woman's suspicions."

"Show me the difference. What about your Mrs. Stephens? Was that instinct or suspicions?"

"Okay. You win, I guess."

She had not won, in the sense of changing his belief that Charley Simmons was faithful to her. But argument was futile and, in the new circumstances, silly. If she wanted to have an affair, and wanted to justify it by calling it revenge, that was her decision. It was reassuring to hear her say that it would always be Charley, for at the present moment he did not like her very much. He would go back to her again, in hours or in days, but at the moment he did not like her very much at all, and he was glad when she wandered away to sit under another umbrella. He sat alone, with a comfortable feeling of possession of her and of her future availability, and the certain knowledge that in her own interests she would avoid being a troublemaker.

He told a waiter to bring him a fruit lemonade, and he sat in the beach chair with his eyes closed and his legs stretched out, getting the last of the afternoon sun. He opened his eyes when a beach chair scraped the concrete near him, but it was not the waiter; it was Charley Simmons.

Charley was dressed in a white gabardine suit, black

and white wing-tip shoes, dark blue shirt, plain white four-in-hand necktie. He was carrying a newly lighted cigar. "'D you have a swim?" said Charley.

"In and out," said Hubert Ward.

"You don't get much of a view from our bedroom. You can see Santa Monica Bay, but for instance you can't look down and see who's in the pool." He pointed with his cigar. "You see what I mean? Our room is set too far back there. Mildred and I talk about using the roof of the diningroom for a kind of a second-story sun porch. Wouldn't cost only a few hundred bucks, and there's all that roof space going to waste and obstructing the view."

"Yes, it'd make a good sun porch. And that space does go to waste," said Hubert Ward.

The waiter brought the tall glass and stood by.

"What are you drinking, Hubie?" said Charley Simmons.

"This is a fruit lemonade."

"Plain? It isn't spiked or anything?"

"If it is, it goes back. I'm not much of a drinker."

"I'm not either, but—waiter, give me something like Mr. Ward's drink only with Bacardi rum in it."

"This is pretty sweet, Charley. Why don't you let him fix you a Tom Collins made of rum?"

"All right. Bring me that, waiter. A Tom Collins made with Bacardi rum."

"Yes sir." The waiter departed.

"I was asleep and Mildred came in to change her dress. We had a few minutes' conversation but then I went back to sleep again. I had a cup of coffee before I came downstairs. You never smoke cigars, do you, Hubie?"

"Very seldom."

"Ulysses S. Grant was supposed to die of cancer from cigars. I understand he was what they call a dry smoker, never lit them."

"I didn't know that."

"Well, that's what I heard," said Charley. "I don't know much about Grant myself. He had a pretty sad life, I know that much. I never been able to pass judgment on him, whether he was a crook at heart or was just taken by his so-called friends."

"How was he taken?"

"Oh, it's a long story if you don't remember your American history. But *there* was a fellow that was a great general, and then he got to be President of the United States. You'd think when you got to be that high up—but then we had Harding only a few years ago. Grant would have been all right if he'd stuck to the army, and Harding was nothing but a small-town newspaper publisher. What the hell am I doing in the picture business?"

"Well, as Herman Mankiewicz says, making a lousy fortune."

"That's all right for Mank to say. Writers can afford to be wisecrackers. But I could have been something else besides what I am, and my wife and children would have been just as well off. What does Mildred get out of all this crap? And sending my kids to private schools, for what? I got Harold at Lawrenceville and he says he wants to go to Yale. A Jewish Dink Stover I got. I got my girls at a Catholic school, and I said to one of them the other

129

day, 'What's that you're singing?' And she says, 'Macula non est in te.' Macula non est in te, for Christ's sake! Sin is not in you, I translate it. Wendy hates the school, because all that religion around her makes her feel like an outcast. Charlene loves it and says she wants to be a nun. So who wins? I ask you. Wendy's miserable, and Charlene makes *me* miserable. But it's the best school we could get them in. The worst of it is, the whole structure is liable to collapse, and I'll be a forty-three-year-old ex-lawyer looking for a job. I'll go in to see my old boss, S. J. Feinberg, the advisor to kings and presidents, and I'll say, 'Well, Mr. Feinberg, can you use a fellow that knows all about the Dunning Process?' You know what he'll say. His dunning and my Dunning might as well be two different languages."

"Charley, you've just got the blues."

"You never spoke a truer word. Well, here's my drink. Waiter, take this cigar and throw it away some place. When a seventy-five-cent cigar tastes like an El Ropo, I'll have one of these cigarettes."

"Charley, why don't you go away some place? Go tiger-hunting in India, for instance?"

"For a change, you're suggesting? Be a change, all right. Take Clive Brook with me, huh? Him and C. Aubrey Smith and I, on top of an elephant? Hubie, I'll give you credit for *some imagination.* You know what I'd see if I went to India? Millions of half-naked Hindus, bathing in the Ganges River and begging for alms, and every minute I'd be wondering when it's going to happen to this country. I know a fellow, when he gets the blues he has

these two Chinese girls, but that's not my trouble, and if
Mildred ever found out, what explanation could I offer?
I've been to a lot of conventions, and for a joke the fellows used to hide a naked broad in my closet, but that's
at a convention, and I don't have to go to them any more.
I guess if I had a piece of tail with five different dames in
nineteen years I've been married to Mildred—five at
the outside. This is confidential, Hubie. You understand
that."

"Sure."

"It never bothered me. After one experience I always
leave the door open in my office. That was a young kid
that she's a star now, but then she used to think if you got
inside a producer's office you had to give. Big star now,
and one of my best friends. Goes around telling people
I'm the only decent man in the whole business, simply because I only wanted her for a part in a picture, not for a
piece of gash. Doris Arlington."

"You passed that up?"

"I never even told Mildred, but Doris did. She told
Mildred that I was the one guy that could be trusted in
the whole business. No, that never bothered me. I was
never a chaser. I was in this business to make money,
pure and simple. I don't mean that as a gag. But the money
isn't going to be there much longer, Hubie. Pictures are
costing so much more and at the same time the public
don't have the money to spend, so you get less back on a
bigger investment. In plain language, you lose money.
And yet at the same time you don't know which way to
turn. What are they going to want, the public? Stars. The

biggest names. But the *money* you have to pay them—if you can *get* them! And making as few pictures as I do, you can't afford to miss. I'll pay good money for a story by W. Somerset Maugham or Louis Bromfield, and I'll go as high as I can for a star. But I can still have a flop picture, if enough people don't go to the ticket window. And the biggest flop will be me, Charley Simmons. One thing I'll never do is borrow money on my insurance."

"I haven't got any insurance."

"The insurance companies will be the last to go. A lot of banks are going, but you don't read about insurance companies folding up. I carry a hell of a lot of it."

"Well, I haven't got any dependents."

"Oh, hell, you'll be all right. You're young and healthy."

"Yeah."

"Keep drinking that fruit juice, and take your time about getting married. But don't count on marrying a rich dame. There may not be any rich dames, Hubie. This is only the beginning."

"The beginning of the end, you mean?"

"It's no joke, Hubie. Babson, Fisher, I don't care who you read. They don't tell *me* anything good."

"Then I won't read them, and I never heard of them anyway."

"I have to read them, just to torture myself."

"Charley, maybe you ought to just get drunk for a couple of days."

"I'll give that a try, tonight. But I have to be at the studio Monday morning."

"Take Monday off. You're the boss."

"That's just the trouble . . . Well, we got some new customers, and you better get some clothes on. Catch a mean cold down here, and you start shooting pretty soon, I read somewhere."

"Week from Thursday."

"I'll be in New York. Pardon me, Hubie. Ruth and Eric."

He walked away a few steps, then came back and got his drink. He made no little joke about it, he said nothing at all.

Darkness came swiftly, and the poolside activity ended abruptly. Some of the house guests went to their rooms to change for dinner; some lingered downstairs. There was a bridge game going on, and four men were at the billiard table, playing pill pool. This was the hiatus between the day party and the night party that was to come. Servants moved about, removing furniture that had to do with the day party and putting in place the furniture that was appropriate to the night party. They put away towels and chairs and umbrellas, and set up the small tables for the dinner party. With the darkness came dampness, so that no one would sit outside during the night party without spoiling a dress or soaking an evening suit. The servants completely ignored the bridge and pool players, who, if they wanted a drink, had to get it themselves. Hubert Ward watched a hand of bridge, but the players ignored him. He watched the pool players, but he was an outsider to them. For no sensible reason he suddenly felt homesick. He had not felt homesick in five years, and he had no explanation for it now. He had not felt homesick in *ten* years. He had never been homesick in his life, but now, for no reason at all, he wanted to cry. He looked at the intent gamblers at the card and billiard tables. He knew them all, they knew him, and he cared nothing about any of them, none of them cared anything about him. He was a very fortunate young man, twenty-five years old—and then he remembered that it was his birthday and it only made him feel worse.

He went back to the kitchen—which was in the front of the house—and the servants who had started to eat their evening meal stared at his intrusion. "You looking for something, Mr. Ward?" said the butler.

"Yes, Harry. Do you happen to have Mr. Barley's telephone number?"

"Mr. Dwight Barley down the road? I think we may have that, sir. Let me have a look." Harry opened a cabinet drawer and brought out a white leather book. "Bara, Theda," he said. "Barley, Dwight. Yes sir, Malibu 6617-J-3. Shall I write it down, sir?"

"Malibu 6617-J-3. I'll remember it, thanks."

"Very good sir."

Hubert Ward went to the telephone booth under the main stairway and gave the operator the number.

"Barley residence," said a maid.

"May I speak to Mrs. Stephens, please?"

"One moment, sir."

Time passed while the maid apparently found Mrs. Stephens, and there was a click as she picked up the extension. "Hello, who is this?" said Mrs. Stephens.

"This is Hubert Ward. I hope I didn't disturb you."

"I couldn't imagine who'd be calling me."

"Does the name register?"

"Of course. But my sister and my brother-in-law are standing right here, just as mystified as I was. This is my first call since I've been in California."

"Are you coming to the party tonight?"

"Afraid not."

"I see. Your sister made other plans."

"Well, not exactly. It's just that—"

"It's just that if you come here then your sister will have to invite the Simmonses, is that it?"

"I'm afraid you've put your finger on it."

"Come anyway."

"I don't think I'd better, really. No, that wouldn't do at all."

"Please come."

"Why? I'm flattered, but why me especially?"

"Because I'm homesick. Suddenly I got homesick, and I got your sister's number and called you."

"Oh, dear. It's hard to say no to that. I know just how you feel. I've been feeling a little that way. Would you come and call for me when your dinner party's over? And what time would that be?"

"Around ten o'clock."

"I haven't got anything very dressy to wear."

"Borrow something from your sister."

"I can see you don't know her very well."

"To tell you the truth, I wouldn't know her if I saw her."

"Obviously. But I'll find something. Oh, this won't be a very late party, will it? Because we're all early risers here, and I think we have to go to Pasadena for lunch. Do you know the Midwick Club? I'm sure you do. That's quite a distance from here, and my sister's calling to me that we have to be ready to leave here at ten o'clock. Sunday traffic."

"I'll be at your sister's at ten o'clock tonight, and I'll bring you home whenever you say."

"Thank you." She rather sang the words, and hung up.

He came out of the booth and saw the butler, Harry, who was shaking both fists in a fit of controlled rage. "What's the matter, Harry?"

Harry shook his head.

"Come on, tell me."

"Oh—one of those *gentlemen*. Insisted on using the ivory cueball. I told him it was against orders. I'm not to put out the ivory cueball for pill pool. But he insisted, and of course he cracked it. This air down here, and you simply can't use an ivory ball in that sort of game. And now *I'll* catch it from the boss. I'm thinking of giving notice."

"Which gentleman was it?"

"I'll leave it to you to guess, sir."

"Mr. Ziffrin."

"Right the first time.'

"I'll speak to Mr. Simmons, Harry. Don't you worry."

"Oh, it isn't only that, sir. It's everything Mr. Ziffrin does. He coughs up in our best linen, wipes his boots on

136

our hand towels, although there's cloths for that purpose in all the bathrooms."

"I'll say it for you. He's a pig. But maybe Mr. Simmons will get rid of him."

"Afraid not, sir. Not the way I *hear*. Not the way *I* hear. Can I get you anything, sir?"

"Not the way you hear? What do you hear, Harry?"

"Excuse me, sir, Mr. Ward. I've said more than I ought."

"If there's anything Mr. Simmons ought to know—"

"It's not my place to tell him, sir. I'm only the butler. Very sorry sir, but please don't pursue the subject."

"Well—"

"Will that be all, sir? Thank you, sir."

The ground floor was now deserted of guests. The diningroom and livingrooms were brightly lighted throughout and in readiness for the night party. Hubert Ward had a last look around, as though he were the host and trying to see how it would all seem to Mrs. Stephens.

If anyone got up hungry from a meal at Mildred Simmons's, it was his own fault. Tonight the dinner began with avocado stuffed with crabmeat and covered with Russian dressing, and then on to mock turtle soup laced with sherry; filet mignon with sauce béarnaise; whipped potatoes, green beans, and asparagus with drawn butter; hearts of lettuce with Thousand Island dressing, and, for dessert, cherries Jubilee. Champagne was the only wine other than the sherry in the soup, but some of the guests spurned the champagne and sipped highballs throughout the meal. There were thirty-nine men and women seated at four tables of ten, ten, ten, and nine persons each. There was music from a combination of piano, trumpet, saxophone doubling in clarinet, bass viol, and accordion. The accordionist was the leader, and he wandered about, spotting executives and stars and nodding and smiling, the nod and smile quickly followed by the playing of a tune or the theme song from the executive's or star's most recent picture. Barney Morse was the leader's name, and he had a very nice sense of protocol; he would not play tunes identified with absent producers or stars until later in the evening, when it was also permissible to play music from Broadway shows. There was some, but not much, dancing during dinner; a man who fancied himself on the dance floor, a woman who wanted no one to miss her Molyneaux original. Dancing during dinner was not encouraged; it was a time to eat and drink and to find out what could be found out about the industry.

Mildred Simmons knew how her guests liked to be entertained. If there was a sameness to these parties it was because it was what these people wanted. It was a seated dinner, with the place cards held in the bills of crystal penguins. "Oh, I got you again. I had you Thursday," a woman would say to the man on her right, and inevitably the man on her left would make some joke on the wording of her remark. The parties offered the pleasure of the familiar; for the unfamiliar, for surprises, for originality the guests could have gone to other parties, but they seldom strayed from their own group, unless there were others straying from it as well. Tonight, for example, some of

them would go to Marion's in Santa Monica, but not before they had put in an appearance at Mildred's.

Hubert Ward was at the table for nine. On his right
was Ruth St. Alban; on his left, Doris Arlington. "Who
didn't come tonight?" said Doris Arlington.

"I think some fellow from the East," said Hubert
Ward.

"That's right," said Doris Arlington. "From Philly.
Sonny Shaplen, S. S. Shaplen's son. I'm glad we're spared
that. Do you know him?"

"I certainly do."

"All I can say is, he better enjoy himself while his
father's still alive. He sure as hell wouldn't get invited on
his own."

"I know Sonny Shaplen. I think he's nice," said Ruth
St. Alban.

"You have a good word for everybody," said Doris.
"And that's just the trouble, Ruthie. Doesn't mean anything. Try rapping a few people."

"But I like everybody, or almost."

"Yes, I guess you do," said Doris. "Well, I take it back.
You stay the way you are."

"I always see the good in everybody," said Ruth.

"I know," said Doris. She cut out Ruth. "Hubie, you
start shooting next week."

"Week from Thursday."

"I just finished one. What's the picture you're doing?
I know it's about aviation, isn't it?"

"Yes. The Royal Flying Corps. It's called *Destroyers
on Wings.*"

"A lousy title. I hope they change that," said Doris. "Have you got a good part? I don't necessarily mean *big*, but *good*? You know, Hubie, you're going to waste because they don't seem to find the right part for you. There goes Arlington, shooting off her face again, but it's true."

"It's a good part, I think. And not very big. But I always wanted to work with Ken Downey. For action pictures I think he's the best."

"Well, you know I was married to Ken for three years."

"I know."

"And a worse son of a bitch to live with doesn't exist. But he's a genius, Hubie. He's like you. He's been wasted. But some day he'll get the right story. Maybe this is it. You know, Ken was a flyer in the war, and he's always wanted to do an aviation picture. But don't lose your temper. He's a practical joker, and the first couple days shooting he'll play some terrible joke. He calls that testing your sense of humor. The man has absolutely no sense of humor. Well—that's not true. He has a sense of humor. But not like Bob Benchley. I mean Bob has a sense of humor, and so has Ken but a different kind. It's hard to explain, but you'll find out for yourself. Bob Benchley would never do anything that would really hurt anybody, and Ken does. He's very cruel. I think the war did something to Ken. He saw a lot of his friends shot down, and he gives you the impression that he doesn't care what happens. That's one of the things that's held him back in this business. You can't get anywhere with men like Charley Simmons, for instance, if you don't at least make a pre-

tense of taking things seriously. Who's the head cameraman, do you know?"

"Yes. Walter Rapallo."

"Oh, then you have nothing to worry about. They
work well together. Walter's the only man Ken will admit
knows more than he does—about the camera, that is.
About anything else—nobody. Love. Art. Philosophy.
Aeroplanes. Poetry."

"Poetry?"

"Oh, God, yes. Poetry. I used to get so fucking tired
of Ken spouting poetry, and then going out and turning in
a fire alarm or something like that . . . Mr. Ziffrin is putting his cigar in the mashed potatoes again. What do you
hear about Ziffrin and Charley Simmons? I hear they had
a row."

"I don't know."

"Come on, Hubie. Open up. It'll get around sooner
or later."

"I honestly don't know anything. I didn't even know
they'd had a row."

"What do you and Mildred talk about, besides who's
screwing who?"

"That's about all, I guess."

"Did you ever screw Mildred?"

"No. And would I tell you if I had?"

"Not in so many words, but I might be able to tell by
the way you answered."

"Well?"

"I'm not sure. I'm not sure you did, and I'm not sure
you didn't. If you haven't, take my advice and don't."

"Why?"

"Not that I give a damn about Mildred. But I'm very fond of Charley, and he's been very good to that woman."

"What about you and Charley?"

"I offered it and was turned down. Everybody knows that."

"Well, I heard that, but would you offer it again?"

"No. Heavens, no. If I had a brother he wouldn't be as safe with me as Charley is. But sometimes I worry about Charley. Tonight, why is he getting plastered? The row with Ziffrin? I'd ask him, but I don't think he'd tell me. There's something going on. A lot of men, including some here tonight, are getting sore at Charley for being so pessimistic. About conditions, I mean. They wish he'd shut up. And I guess I do, too. You don't put out a fire by pouring gasoline on it, and Charley's one of the few educated men in this business. He isn't only U. S. Films, Incorporated. The things he's saying, if the *Wall Street Journal* got hold of them, stocks in every company would collapse. This is the third largest industry in the whole United States, or the fourth. Third or fourth, it doesn't do any good to cry the blues that way. Do you think it does?"

"No, but I don't know much about that. I don't put my money in stocks."

"I wish I hadn't. Not that I don't like working. I'll never stop as long as I can get a job. But, boy, I took a shellacking in the market. Twice, not just once. From now on, annuities and government bonds for little Doris. And bridge with my friends that haven't caught on to contract. Do you know what I did the last time I was in New York? I was there for two weeks, and I had ten lessons from Ely and Josephine Culbertson. I wish Mildred played bridge. I'd love to take some money away from her. How about you, Hubie? Would you like to start a game after dinner?"

"Not with somebody that just took lessons from the Culbertsons. Half a cent a point is my limit."

"Oh, then I withdraw the invitation. Joe Ziffrin. He'd play for a nickel a point, and he fancies himself. Our hostess is signaling to you."

Hubert Ward turned around, but Mildred was not looking in his direction.

"She gave up," said Doris. "I don't know what she wanted. Be independent, Hubie. Make her come to you."

"That's what I'm going to do."

Doris looked at him and half smiled. "You know, I'm still not positive, but I *think* you and Mildred. I only said I *think*."

"Lay off it, Doris. You could start something where there *is* nothing."

"Oh, if you only knew how many times *I've* said that, in those very same words. I fooled Ken Downey with that line for six months one time."

"I'm not trying to fool anybody."

"And you're not, Mr. Ward. Not little Doris. But I'll keep my suspicions to myself. I'll do that for Charley, not for Mildred, or even you. Oh, shut up."

"I didn't say anything."

"You were going to."

"You won't mind if I see if I have better luck with Ruth—conversationally, that is."

"Oh, with Ruth you don't need luck as far as anything else is concerned. But of course you found that out a long time ago. No, go right ahead. I'll see what I can extract from Eric."

Ruth St. Alban was at least a simple chatterer, and for the remainder of the meal she held forth on the subject of her diet, which was guaranteed to slim you down without leaving wrinkles, owing to a high calcium content. At the end of dinner the women went upstairs, and the men sat around the tables as they were being cleared. Hubert Ward made his way to Charley Simmons's table.

"Hello, Hubie. You don't have a drink. Take a Benedictine frappé. It goes good after a heavy dinner."

"No, I'll have some coffee, that's all."

"Sit here next to me before Joe Ziffrin gets a chance. He's maneuvering his way over, and I got nothing to say to him. Who'd you sit next to tonight?"

"Doris on the one side and Ruth on the other."

"I hear Doris just finished one for Paramount that's going to make her bigger than ever, if that's possible. That's a real woman, Doris. If she'd of been a man and maybe just a little education, she could be the head of any studio in town."

"They say that about Mildred, too. Practically that."

"What they say about Mildred is that half my brains belongs to her. That's a little different. That's the same as if you said teamwork. But Doris is a lone wolf type of operator. And not saying anything against Mildred, or de-

144

tracting in any way, but Mildred isn't as good as Doris when it comes to judging people. That's because she had it tougher all the way, Doris. Chottie Sears and Doris Arlington would be my pick if I were asked to name the two brainiest women in town, but Doris I know better. I don't see as much of Chottie, so that leaves Doris. Mildred is mixed up in this business because *I* am, but Doris is strictly pictures. Strictly. She has a good story sense, she knows camera work, and she could cut a picture if she had to. And pictures are her life, and not just her living, if you know what I mean. She likes the men, all right, but the men come second with Doris. She arrived at the point a long time ago where no man is as important to her as her career. I wonder what would have happened if she and I got together that time. It's interesting to speculate that. She was awful pretty then. She grew into a handsome woman, chic. But if I would have screwed her that time, there was something very appealing to the kid. The brains I didn't know about till later. But what if I fell for her then, and then the two of us pooled our brains? We could have changed the entire history of this town, the entire industry."

"Probably. Charley, will you excuse me? I have a date that I'm bringing back here. You're all right. Ziffrin's got an audience."

"Who's your date, if I may ask?"

"She's Mrs. Dwight Barley's sister. A young widow named Stephens. I said I'd pick her up at ten o'clock. And Charley, I know you're not drunk, but go easy."

"I can't *get* drunk, Hubie. Not that it's any your

business. I just stay the same. See, that's the difference between those sweet rum drinks and whiskey. The rum knocked me, but the whiskey has no effect."

"Famous last words," said Hubert Ward.

"I appreciate your good intentions, but don't start taking liberties, Hubie. Go get your date."

Dwight Barley and his wife were reading magazines, and Hubert Ward, when he rang the doorbell, could see the Barleys simultaneously removing their reading glasses, with Barley the one who came to the door. It was an ugly yellow house, more suitable to a New Jersey seashore resort than to Malibu, California, but so was Dwight Barley. He was wearing a tan gabardine jacket and grey flannel slacks, polka-dot bow tie, and plain white buckskin shoes. "Good evening. You're Mr. Ward? Will you come in?"

"Yes, good evening. I've met you before—"

"Well, I didn't think you'd remember. Come in, my sister-in-law will be down in a minute. I'd like you to meet my wife."

"I've also met Mrs. Barley."

"Oh, yes indeed," said Josephine Barley. "Sit down, won't you? Nina will be down any minute. She had to borrow an evening dress from a friend of mine. Nothing of mine would fit her, of course."

"How about a drink, Mr. Ward? What would you like? We have whiskey, gin, and brandy. And tequila."

"Not a thing, thanks. I'm not much of a drinker."

"That's a load off my mind," said Josephine Barley. "I had visions of Nina left all by herself at a movie celebrity party."

"You underestimate your sister's attractiveness."

"Not a bit. It's just that I *know* Nina, and her shyness among strangers. And I suppose all the big stars will be there, they usually are, aren't they?"

"No."

"They're not? Who is, then?"

"Big stars, but not all of them by any means. A lot of them are never invited to the Simmonses'."

"Oh, then there's an inner circle, you might say?"

"Very much so. A lot of big stars would give a year's salary to be invited to the Simmonses'."

"Oh, dear. There's that much prestige? I didn't realize that. I didn't realize that at all. I thought all movie people more or less went around together."

"No."

"Then tell me, Mr. Ward," said Barley. "How do you get admitted to this inner circle? I mean, why are some in it and some not?"

"It's hard to say, exactly. I'm not a big star. There are lots much bigger, but I was invited to these people's parties before I realized that—well, I was like Mrs. Barley. I thought all movie people went around together. But we had the same thing at home."

"Where was home, Mr. Ward?" said Josephine Barley.

"North Montclair, New Jersey. There were some people that belonged to the club, and some that didn't."

"Oh, you're an Easterner?" said Josephine Barley.

"Very much so. I'd never been west of the Delaware River till I came out here. Chicago was practically the western frontier, to me."

147

"Oh, *really?*" said Josephine Barley.

"Do you mind if I ask you—well, an impertinent question. But is Hubert Ward your real name?" said Dwight Barley.

"No," said Hubert Ward. He paused just long enough for them to begin to triumph. "My real name is Richard Hubert Ward. Why?"

Barley was quick to recover. "If it comes to that, my name isn't Dwight Barley. It's Timothy Dwight Barley, but I stopped using my first name long ago. Timothy Barley—if you know anything about farming. I could have been called Timothy Alfalfa Oats Barley. In fact my nickname in college was Farmer."

"Where did you go to college?"

"I went to the University of Michigan, at Ann Arbor."

"And before that, Exeter," said his wife. "Where did you go, Mr. Ward?"

"Well, I went to Andover for a while, but I didn't last very long. I didn't go to college at all."

"Oh, you went to Andover? I broke my leg in the Andover game. You're too young to have been on that team—"

"Not only too young. I never went out for football."

"It's a great game, Ward. You learn things on the football field that last you through life."

"Not anything I wanted to learn."

"Well, of course you were going to be an actor."

"No, I was going to be a banker. That's what I was headed for. But my father fixed that."

"Why? What did he want you to be?"

"A banker. But he did a little high-powered embezzling."

"Are you joking?"

"No. I wouldn't joke about that. He got caught, and he shot himself."

"Is that true?" said Barley.

"You're a businessman, although I don't know what business. But you could find out without much trouble. And you probably will, so I'm telling you myself."

"Why do you say I probably will? Frankly, I had no such intention."

"But I'm hoping to see more of Mrs. Stephens than just tonight, and I'm sure you and Mrs. Barley will want to find out all you can."

The Barleys looked at each other, each willing to let the other make the reply. Josephine Barley accepted the duty. "My sister's returning to Chicago next week, so I guess that won't be necessary, Mr. Ward."

"Maybe not. But now you know that much, at least. Ah, here she is."

"Hello," said Nina Stephens. "You were late, so I won't apologize for keeping you."

"Very pretty dress," said Hubert Ward.

"Borrowed, but I'd like to buy it from the owner. Maybe if I spill something on it she'll be willing to sell it cheap."

"*Nina!*" said Josephine Barley.

"Now I don't mean it, Josephine. Well, are we ready?" Nina Stephens looked at her sister and brother-in-law and frowned a little. "Yes, I think we're all ready. I left a note in the kitchen to be called at half-past eight. Is that early enough, Josephine?"

"Yes. Goodnight."

"Goodnight, Nina," said Dwight Barley. "Mr. Ward."

"Goodnight, Mrs. Barley. Mr. Barley. The bank was in Newark. Newark, New Jersey. His name was Sanford Ward. Goodnight."

In the Lancia, even before he started the engine, she said, "What was that all about? You didn't hit it off, I could tell that. I always know when Josephine doesn't approve of somebody. And Dwight, too. Not that they were going to receive you with open arms anyway. If you don't belong to the California Club, don't expect much cordiality from my brother-in-law. He says that's the only place where he meets his kind of people. And he may be right."

"Well, it isn't the only place, but I know what he means." Hubert Ward reported the gist of the conversation as he drove slowly to the Simmons house. She was silent throughout, and when they stopped at the house she made no move to get out of the car.

"This is where we get out," he said.

"I'm not so sure," she said. "I only met you this afternoon."

"I only met *you* this afternoon."

"My sister is quite a bit older than I am, and she's been very worried about me. She insisted on my coming to California because—I wasn't—I was taking too long snapping out of it. My husband's death. If you don't mind, Mr. Ward, I think you'd better take me back."

"But I do mind. I mind very much."

"Please. Get me a taxi. Or there must be one of these chauffeurs that will take me home."

"You know damn well I'd take you home, and not any taxi or somebody else's chauffeur. But you also know damn well . . ." He stopped abruptly, the thing that happens when an idea is so new that it has never been confined by words.

"What?" she said.

"I don't know, Nina. I don't know. I said more to your sister than I can say to you."

"You said much too much to my sister."

"Yes. I did. But what I said I meant. I do want to see you more than just tonight. I don't want to see anyone else. I never want to see anyone else. And I've never said that before, to anyone."

"There's an explanation for that. An easy one." She waved her hand in the direction of the house, brightly lit, music coming from the diningroom at the other end. "I'm not a part of that, and you told me this afternoon you were bored."

"Yes, that's the easy explanation, all right. But give me credit for thinking of that one myself. I did. But it wasn't enough, not good enough."

"Evening, Mr. Ward? Park it for you? You want me to cover it for the night?" said the Simmons chauffeur.

"No thanks, Leonard. We're not ready to get out yet."

The Simmons chauffeur went away.

"We could talk about this inside. Your shawl isn't much protection from this damp air, and I'm told the dampness raises hell with a permanent wave. You'll spoil it for Pasadena tomorrow."

"I don't give a *damn* about Pasadena tomorrow. Can we talk inside? We *ought* to talk, so that there'll be no misunderstanding."

"Although I know what you're going to say."

"Yes, I guess it's pretty obvious."

"You're going to tell me that we're not going to see each other again. But Nina, you're not going to mean it. I *know* that. You can't mean it, because at least some of what's happened to me has happened to you, too. I believe that as much as I believe in God. Or more. If I'm wrong, tell me, and I'll turn the car around and drive you home."

"No, you're not wrong."

"That's all I want you to say now. Let's go in and I'll show you the animals in the zoo, and when you get tired of them I'll take you home."

She turned to him and smiled.

"You know, that smile was as good as a kiss," he said.

"Strange man," she said. "Nice, though. In some ways."

He had not prepared her for the stares. Other men, and he himself, had brought an occasional bit player and non-professional to parties of the group; and from time to time there would be visitors from the worlds of Los Angeles, Pasadena, and Santa Barbara, three worlds in one outside world. But Nina Stephens, whom some of them had seen in the afternoon (and mistaken her for a new governess) was now stared at with hostility. The actresses were sure she would not photograph well; the non-acting wives noted the absence of jewelry and the dress that was a "Ford"; the men thought she might be some German actress whom an agent would bring to their offices on Monday. One non-acting wife said she understood the young woman was Hubie Ward's sister. One man said he had laid her two weeks ago in the most reputable Hollywood brothel, and he thought Hubie Ward had a hell of a nerve to bring her here.

"Let's find our hostess," said Hubie Ward.

But their hostess found them. "Good evening, I'm Mrs. Simmons. I met you this afternoon, didn't I?"

"How nice of you to remember," said Nina Stephens.

"Mrs. Stevenson? Did I get it right?"

"Without the son. Stephens."

"I hope you told Dwight and Josephine. Are they coming, or maybe they're here."

"They have to be up very early, but they asked me to thank you and could they have a raincheck."

"I bet it was Dwight that said that, not Josephine. Slang."

"No, I think it *was* Josephine."

"Well, make yourself at home. Drinks are over there, and if you get hungry, just tell the waiter. The buffet won't be ready till around twelve." Mildred left them.

"She never said a word to you," said Nina Stephens. "I don't think she's very happy about your bringing me."

"I don't think she is either."

"I guess no more need be said about *that*," said Nina.

"I guess not."

She smiled at him again. "We've gotten pretty far in a very short time."

"Yeah," he said. "I was thinking the same thing."

"And with not much said. We're going too fast."

"Not for me."

"For me, though," she said.

"All right, we'll slow down. Just as long as I can be with you, that's all I care about."

"I recognize a lot of the women and a few of the men. But who are the others?"

"Producers. Directors. And their wives. And some wives and husbands of the men and women you recognize."

"This is Hollywood society, I take it?"

"Yes."

"When does the excitement begin?"

"The biggest excitement will be around four o'clock in the morning."

"What happens then? A naked girl comes out of a cake?"

"Sorry to disappoint you. No, the biggest excitement will be in the poker game. They'll raise the stakes, and play stud, and maybe some guy will have a possible straight flush. Something like that. And you'll see a pot go to, oh, fifteen or twenty thousand dollars. Maybe more."

"I know people that play for that much in Chicago."

"Well, that's the big excitement in this group. I grant

you that all these men have been to parties where the naked girl comes out of a cake. And plenty more than that goes on. But not at these parties. And I guess some of the women in this room have been the girl that came out of the cake. But not any more."

"Mrs. Simmons looks as though she might have been a madam. Maybe I shouldn't have said that, but was she?"

"She'd love you for that. No, she was a stenographer in her husband's law firm, before he got in the movie business."

"*There's Doris Arlington!* Oh, do you suppose I could meet her? Is she going to hate me because I came with you, like Mrs. Simmons?"

"No. Doris and I were never that way about each other. I'll get her to come over. She's looking for some suckers to play bridge."

"Doris Arlington playing bridge? Don't disillusion me. And she's good?"

"Yes, and she's been taking lessons from the Culbertsons. She saw me wave. She's coming over."

Doris Arlington slunk over to them. "Hello. I'm Doris Arlington. I see Hubie's not introducing you around." Doris sat beside Nina.

"I'm Nina Stephens."

"How do you do," said Doris. She lowered her voice. "Hubie, Mildred and Charley have had a knock-down-and-drag-out. I thought I ought to tell you."

"Where is he?"

"I haven't seen him for about a half an hour. I think he may have gone upstairs."

"Will you talk to Nina while I go look for him?"

"I'd be most happy to, but are you sure you want to do that? I'm not sure it's wise."

"Were you there when they had the fight?"

"At the beginning. She told him to stop swilling the booze and then they went out in the hall and closed the door behind them. Then she came back, but I haven't seen him since. So I guess he retired to his bedroom. It was a bad one, I'll tell you that. She came back and the first thing *she* did was have a great big rye highball. 'If he can get drunk I guess I can too,' she said."

"And you haven't seen him for a half an hour."

"Nobody has, at least nobody in this room. He completely disappeared."

"He doesn't want to have to talk to Ziffrin."

"This wasn't about Ziffrin."

"How do you know?"

"Those two wouldn't fight that way about Ziffrin. I'd stay out of it if I were you."

"I know what you're trying to say, Doris, but I'm going to find Charley. Excuse me, Nina? I'll be right back."

Hubert Ward went upstairs and knocked on Charley's bedroom door.

"Who is it?"

"It's me, Hubie Ward."

The door was opened. Charley Simmons did not wait at the door, but walked to a chair, beside which, on the floor, was a whiskey bottle. He had a highball glass in his hand. "Shut the door," he said.

"What is there I can do, Charley?"

"You've done it. Thanks."

"What are you talking about?"

"Don't make me throw up. Mildred told me."

"Told you what?"

"Yeah, I got her mad enough and she told me. She thinks I have a woman some place, so today she had her man. You. I don't have a woman. But she *thought* I did. She wouldn't ask me. No. No, she wouldn't ask me. That would have spoiled her excuse. Well, Hubie, you and her talking dirty God knows how many years, you finally got her in heat. Something to see, isn't it? Now you know why I never wanted anybody else for nineteen years. But now I don't want her either. Now she's nothing but an ugly woman with a shape, and all the fancy things you told her and she read about and maybe I told her. Yeah, maybe I told her too. But I don't want any more of it, Hubie. You help yourself. Not that I blame you. If it's there, grab it. But do me a favor. Pack your God damn bag and don't sleep here tonight. Go on downstairs, join the party, and I don't even care if you take her with you. But no more screwing my wife in my house. I have enough trouble. Go on, beat it, Hubie. Get out, out, out, out, out of my sight. And don't stay here tonight."

"What are you going to do? Are you going to divorce Mildred?"

"I don't know what I'm gonna do. We got the kids to consider. Stover at Yale, and the daughter that wants to be a nun, and the one they didn't spoil. I don't want you to spoil her, too, Hubie. And you would. You're the kind that would. You can't help yourself. I know *all* about you. All about you. Marty Ruskin told me all about you a long time ago, Hubie. So go away, will you?"

"I'm sorry, Charley."

"Yeah, I wouldn't be s'prised. But you stink, Hubie. You honest to God stink." He picked up the bottle and poured whiskey to the top of the glass.

"I agree with you," said Hubert Ward. "Charley, Doris is worried about you. Do you want me to send her up to talk to you?"

"I'll be a son of a bitch. Do you think I'd let Doris get mixed up in this stinking mess? No, you wouldn't understand how I feel about Doris. Do you know what I think about Doris Arlington? Married three times? In six hundred beds? The straightest woman in Hollywood. The only one. The only one that's on the level. You wouldn't understand that. And neither would your mistress, Mrs. Charles Simmons. Go 'way." He looked at the glass and started to drink, and he did not see Hubert Ward.

Doris Arlington was engaged in chatty conversation with Nina, but when she saw Hubert Ward she stopped.

"How is he?"

"He's in very bad shape. But if he finishes the drink he just started he'll pass out. Straight whiskey, a highball glass full."

"I think I'll go up."

"No. Don't," said Hubert Ward. "I said don't, Doris. He doesn't want you to. He said so."

"Me in particular?"

"You in particular."

"I want to help him."

"Tomorrow, but don't go up there tonight. I won't let you."

"*You* won't let *me?*"

"Cut the movie-star stuff, Doris. You don't frighten me a bit. The best thing for him to do is pass out, and he's ready to. Let's go out and get a breath of fresh air. Come on, Doris. You come with us."

"No."

"Come on, the three of us. Clear the brain before you start your bridge game."

"All right," said Doris Arlington.

They went out together and walked toward the pool. He lit cigarettes for the women and for himself. "Maybe I can get a towel and dry off a couple of chairs. Wouldn't you rather sit out here a while?"

"Not after what you said about the dampness and my permanent," said Nina.

"Let's just finish our cigarettes. Standing that long won't hurt us," said Doris. She looked up toward Charley Simmons's bedroom windows. "I hate to think of him up there, all by himself, feeling lousy."

"He's probably passed out," said Hubert Ward.

"He was telling me earlier, he's going to make a sun porch of the diningroom roof," said Doris.

"Yes, he told me that this afternoon."

They all looked toward the diningroom roof, imagining a sun porch, then Nina spoke: "There's someone up there."

"Sh-h-h," whispered Doris. "Do you see who it is, Hubie?"

"Yes."

"Don't make any noise," whispered Doris.

They made no move or sound as they watched Charley Simmons, walking unsteadily, staggering now and then, now and then stopping to look out at the sea. He was in evening shirt and trousers, without the jacket, and they could see him plainly. And slowly they began to hear him. "We can put the God damn wuddia-call here. Here, we'll put the God damn, the God damn umbrella." He was talking to himself.

"He's getting close to the edge," whispered Nina. "Can't we stop him?"

"He'll be all right if he goes back, but we mustn't startle him," whispered Doris.

"Put the God damn railing—" they heard him say, and then he took a step and toppled forward. He stayed still where he fell, on the concrete terrace. They ran to him, but he remained frozen in the same position and did not answer them because he could not. "Don't move him," said Nina. "Don't touch him. I think his neck is broken, but he may be alive."

Doris shook her head. "No, but we can get a doctor."

"I'll get a doctor," said Hubert Ward.

"Send someone out with a blanket," said Nina. "He *may* be alive. But we mustn't touch him. We could do just the wrong thing. Ah, the poor man. It's Mr. Simmons, isn't it?"

"It *was* Mr. Simmons," said Doris. She stood and stared down at him, and on an impulse Nina Stephens put her arm around Doris Arlington's shoulders.

"It was so quick," said Nina.

"For him, not quick enough."

"We couldn't have stopped him," said Nina.

"I guess not. And even if we had." Doris Arlington put her hand to her lips and made the gesture of throwing a kiss to the figure on the concrete.

"Were you in love with him?" said Nina.

"No, girl. I was better than in love with him. He was somebody I really liked."

Suddenly five or six men and women burst out of the house, Mildred Simmons among them. "Where is he? Where is he?" she shouted. Then she saw him on the concrete, ran to him and knelt, and drew him up, and his head rolled of its own weight.

"Mildred, don't! His neck!" said Doris Arlington.

"I hope he *was* dead," Nina whispered to Doris. "He has no chance now."

"Here's a blanket," said a man.

Mildred Simmons held her husband to her bosom and rocked from side to side. "Poppa, poppa," she repeated. She looked in the faces of the people gathered around, from one to another, but gave no sign of recognition, not even to Hubert Ward when he appeared.

"There's a doctor on the way, he's staying at the Lewises', and the sheriff's patrol are getting an ambulance," said Hubert Ward. It was an announcement more than a message to Mildred. He went over and stood beside Nina Stephens, and now Mildred followed him with her eyes, but kept rocking from side to side with Charley's head crushing her breasts. Now there were more

161

people, and again more, speaking softly but creating by their number a steady muttering.

"We can't do anything," said Hubert Ward to Doris Arlington. "I'm going to take Nina home."

Doris Arlington nodded. "Yes, you ought to," she said.

From the edge of the group someone said, "Here's the doctor," and it was repeated by others.

"Let's wait," said Nina. People crowded in front of them and they could not see or hear the doctor, a thin young man in a dinner jacket. Then they saw him stand up and they heard a wail from Mildred, and now the others, no longer speaking softly, uttered words of comfort.

"Shall we go now?" said Hubert Ward.

"Yes," said Nina.

They walked through the house and Hubert Ward told a boy to bring his car. "Would you mind waiting in the car? I won't be long."

"All right," said Nina.

He went up to his room and put his clothes in his bag and returned to the car. He tipped the boy, and drove out to the road. "It's still quite early," he said. "It's only a little after eleven. Shall we go for a drive? Put my coat on and let's drive somewhere."

"All right," she said.

They drove toward Santa Barbara, the first ten miles in silence. "Are you warm enough?" he said.

"Yes, are you?" She was huddled in his polo coat.

"Yes."

"You don't have to talk," she said.

"Thanks," he said. "I just don't want to be alone."

"I know."

"And I suppose you know why."

"It isn't hard to guess," she said. "But don't talk, unless you want to."

"All of a sudden I do want to. Will you let me?"

"Yes."

"And not hold against me anything I say?"

"I won't promise that."

"You don't think much of me, do you?"

"If I say no, you won't talk, and I think you ought to talk. It'll be better to talk to me than to somebody in the movies."

"Quite the opposite. You're the only one whose opinion I give a damn for."

"You mustn't think that. This is your life, and I'm leaving here in a few days. I'm going back to where I belong, and you're staying here. Their opinion is very important in your life."

"There's nothing important in my life except you. Whether you like it or not."

"That will pass. Everything does. Nearly everything."

"I slept with Mildred Simmons just once. That's all."

"Well, now the coast is clear . . . I'm sorry, I shouldn't have said that. I don't know any of the circumstances, and I don't want to know."

He was silent.

"Listen, you don't owe me any apology. I mean explanation."

"The strange thing is that I feel that I do. For that and everything else I've ever done that you wouldn't approve of."

"We're going too fast again, and you're driving too fast, too, by the way."

"Sorry."

"I'm getting out of your life and you out of mine—tonight."

"No!"

"Yes. I've been married, I have a child. And some day I expect to marry again. But until then I don't want to have anything messy."

"Have I suggested anything messy?"

"No, but what you wouldn't consider messy, I do. No matter how you'd dress it up, or even if I dressed it up, it would still be messy."

"Would you consider marriage messy? To me?"

"I haven't even known you twelve hours, half a day. Don't speak of marriage. Yes, that kind of marriage *would* be messy. When I was married it was for life. My husband was killed, but the next time I marry will be for life, too. Anything else I consider messy."

"Staying married can be messy, too."

"Not very often. That's the Hollywood idea. When it's unpleasant or uncomfortable, or inconvenient, you get a divorce. No wonder you have so many divorces, if that's the way you enter into marriage. It shouldn't be that way. You shouldn't admit that you may be making a mistake. As soon as you have any doubts you should break the engagement."

"You were lucky. You happened to have a good marriage."

"It wasn't all luck. The trouble is people leave too much to luck. They get married and then trust to luck. They should be sure in the first place."

"Do you go to church?"

"Of course I go to church. And not just on Easter. I go two or three times a month. Sometimes oftener."

"You're not a Catholic, are you?"

"Heavens, no. What ever gave you that idea? I'm an Episcopalian, and very Low Church. Are you Catholic? I went to school with a girl named Ward and she was Catholic."

"No relation, I'm sure. No, I'm nothing. I was christened an Episcopalian but I was never confirmed."

They were silent again until he said to her, "Are you asleep?"

"No."

They were driving with the top down and the windshield wiper was swinging back and forth. The arc it made was the only clear area on the glass; the rest was as untransparent as if it had been frosted.

"It looks like a pendulum, the windshield wiper. The clock of life, time passing much more quickly than we realize," she said.

"Yes, I see what you mean," he said.

"That man tonight, I feel as though I wanted to apologize to him."

"Why?"

"Several reasons. My lack of feeling, for one. I ought

to be feeling more than I do, to see a man take a wrong step, and a second later he's dead. All life has gone out of him. A drunken man, walking on a roof, talking to himself. Do you know what's so terrible about it?"

"What?"

"I'm almost ashamed to say this. But I've seen the same thing in comedies."

"Two-reelers, yes."

"There's a Jewish comedian with a big nose, I can't think of his name."

"Jewish comedian with a big nose."

"A long nose. A nose like an ant-eater, almost."

"Larry Semon."

"That's his name! Do you see what I mean? This man tonight was like Larry Semon. He even looked a little like him. I must have seen hundreds of comedies of people walking off roofs."

"Yes."

"Stepping off into space. Except that usually someone pulls them back."

"By the seat of the pants."

"Or else they almost fall but not quite, and then they look down and realize how high up they are. That's all I can think of."

"It would give Charley a laugh."

"It would?"

"Yes, I think it would. He had a sense of humor, and I guess—I don't know."

"What?" she said.

"Well, it's sort of grim humor. But Charley was a big

166

shot, one of the biggest. And it's kind of ironic, a big shot in pictures ending up doing a pratfall. I can't laugh about it, God knows. But it's ironic. It's like—I don't know. As though Tom Mix got kicked to death by a Shetland pony."

"And those who live by the sword shall perish by the sword," she said.

"I guess so, yes. Charley Simmons never made any comedies, of course."

"But he made movies, and I never have taken them seriously."

"God knows *he* did. Especially the last few months. He took the whole world seriously."

"Was he nice?"

"Was he nice? Yes, he was nice. I always liked him. He didn't like me."

"Naturally."

"No, that wasn't why. I only slept with her once, and that was—so recently that—no. He didn't like me, because big shots, the Charley Simmonses and the big directors, they're the real big shots. Actors and actresses are better known to the public, but when the big shots crack the whip, we go through the hoop. We're cattle."

"I see. And for the same reason *you* don't like *them*."

"I guess that's true. Except in the case of Charley Simmons, I damn near had a friend. I don't know *why* he began confiding in me, but lately he did. Maybe because I wasn't a big shot. I guess that was it. The things that were worrying him, he didn't dare confide in another big shot, because when he tried to talk to them they got sore. Charley was in trouble that had nothing to do with

Mildred or me. Charley was worried about the world."

"I don't believe that people worry that much about the world. I think when they worry about the world they're really worried about something inside themselves."

"You happen to be right in his case. He was fed up with picture business, and secretly he wanted to go back to practising law. He was a lawyer. A Phi Beta Kappa. And he was never at home in Hollywood. You hit it right on the nose, at least in Charley's case."

"Where are we going?" she said.

"We're headed toward Santa Barbara, but we don't have to go there. I'm just following the highway. Are you cold? Shall we stop and get a cup of coffee?"

"No, your coat is very comfortable."

"It's very unusual, too. It's ready-made. And it's three years old. In fact, it's a polo coat that I've worn on the polo field. A very unusual coat."

"Belonging to a very unusual man."

"I don't know how you meant that, but you're right there, too. I am a very unusual man." He held out his wrist. "Can you see what time it is?"

"It's ten past twelve," she said. "Why?"

"I can relax. My birthday is over."

"Was today your birthday?"

"Yes. I was twenty-five. It's supposed to be an important birthday, but I hardly thought about it all day. I had a lot else to think about."

"Why do you say you're a very unusual man?" she said.

"Because I am. Take the opposite of an unusual man, and you've got Dwight Barley."

"And my husband, if you mean conventional."

"I mean conventional. And that's what you like, isn't it?"

"Decidedly."

"Because you're a very conventional woman?"

"Decidedly."

"But you're not, you know."

"In every conceivable way," she said.

"No. You've made yourself that, but you've done too good a job. The conventional women are Doris Arlington. Ruth St. Alban."

"Was she there tonight?"

"Yes. Why?"

"I heard some story about her, when she was stopping over in Chicago one time. A boy I know was introduced to her. Oh, it was one of those messy things. But how can you say they're conventional?"

"Because they're dying for respectability. They love all the excitement and publicity, but every time they fall for a man they always say this is the real thing at last."

"You were saying something like that yourself, earlier this evening."

"I know. That's why I understand these women. I'm a very unusual man, but that doesn't say I'm not fed up. If we'd stopped for a cup of coffee, the man behind the counter would recognize me. All the other customers would recognize me. We'd get special attention, and then I'd be expected to put down five bucks for two hamburgers and two coffees, forty cents' worth of food. Five dollars, keep the change. Live like that a few years and the novelty wears off. And they'd all stare at *you*."

"As they did tonight."

"Yes, but in a diner some son of a bitch would decide to make a play for you, just to show off. 'Hey, Hubert Ward, introduce me to the girl friend.' And because they didn't recognize you they'd think only one thing."

"That I was a chippie?"

"Yes. Write your own script. If I had a fight, it'd get in the papers and maybe I'd be sued. If I didn't fight they'd all call me yellow. And you'd think I was yellow for not protecting you. If I try to do anything interesting, or worth-while, they say it's to get publicity. If I don't do interesting or worth-while things, I'm just another movie actor. No brains. No taste. You see, I'm not big enough yet to be allowed any independence. If you were going to be staying here, and had dates with me, I'd hear from the studio."

"Why?"

"They'd say, 'Lay off that society dame, Hubie. Start taking Sandra Stafford out.' Sandra's in my next picture. Publicity."

"Well, do you like her? She's pretty."

"Very pretty—and living with a press agent named Murray Bax, who happens to be a friend of mine. I was in a picture with Sandra and I made an honest play for her till Murray wised me up. He's separated from his wife, back in New York, and living with Sandra in Laurel Canyon."

"Sounds primitive."

"Laurel Canyon? It isn't. It's all culture in their house. Thousands of books. Symphony records. Socialist magazines. I'd take her to the Grove, drive her home, and then Murray and I'd sit and talk till it was time for them to go to bed. Next day in the papers, Sandra Stafford and Hubert Ward at the Grove again. So if you read about Sandra and I having a big romance, that's the romance. By this time the columnists know about Sandra and Murray, but they print it anyway. And laugh at me because they know I'm not getting anything."

"You're not getting anything? Oh."

"I'm not even getting a goodnight kiss."

"But all the actresses aren't living with Murray Baxes."

"Thank God."

"I see."

"Don't be haughty about it."

"Not haughty. Just conventional."

"What do you expect me to do?"

"I expect you to find some Sandra Stafford that isn't living with a Murray Bax."

"Well, that's what I *do* do."

" 'Do do do, what you done done done be-fore, baby,' " she sang.

He laughed. "I love you," he said.

"Just as soon you didn't say that," she said.

"Oh. All right," he said.

There was a brief silence, and then she said, "I guess we ought to think about turning around."

"All right," he said. Expertly he made a U-turn without slackening speed, and they were headed toward Los Angeles. He began to whistle the Gershwin "Do-Do-Do," and he continued to whistle it without being aware of it. For ten minutes he whistled it.

"I have that record, played by George Gershwin himself," she said.

"What record? Oh, 'Do-Do-Do.' I didn't know he made a record of it," he said.

"It's a piano solo. Columbia, I think."

"Is that so? I must get it."

"It's not a new record, you know."

"Oh, I can get it through the studio. You can get anything through the studio."

"How convenient. A Sandra Stafford without a Murray Bax?"

"Oh, that's no problem. I'll look around and see who they have under contract."

"They put them under contract, do they?"

"Seven years."

"They must be worn out after seven years."

He laughed. "And you call yourself conventional! That's the kind of a crack you'd *never* hear from Ruth St. Alban."

"Thank you very much. I'm *sure* you intended that as a compliment."

"Why of course."

"Are we having a quarrel?"

"Of course not, Nina. How could anyone quarrel with you? How could anyone *any*thing with you? Have you read a book called *A Farewell to Arms,* by Ernest Hemingway?"

"Yes, he comes from Chicago."

"At the ending he says something about it was like saying goodbye to a statue."

"I remember. It was—"

"With you it's like saying hello to a statue. No, we're not having a quarrel. Me, a dumb movie actor? I don't want to mislead you. I read the book because I'd like to play the part of Lieutenant Henry."

"I'm sure you'd be very good."

"So am I, but I'm not a big-enough dumb movie actor."

"You will be."

"That man we saw killed tonight. Charley Simmons."

"Yes?"

"He knew all about me, and he kept it to himself. The kind of things he knew about me would have kept me out of that crowd. They're all up from nowhere, those people. But they're *up.* I'm not up. Only part way. And there are some that are farther up than I am, much farther, but they never made it with that crowd."

"I don't follow you. What are you leading up to?"

"I'm not sure. Not even sure if I'm leading up to *anything.*"

"It has something to do with Mr. Simmons not telling what he knew about you."

"Yes. And with his state of mind. And with my being a dumb movie actor. I wish we could drive all night and I could talk to you."

"I'd like to help you, but that's impossible."

"I know."

"But do you want to stop for a little while and talk?"

"Would you let me? I won't make a pass at you, I promise you that."

"I know that."

He stopped the car at the edge of a town, under a street light. He got out and opened his bag and exchanged his dinner coat for a tweed jacket that latched at the throat.

"You were cold?" she said.

"A little." They lit cigarettes, and then, beginning with the suicide of his father, he told her truthfully the story of his past ten years. He talked for more than an hour. They were interrupted by a deputy sheriff in a car.

"You folks in trouble?"

"Just talking," said Hubert Ward. He handed his driver's license to the sheriff.

"I thought I recognized you," said the sheriff. "You did right to park under a light. We had some lover's-lane stickups this past month, you probably read about. Tell you, Mr. Ward, if you just want to talk I suggest about a quarter mile down the road you can park in front of our headquarters and nobody'll bother you there."

Hubert Ward started his car and followed the sheriff, who waved to him and drove off. "A nice cop," said Hubert Ward. "Where was I?"

"You had talked yourself into a job in a play. Ruskin got you a room in a hotel."

He resumed the story and continued until he was

able to summarize his motion picture career with the naming of the pictures and the stars he played with, his acceptance in the power group, and the onset of restlessness and boredom. "And tonight one of the nicest guys in the whole business is dead. I don't know how much of it is my fault. Probably a lot."

She made no immediate comment. She smoked her cigarette. "Most of this was confession," she said. "But the only part you seem sorry about is Simmons and his wife, and that's the only part you skipped over. You had an affair with her. That is, you slept with her just once. That must have been very recently."

"Yes."

"And that's the only thing I want to ask you about. When did you sleep with her?"

"Yesterday afternoon."

She nodded. "Yes. I guess I could have told that. She was very possessive. And she had every right to be, after being faithful to him all those years. But I don't think you'd better see her again, unless you plan to marry her."

"I don't plan to marry her. I told you this messy story because some day I hope to marry you."

"I realized that, halfway through it. Called making a clean breast of it. Heaven knows there was no other sane reason for painting such an ugly picture of oneself."

"No, nothing anybody else says can top what I've told you."

"What a strange way to express it, but I guess that's theatrical language."

"It is."

"You make me long for the humdrum life of suburban Chicago. The only trouble is, it isn't so humdrum, not when I think of some of my friends. And maybe it could have happened to me. If Wayne—my husband—had ever been untrue to me, I don't know what I'd have done. If he had been I'd have been so desolated that I couldn't have gone on living—but you do go on living, and I've known girls like myself. Terribly in love with their husbands. Then the husband makes a slip, and the girl almost seems to have been waiting for that one slip, to give her an excuse. Naturally I'm thinking of one in particular. And what an unholy mess she's made of her life. For five years she'd hardly dance with anyone but her husband, and then she discovered that he'd had an affair with an art student. You'd hardly call it an affair. Two weekends on his boat with a friend of his and another art student. But it was enough, and who am I to judge?"

"In this case, you *are* the judge. You're the whole works. Judge and jury. I told you about myself so that you *would* judge."

"Hubert Ward, you told me about yourself so that— you sort of tied my hands. You disarmed me. You make it impossible, or tried to make it impossible, for me to judge you without making me seem like a prissy old maid."

"No, that wasn't my intention."

"Well, maybe it wasn't your intention. Possibly it wasn't. But that's the effect. You've made a full confession of all the bad things about yourself, and therefore

I'm supposed to be lenient. But you've been or done just about everything that in my opinion constitutes being a complete son of a bitch. The last time I used that expression was about a gangster that poured gasoline all over a horse and set fire to it."

"Good company you put me in."

"No, you're not in that company. Just happens I don't often swear. Anyway, telling me all about your sins and peccadillos, you came very close to bragging several times. And no penitence. No penitence except over Mr. Simmons. Even the Catholics are supposed to feel sorry when they confess. I got that from your namesake, the Ward girl."

"Well—there I am."

"I know. And you're putting it all up to me. Do I see you again, knowing all about you? Or don't I? I'm afraid the answer is no."

"Okay, Nina," he said. He started the engine, which was set low in the chassis and gave off a heavy sound.

"I'm sorry," she said. "But you know I'm right. We're worlds apart."

He put the car in gear and eased it forward. "You don't have to say any more," he said. "As a matter of fact, I don't want to hear any more."

"You won't listen if I talk?"

"This windshield folds down. If I fold it I couldn't hear you even if I wanted to."

"Not if you went fast, but if you went slowly."

"But we're not going to go slowly. I'll have you home in a half an hour."

"All in one piece, I hope."

"Don't worry about my driving. I've only killed one person, so far."

Neither spoke again until he drew up to the Barley house. They got out and she took off his polo coat and handed it to him. "That was a horrible thing to say," she said.

"What?"

"That you've only killed one person."

"You've been thinking about that all the time?"

"Yes. Goodnight, and goodbye."

"Goodnight and goodbye it is."

"*Just a minute, Mr. Ward. Young lady.*"

They turned in the direction of a flashlight beam.

"Magruder, coroner's office. Few questions I'd like to ask you relative to what happened tonight." Magruder turned his flashlight on a badge in a leather case. He put the case back in his pocket, and directed the beam at their faces. "All right if we go inside?"

"Why can't we talk out here?" said Hubert Ward.

"We'd be more comfortable inside, but as far as that goes, Ward, I have a car here and we could go all the way into L. A. I was making it easier for the young lady and yourself, but that's the way you want to be, suit yourself."

"Let's go inside," said Nina.

"You're more sensible," said Magruder. "I've been waiting here for three hours, and I don't mind telling you, it was no pleasure. You're Mrs. Wayne Stephens, the sister of Mrs. Dwight Barley. First name Nina. Age twenty-five. Occupation, housewife. Widow. Home town, Lake

Forest, Illinois. Maiden name, Nina Parsons. Ward, I got everything on you I need. Shall we go in?"

The questions were deceptively simple but numerous, and Magruder wrote the answers slowly in a notebook. Then he began to ask the same questions over again, phrased slightly differently, but apparently essentially a repetition of the first examination.

"Are you trying to trap us?" said Hubert Ward.

"What makes you say that, Mr. Ward? Why would I want to trap you?"

"Into giving different answers," said Hubert Ward.

"Nobody's trying to trap anybody here, but why did you ask me that question?"

"Listen, Magruder, obviously you asked Doris Arlington all these questions, and then you asked us and you got the same answers."

"Why are you so sure I asked Doris Arlington the same questions? Or any questions? You been in communication with Miss Arlington?"

"You know damn well I haven't."

"I'm an officer of the law, Mr. Ward, and you don't have to swear at me. As it happens, there's one or two things about this death tonight, if we don't get satisfactory answers, this thing could drag on for weeks, making headlines. On my recommendation to my boss, this thing could be kept open, depending on his decision in the matter. Nobody wants that, do they? All right, you just let me do my work my own way, will you? We don't have Philo Vance in our office. Just fellows like myself, trying to protect the public and doing a pretty fair country job of it. If we don't find any suspicious circumstances, it's accidental death. But if it isn't accidental death, I don't have to tell you what the papers will make of it."

"They will anyway," said Hubert Ward.

"How can they? We saw him fall, and he was killed instantly," said Nina.

"Mm-hmm. All right. Let's go over one or two of these things once again. The last thing you heard Mr. Simmons say was something about the railing, putting the railing somewhere. Can I have that again, Mrs. Stephens? Just remember it the way it was, don't try to repeat what you told me. We're all human and memory plays strange tricks."

Half an hour later Magruder closed his notebook, put it in his inside breast pocket, and gently slapped his coat above the pocket. "I guess that will do it, for tonight anyway. Understand you were planning to go back East next week, Mrs. Stephens. Your sister said."

"Yes, can't I go?"

"I don't think there'll be an inquest. I think you can count on going. We'll let you know definitely some time tomorrow. Thank you for your cooperation, but you know how these things are? We have to weigh every morsel, every scrap."

"I know, Mr. Magruder. I know. My husband was killed in an accident."

"Yes. I didn't want to bring it up, but I knew that. This is certainly a nice place your sister has here, and Mr. Barley. You know I had a brother-in-law played football against your brother-in-law. My brother-in-law played guard for Minnesota. Two games they were in against each other. Mr. Barley and I got talking, but I knew he wanted to go to bed or we'd have been here all night, swapping stories. Very nice fellow. Well, goodnight."

They saw him to the door, and watched his car light up and drive away. "There were two of them. Magruder and someone else."

"Yes. Why?"

"I don't know. I never even saw his car, did you?"

"No."

"I'll bet they've been wondering where we were."

"I'll make you some coffee," she said.

"No, never mind, thanks. I've caused you enough trouble. You realize your name is going to be in the papers. The Chicago papers."

"I was wondering about that."

"It's not going to be so easy to shake me, Nina. You'll find out when you go back to Chicago. They'll all want to know how you happened to be there with Doris Arlington and me, just when Charley fell. You said we were worlds apart. We're not any more. You'll find out."

"I think you exaggerate. But let me give you some coffee."

"All right. God knows, I don't want to go."

She went home to Lake Forest on schedule, and a week later she wrote to him. "You were right," she wrote, in part. "I don't mind so much for myself, but the other children, in all probability encouraged by their mothers, continually ask my daughter for details concerning Hubert Ward . . . My own friends have taken to 'kidding'

181

me about Hubert Ward, but behind the 'kidding' are implications that I do not like. There is no doubt but that some of them believe that I was a very different person in California from the one they know here. I don't know which are worse—the men or the women . . . Have you started work on the aviation picture?"

Their correspondence was regularly spaced: a letter from him would be answered a week later by a letter from her. Each letter had to be to some degree a reply to its predecessor; the contents of both were chatty and superficial, and expressed nothing of what he or she might be feeling. They were self-conscious about intimacies. She admitted that she looked for his name in the Hollywood gossip columns, and the first break in the regularity of their correspondence occurred after several of the columns reported that he was having a romance with Patricia Stanford, the English actress who was making her American debut in *Destroyers on Wings*. Hubert Ward heard nothing for two weeks, and he found that Nina's letters, which of themselves had begun to bore him, had nevertheless become a part of his life. He guessed the reason for her silence, but he could not tell Nina that Patricia Stanford was nothing in his young life. Patricia Stanford was not quite nothing in his young life. She had willingly cooperated in the studio's suggestion for a publicity romance with Hubert Ward, and she had immediately assumed that she was to go through all the motions of an affair. She was not at all reluctant; she had come to Hollywood with his name on her private list of four or five actors whom she would rather like to sleep with. For his part she was beautiful and easy, and her manners and speech distinguished her from the pretty and easy American girls he played around with. But he discovered that she was fascinated by scatological humor, particularly jokes about flatulence and uncontrollable bowel movements, which she exchanged with members of the camera and stage crews in a spirit of intestinal democracy. The technicians laughed with her, but when she was not looking they laughed at her and made the gesture of pulling the chain. Hubert Ward was delighted when she was compelled to break a date with him for a legitimate reason. "Nobody breaks dates with me," he said, and the affair was terminated, to the unhappiness of neither party.

He had not gone to the gatherings of the power group after the death of Charley Simmons. He had stayed away from Charley's funeral on advice of Doris Arlington. "Maybe you'll be criticized, Hubie," said Doris. "But maybe you won't even be missed, there'll be so many there. And it isn't worth taking a chance."

"What chance?"

Doris took a deep breath to keep from losing her temper. "The chance of Mildred seeing you and making a scene. Mark her down as an enemy, because that's what she is. I'll never forget her holding Charley squashed against those tits of hers, and staring at *you*. She's gonna blame you the rest of her life. Stay away from her—unless you're in love with her, which you're not."

After the convenient ending of the Patricia Stanford affair he had an impulse to see Doris Arlington.

"What for?" said Doris. "I'll be glad to go out with you, Hubie, but strictly Platonic. I have somebody."

"Hell, I know that. I hear he's part Cherokee."

"All right. Thursday night. Pick me up around eight."

"Beverly Derby? I'll have to reserve a table."

"Not if you come in with me you won't, but all right."

They ordered dinner after Doris had made her entrance and distributed graciousness. "I hope you're not taking me out in the expectation of pumping me about Ken. How are you getting along?"

"Fine. No practical jokes so far."

"Lulling you into a false sense of security. You go on location on this thing, don't you?"

"We have a week at the ranch, for some exteriors."

"Will you be coming home nights, or are you staying out there?"

"We're staying out there six nights."

"Don't be surprised if you find a snake in your bed. If I were you I'd carry a pistol."

"I do anyway, in costume."

"Well, if you come across a snake in your bed shoot the God damn pistol, empty it. Then Ken will think *you're* a little crazy and he'll go easy on the jokes."

"I'm glad I didn't try to pump you."

"Oh, that was just a friendly warning. I'll *talk* about Ken Downey. What I hate is being pumped. Anyway, it's usually women that try to pump me about him. Let them find out for themselves. I did. Now, what's on *your* mind?"

"You're so smart."

"You bet I am. Is it Mildred?"

"I haven't seen her or heard from her. I think she's in New York, I read somewhere."

"She is. Charley's estate, and seeing the boy at Yale. She'll be gone for another two weeks. What about this English dame, Stanford? I met her the other night and she told a story I wouldn't tell to a plumber. And it was that kind of a story. I don't go for dirty stories much anyway, maybe because everybody expects me to have a repertory of them and I never remember a one. I'm more practical about that. If I want to go to the bathroom, I go. And if I want to go to bed with a man, I do. But I don't collect stories about it. I mean jokes. I have plenty of stories, but they're true ones, actual facts. I know one about you, now that I think of it. Did you get in bed with Ruth St. Alban one night and it turned out to be her maid, not Ruth?"

"Yes."

She imitated Ruth St. Alban's voice and enunciation: "'He was expecting *some*body to be there, and I was just *so* tired but I *couldn't* disap*point* him. So I asked Lottie if she'd mind, and she was *thrilled*.' If I were a man I'd prefer Lottie, too."

"I knew the difference right away."

"It makes me wonder, how many guys have thought Ruth was wonderful with the lights out and it was Lottie all the time."

"None."

"How are you and Lottie since then? How did it affect her manner toward you?"

185

"Oh, she gives me a little smile when nobody's look-ing, and I smile back."

"Have you ever gone back for a retake, on purpose?"

"No."

"You draw the color line?"

"Lottie has a boy friend, I think he's a middleweight. Anyway, a prizefighter. Ruth really oughtn't to tell that story, because the boy friend's very jealous. Lottie made me promise not to blab, and I never did. I guess I could go back for a retake, or could have. I wouldn't now, and anyway let's change the subject."

"What's the matter? There's something eating you."

"It's something I don't know anything about, a new experience for me. I may be falling in love."

"Am I privileged to know this unfortunate creature?"

"The girl we were with when Charley broke his neck."

"A non-professional. She went back East, didn't she? Chicago or some place? I thought she went right back."

"She did. I haven't seen her since that night. Spoken to her on the phone, just before she left. And we've been writing letters once a week or so, but that's stopped."

"Then let it stop. She's too good for you. You shouldn't take a girl like that out of her kind of life, away from her friends, and dump her into this place. And that's what it would be. Marriage or nothing with her, if I'm any judge."

"Good sound advice."

"What if you told her that you'd laid a colored girl?"

"I did tell her just about everything else."

"The truth? I've heard that you've been a bad boy, Hubie."

"You mean in my past?"

"Oh, nothing lately, if you don't count having an affair with Mildred Simmons."

"Not admitting anything, Doris, but Mildred is surely old enough to take care of herself. If she had an affair with anybody, she knew what she was doing."

"I agree with you. I was sore at you, but who am I to judge?"

He smiled.

"Well, who is anybody to judge, after all?" she repeated.

"That isn't what I was smiling at. Not the idea, but the words, the question. The girl I'm in love with said exactly the same thing when I gave her my life history. She also said I was a complete son of a bitch."

"You didn't get anywhere, is my guess."

"Did I sleep with her? No."

"What about her husband? Or did I read in the paper that she was a widow? Yes, I did. She got children?"

"A little girl, six or seven years old."

"Money, probably."

"Probably. Not poor. It takes money to live in Lake Forest, doesn't it?"

"It did, I don't know if it still does. Of course the rich aren't as rich as they used to be. I just lent two thousand bucks to a man that a few years ago used to spend easily that much in a month, just calling me long distance. I'll never see it or him again, but he spent plenty on me, and not just jewelry. He used to take me to Saratoga, Palm Beach, the opening night of the opera. Kind of a chump in a way, but a nice chump. A gentleman. He knew all those Whitneys and Wideners, and he never gave me any of that horseshit about marrying me. He was single. But I realize now that he wasn't as rich as the people he went around with. He was having a high old time spending capital, and quite a bit of it he spent on me. So I let him have the two thousand and he got all choked up over the phone. He said he'd pay me back five hundred a year as soon as he got a job, but I know when that will be. Never. You've been pretty careful with yours, haven't you?"

"Yes. Still paying a hundred and fifty a month rent. I spend a little on clothes, but not like Georgie Raft or Menjou. I have no servants. I don't need any. Don't drink, don't gamble. One car, I bought second-hand from a writer out at Warners'. His wife wouldn't ride in it. She said it looked as if a steam-roller ran over it."

"It does. She's right."

"A fine Italian car. If I have to go some place in a limousine I hire one, and half the time the studio pays for it."

"And you have no family."

"I have a family, but they won't have me."

"Yeah, I understand. In Hollywood that makes you— unique I guess is the word. I never knew anybody else out here that didn't have a family payroll. Your people must really have it in for you. What have you got? Your father was in prison or something?"

"He committed suicide. I have a mother and a married sister, and an uncle. And a lot of cousins, some rich."

"In other words, you're the black sheep. Think of that. I was the black sheep, too, but I was allowed to return to the fold. The minute I signed a contract they all moved to the Coast. My mother, my father, two brothers and their wives, my sister, and my grandfather that since died."

"And they all went on the payroll?"

"Like hell they did. I said I'd rent them a house in Van Nuys, but if they wanted to eat they had to work. Not a nickel from me. They soon got tired of all living in the same little bungalow in Van Nuys and the men went out and got jobs. Best thing I could have done for them. I support my mother and father, but the boys are working and my sister opened a beauty parlor in Pasadena, and now *she* has a husband that *she* supports. I hardly ever see any of them. Once in a while a friend of theirs wants to visit a studio, and as long as it's some lot where I'm not working, I arrange it for them. I give them a hundred bucks apiece at Christmas, and the hell with them. My old man keeps a scrapbook, and gives it to me for Christmas every year. Clippings about myself. Schallert, Parsons, Harrison Carroll. You'll be in it this year, on account of Charley Simmons. My mother bakes cakes for weddings and anniversaries in the neighborhood. She charges a little extra because the cakes are baked by Doris Arlington's mother. A hell of a recommendation for a wedding cake, if they ever stopped to think. But they're all right, my family. They came here to sponge off me, and I said nuts to that. When I ran away from Spring Hill, P-A, at the age of sixteen, they didn't even bother to get the cops after me."

"Who did you run away with?"

"You won't believe me."

"Sure I will. Who? Tell me?"

"A trombone player in Sousa's Band. He came from Spring Hill and he was home on vacation, and I had my first high heels. Black lisle stockings. Middy blouse and skirt. Took me out to the picnic grove and I got exactly what I was looking for. I followed him to Chicago and then he left me. He didn't walk out on me, but I couldn't travel with the band."

"Didn't your family know you'd gone away with him?"

"I didn't go away with him. I followed him. No, I never made any trouble for him. Karl Botzhoffer. Romantic name, wasn't it? But he was a looker. I used to see his picture in ads for trombones, but I think he must have died. I asked about him on the set one day when they had a lot of musicians, and they all seemed to think he was dead. All the brass section recognized his name right away. Karl Botzhoffer. Sure. Well, he started me out in my career."

"I thought Griffith discovered you."

"That's the story. But Karl Botzhoffer discovered me, in the picnic grove in Spring Hill, P-A. Tender memories. Mickey Neilan gave me my first job, and then D. W. discovered me. That is, he gave me a small part. Harry Zimmermann was the first to put me under contract. I hear Harry's in hot water. Some Eastern writer is suing him for sixty million dollars for plagiarism. Or six hundred million, I don't know. Harry shouldn't read so many books.

He'll read a book by Theodore Dreiser or Sherwood Anderson or one of those, and then a week or two later he has a wonderful idea for a picture. Tells it to Martha Kensington and Joe MacDuffie. They write an original around the idea, Harry buys it for the studio, gets a kickback from Martha and Joe, and lo and behold, they have a big new picture on the way. A Harry Zimmermann Production, no less. He gets away with it most of the time, but one of these days some writer is going to sue for an *accounting,* instead of just taking five or ten thousand in settlement. And then Harry'll really be in trouble, because no studio wants any outsider to have a look at their books."

"How do you know all these things?"

"I like money, and the things Ken used to tell me about studio finances would curl your hair. If you keep your ears open and look dumb you can learn a lot, too. Parties at Mildred and Charley's, my house, the rest of the crowd. You knew Joe Ziffrin was getting Charley's old job."

"I thought he was out."

"People thought so because they thought Mildred would vote her stock against him. The trouble with that was, Mildred has no stock. U. S. Films, Incorporated, had options to buy back Charley's stock if and when he died. And they exercised that option. So Ziffrin snuck off to New York and London and talked to the principal stockholders, and in a week or two you'll see the announcement. Poor Charley must be spinning."

"How do you know this?"

"My part-Cherokee, as you call him. He was talking to his people in London yesterday and they happened to mention it. Then he happened to mention it to me, so I called my broker this morning. I expect to make a nice little profit."

"How about if I bought some?"

"I advise against it. You never play the market, do you?"

"Not so far."

"Don't start now. I bought some U. S. Films stock because I had a good tip. And I'm going to be told when to get out. But you won't know when to get out, and I won't tell you. Playing the market isn't only knowing when to buy. It's knowing when to sell. Stay out of it, Hubie. I don't want that on my conscience."

"All right."

"And don't blab about Ziffrin. There have been rumors, but only a few know he went to London."

"You're a hell of an advisor."

"I know. You wanted to be told to marry this girl, and you want to get rich quick in the market. Well, if you want me to, I'll pay for the dinner. I don't want you to be out four dollars, poor boy."

"It'll be closer to eight, with the tip. And now where do we go?"

"Do you want to come back to the house and gab for a while? What time are you on the set?"

"Tomorrow, half-past seven."

"Means you get up at six."

"Five-thirty. I'll drop you at your house."

She signed some autographs, he signed some but fewer, and he drove her to her house. He walked to the

door with her and she put out her hand. "Thanks, Hubie,
I enjoyed myself," she said.

"So did I, to tell you the truth."

"We could be friends. It might be very good for both
of us."

"But if you said come in, I'd come in. And if you said
stay, I'd stay."

"Well, I should hope so. But I'm not going to say it,
now or any other time. On that basis, will you take me out
again soon?"

"Sure."

There was a flashing moment of opportunity, but it
passed. She looked away from him. "Goodnight, Hubie,"
she said, and turned her back.

"Goodnight, Doris," he said.

She closed the heavy door firmly and he went back to
his car.

Sometime during the next two or three weeks—one
day, one afternoon, late one night, early one morning—the
actors and the camera and stage crews on the set, and then
the people who did not ordinarily go on the set, and then
the studio, and then a goodly number of the men and
women who made their living in motion picture production, and friends of assistant directors, and waiters at the
Brown Derbies, and dealers in second-hand foreign cars,
and high-priced prostitutes, and some of the writers of the
chatter columns, and Vine Street astrologists, and Mildred
Simmons, and a one-legged man who sold newspapers,
and a Catholic priest in a poor parish in downtown Los

Angeles, and Barney Morse, who played the accordion at stylish parties, and Philip W. Carstairs, who was conducting a school for acting in a bungalow on North Cahuenga, and Martin Ruskin in an office in the Bond Building in New York City—they all began to hear the very first hints that a miracle was happening on the set of *Destroyers on Wings*. No one was saying much; it was too early to tell; and the rumor was actually a hundred small rumors, not yet generally known or talked about in large gatherings or talked about very much in person-to-person conversations. Sometimes the rumor consisted of a single sentence: "They say watch out for a performance Hubert Ward is giving in Ken Downey's picture," and ended there.

But people began to want to go on the set; actors from other studios as well as men and women on the lot; make-up men and women, writers under contract, agents of other people in the *Destroyers* company. "How it got around I don't know," said Ken Downey. "But let's keep the bastards the hell out of here. And that includes you, Eddie."

Edmund Greenhill had directed a few pictures before becoming a supervisor. "I have no desire to interfere, not the slightest," he said. "Put up a sign if you wish. Visitors barred."

"That's what I don't want to do if I can help it. That's announcing it."

"Well, you're not asking me to have Murray Bax spread the rumor that Ward stinks. That I won't do."

"That I'm not asking. Just discourage the front office

from dropping in, and tell Murray no interviews till we're finished shooting."

"That's easy enough. Personally I hate the son of a bitch and always did, but if you're getting a picture out of him . . ."

"It's not only me, Eddie. I hate *all* actors, not just Ward."

"That's what I thought."

"And this prick isn't really an actor, but here we go again, the unbeatable combination, the actor for the part. Ward has sense enough to realize that I can only do so much, and after that it's up to him. To play a shitheel, a real yellow-belly, the actor has to let go. He can't hold back and protect himself, so the people in Peoria will know he's only acting. If he does that, he might as well step out of character and wink at the God damn camera. But Ward isn't holding back. He's playing the shitheel that he really is, as if he just discovered he was a shitheel."

"I could have told him that a long time ago."

"It wouldn't have done any good. He had to discover it for himself, and maybe be a little proud of it. Maybe that's it, I don't know. But for instance yesterday, the officers' mess sequence, where Norman Travis gives him a punch in the mouth and he doesn't fight back. I said to Ward, 'Now, Hubie, we're going to come in on you and hold on you for ten seconds. Ten seconds, that's a long time. And you're holding your hand to your mouth. I don't want you to take your hand away from your mouth and look at the blood. We'll do that later, but for ten seconds it has to show in your eyes, that you're a coward and can't *make*

195

yourself fight back. All the other pilots have seen you take a punch, and they're waiting to see what you do.' He stopped me. 'I know, I know, Ken,' he said. 'Just let me do it.' So he said he was ready and we began to roll. He got up from the floor, holding his mouth, and I held on him for sixteen seconds. And I'm going to use it all. One take, and it was perfect. Absolutely perfect. He got everything in it I wanted him to, and more. The shame and the *pain*. We faked the punch, of course, but you won't know that when you see it. You'll think Norman really punched him, not because of the action, but because of what goes on inside that face. I wonder if this guy can ever do anything else? I doubt it, but he won't have to. They're going to remember this performance for a long time."

"I guess maybe you're right. Norman was in to see me."

"I knew he would be. He's been trying to talk to me, too, but I won't let him. He wanted Ward to play the yellow-belly, and now he's got him. The troublemaker is Stanford. Norman, all he cares about is top billing and the most money, but Stanford wised him up about Ward. She's an actress and she's sore at Ward for giving her the air. She knows Ward's going to walk away with this opera, and I think you'd better have a talk with *her*. She's bad news, that dame. I'll tell her off when the picture's finished, but you better talk to her now, today."

"What shall I tell her?"

"Just say to her, 'Listen, you English cunt, you stop fucking around with Ken Downey's picture.'"

"You can just hear me saying that."

"You know, the funny thing is, it might work."

"Maybe, but *I* couldn't say it to her. I honestly couldn't."

"I know. But you can get the idea across to her that Hollywood money is very nice, and she's a long way from stardom. Her first American picture, and could be her last."

"These are things I *can* say."

From the earliest public exhibitions of the picture there was never the faintest doubt that *Destroyers on Wings* was a hit. The dogfights between German and Royal Flying Corps planes, the heroism and horseplay of the gallant young pilots, and the romance between Norman Travis and Patricia Stanford (as the Canadian athlete at Oxford and the daughter of an English lord, respectively) were highly satisfactory to the audiences in Glendale and Long Beach; but the astonishing tributes to *acting* by Hubert Ward as a cowardly weakling confused the studio. Comments on acting were rarely made by the Glendale and Long Beach audiences, and when made they usually referred to performances by character actors, horses, and dogs. "Hated Hubert Ward but it was good acting . . . Hubert Ward a good actor . . . Good acting by Hubert Ward . . . For acting give me H. Ward. Makes others look like an amateur . . ." The comment cards from the Glendale and Long Beach theaters were not strewn about the theater lobbies; an abnormally high percentage of the audiences wrote on the cards and registered their critical convictions by dropping them in the baskets hopefully provided for the purpose.

"What I always said about Hubie Ward," said Harry

Zimmermann, now a maker of bread-and-butter Westerns at RKO. "A fortune for the studio that put him in the right part."

Eddie Greenhill telephoned Hubert Ward after the Glendale and Long Beach previews. "If you don't have an engagement tomorrow—next day, come have luncheon with me in my office?"

"Fine, Eddie. Tomorrow?"

"Good. Excellent. Excellent, Hubie."

"Eddie?"

"Yes, Hube?"

"Now is it all right for me to drive my car on the lot?"

"Why, of course, Hubie. I'll issue instructions."

"No. Just countermand the old ones, that said I *couldn't* bring my car on the lot."

"You'll have a special place of your own, with your name on it. Just say where you want it and it'll be there tomorrow. Now don't make it too tough, Hubie."

"How about next to the bootblack's stand?"

"That's reasonable. I was afraid you were going to want Norman Travis's place, and that's in his contract."

"Oh, I wouldn't do that, Eddie. I'm not a star yet."

"A mere technicality now," said Greenhill.

Luncheon began with caviar and champagne and Greenhill's disappointment that Hubert Ward did not like caviar or champagne. "But you go right ahead, Eddie," said Hubert Ward.

"Well, being's it's open," said Greenhill. "I hope you like filet mignon."

"I do."

198

"That's what I ordered."

"And what do you want me to do, Eddie? Why am I here?"

"You can be blunt, all right. Well, why not? No use beating about the bush, they say. Hubie, New York is beckoning to Hubert Ward. It's in your contract you have to go, but forget that. You been in the business long enough now that you can foresee that the studio's going to renegotiate your present ticket. We want you happy and content."

"I know. And my present contract expires in January. We're on the last option, Eddie. Which is why you didn't mind putting me in *Destroyers on Wings* as a miserable shitheel."

"Well, did it turn out good or did it turn out bad? Results are what you have to take into consideration, Hubie. This lot is where they gave you your best role of your career."

"Accidentally. And my worst, one after another. I never got the girl if there was a big star in the picture. And if I got the girl it was never anybody like Doris Arlington or Ruth St. Alban."

"Be big, Hubie. Be big, don't be picayune. This studio is your home lot, your home base. You don't want to be picayunie now, especially now. Wouldn't you rather be the king here, where you made so many pictures, good, bad and indifferent? That's the way I'd feel about it if I were you."

"Fortunately you're not me," said Hubert Ward. "But I don't want to talk contract. I pay a man ten percent for that, and it's a long time since he earned it. What about New York?"

"Beckoning. They're getting calls for you. Interviews. Publicity. Your contract says you have to go if we tell you to, but that's not what I'm doing. We won't make you. We won't invoke the contract. But on the other hand, all expenses paid. The shows. The night spots. And you'll have it all to yourself. By that I mean, Hubie, if you say you'll do it, we won't send Norman or Stanford. It's all yours, a clear field. Murray Bax says this'd be your first trip since you've been in pictures. Tell you what we *could* do. Stanford and you I know were pretty cozy there for a while. If you decided you wanted to take her with you—we'd pay her expenses also."

"Thanks, but no thanks."

"Well, just an idea. There'll be plenty waiting for you there in New York, especially with the build-up we'll give you before you get there."

"What about Chicago?"

"Listen, Chicago, sure! I didn't even think to suggest it. We didn't even dare to hope for Chicago, but if you'll go—mister!"

"All right. A week in New York, and a week in Chicago."

"We'll get to work on that right away. The week of the twentieth in New York, and the week of the twenty-seventh in Chicago?"

"Chicago first."

"Any way you like. How about Cleveland? Detroit? St. Louis? Hubie, you know we could book you into theaters for personal appearances in all those places and you could make yourself a nice piece of change."

"No. A week in Chicago, a week in New York. No theater bookings."

The photographers and the press kept him well over an hour in the trainshed in Chicago, and the grateful studio publicity people said no star, not even Joan Crawford, had been so cooperative. He posed until the photographers ran out of ideas, and by the time he had had a bath the early editions were delivered to his room and he was on Page One of them all, with pictures, stories, or both. The studio had assigned a publicity man, Frank Terry, as all-around equerry.

"This phone's going to be ringing like this all day," said Terry. "But I'll brush them off for you."

"There's one I don't want you to brush off. If a Mrs. Stephens phones, I want to speak to her."

"Oh, Christ. A lady by that name did call. She said it was personal, but they all say that."

"Did she leave a number or anything?"

"No, nothing."

"Can you get me a car that I can drive myself?"

"Sure, but how do you think you're going to get out of the hotel? They're out there in the corridor now. High school kids. Elderly women. Some queers."

"Before the picture opens?"

"Oh, we did a job here in Chicago, Mr. Ward. If you gave us a little more time you'd be the biggest thing since Paul Ash."

"Get me a car. Something like a Buick coach, or a Chevy. Inconspicuous."

Terry arranged for the car. "This is some private thing and I guess you don't want me along, but I'll tell you what we do. We go to the elevators. Don't wear an overcoat or a hat. The fans will follow you. We wait for an Up elevator. We go up a couple floors, get off, and then take a Down elevator. We'll go all the way down to the Grill without stopping. They know me here. And you can wait down there some place while I get you your hat and coat. The car's parked at the side entrance."

"Never mind my hat and coat."

Hubert Ward evaded the fans and followed Terry's plan. He got to the car without being recognized, simply by holding a handkerchief to his nose. And then he drove to Lake Forest.

She was home. A maid answered the doorbell and said, "My goodness. Ain't you Hubert Ward the movie star?"

"Yes. I'd like to see Mrs. Stephens."

It was not necessary to announce him. Nina, in a blue silk-and-wool suit, came out of a side room with a sheaf of papers in her hand, an opened fountain pen clenched in her teeth. She saw him and at first she frowned, unable to trust her recognition of him.

"Hello," he said.

"Why hello. *Hello*." She smiled. "It *is* you."

"It's me." He went to her and put his arms around her and kissed her, although they had never kissed before.

"Let me put these things down," she said. She laid the papers and pen on a table, and with her hands now free she put her arms around him and held him close, and put back her head to be kissed again. She held on to his hand and led him to the room from which she had first emerged.

"Did you know that I telephoned you?" she said.

"Yes I did. Did you know that the only reason I came to Chicago was to see you?"

"No, I didn't."

"Well, it was."

"I was just checking some bills for The Children's Aid Society," she said, for something to say.

"Did they come out right?"

"I don't know. I haven't finished. How long are you going to be in Chicago?"

"As long as it takes me to persuade you to leave it."

"Well—goodness." She sat on the sofa.

"You stopped writing to me," he said.

"Yes." She brushed something off her skirt. "Yes, I stopped."

"But just now, when you saw me—"

"I know. I know," she said.

"That's the only reason I came to Chicago."

"Well, I don't know. I really don't know."

"Yes you do, Nina."

"I thought about it. I admit I thought a lot about it. But then I read about you and some English actress, and that brought me to my senses."

"I don't get the Chicago papers. Was there anything in them about you? You and some meat-packer, some stock-broker?"

"I've seen a few people, if that's what you mean. I've been going out more."

"You've completely lost your tan."

"Yes, I know. We're going to Florida next week and I'll get it back."

"Who's going to Florida?"

"Well, actually just me, but there I'm meeting some friends of mine that have a boat, and we're going cruising."

"Who's the man?"

"Oh—a lawyer from downstate."

"Then I have practically no time at all, have I?"

She had recovered her poise. "That was just something to say."

"You know better than that."

She shook her head. "Different worlds, Hubert. Not so much different worlds as wanting to live different ways. I was in town for lunch today and I saw your picture."

"It's in every paper in Chicago. I made sure none of them missed me. I wanted to make sure you didn't fail to be informed of my presence in your great city."

"Only saw the one paper. But then when I telephoned you I was rather glad you didn't come to the phone."

"What would you have said if I had come to the phone?"

"Oh—welcome to Chicago. How are you. Have you seen my sister. Chit-chat."

"It was much better this way."

"Was it? Yes, it was more honest. But honesty isn't always the best policy. It isn't always the only policy. You'll be here a few days and I'm leaving next week. If you'd telephoned me I'm not sure I'd have seen you, and that would have been that."

"Do you love me, Nina?"

"I haven't heard you say that you love me."

"But I do."

"Yes, I love you. At least I guess it's love. The customary symptoms. I thought about you all the time, even when I didn't want to."

"Regardless of the messy things in my life, as you call them?"

"No, not regardless of them. But in spite of them. I don't happen to want messy things in my life, but they happen to friends of mine, people I like. And in your life I guess it's par for the course. Hollywood. I guess you couldn't avoid it if you wanted to—and why should you want to? If women, girls, want to make fools of themselves. It's very easy for a woman to get a man, for a while at least. But how long does that last? And is it worth it? It wouldn't be to me."

"Did you have an affair with the lawyer from downstate?"

"No. But he'll be on the cruise, and I knew what I was doing when I said I'd go."

"You wouldn't consider that messy?"

"He's asked me to marry him. And there's no very good reason why I shouldn't."

"You don't love him."

"No, but I'm sure I would, eventually."

"Then I got here just in time."

"I'm not sure that you did, Hubert. You may think me

a cold-blooded woman if you like, but it doesn't really matter what you think of me, does it? This man, I know, thinks I had an affair with you, for instance. A lot of people here do. But in those matters I don't really care much what people think. It's what I think that matters. I can have a man if I want one. Or men. They try. I'm not repulsive. And I will. I know what happiness there is with a man. And the physical. I'm a very healthy person. But I don't want just the physical without the rest, or the companionship without the physical. I have a very high opinion of myself and I want to keep it. I think it was instilled in me by my father. He was quite a ladies' man, but possibly for that very reason I believed what he told me about promiscuity. Consequently I've been to bed with exactly one man in my whole life. Some of my best friends don't believe that, but they can think what they please."

"You were married very young."

"Yes, I was eighteen. But I'm sure I could have held out much longer. I was completely faithful to my husband, and I didn't go dashing about when I was free to, after he died."

"Well, do you want to risk having Chicago convinced that you had an affair with me?"

"Meaning, will I see you again? Yes. I have two dinner engagements toward the end of the week, possibly three."

"With the lawyer from downstate?"

"One of them is with him and possibly the third. He has to finish up some last-minute work."

"Will you have dinner with me the other nights?"

"If you want me to."

"That's what I came here for."

"Yes, it'll be nice to be with you."

"You know what I'm going to do, don't you?"

"I guess I do, but I'll be on my guard."

"And you won't mind the publicity? There'll be plenty of it."

"I'd almost rather have it than secrecy. By the way, what did you ever do to a man called Phil Sturtevant? He works for *Time*, and let me tell you, he certainly cautioned me about you."

"He's the one I gypped out of a month's rent. Remember my life story?"

"You must have done something more than that to make him hate you so much."

"I did. I humiliated him in front of a couple of dames."

"Oh, then I can understand it. I never knew what to say to him."

"Did you defend me, Nina?"

"You could call it that, I suppose. He was so vague. He just said you were the worst man in New York, had a terrible record going back to prep school. But he was vague about it, and I said you can't say a man is the worst man in New York without giving some details. All he'd say was that if I was infatuated with you, there was no point in giving details."

"Were you infatuated with me?"

"Actually he said hypnotized."

"Were you hypnotized?"

"Maybe he did say infatuated, too. Yes, he did."

"Were you infatuated, or hypnotized?"

"Well, he seemed to think I was."

"And that's all the answer I'm going to get?"

"You want everything. I've already told you I love you. No, I wasn't hypnotized *or* infatuated. I have much too much sense for that."

"It doesn't show much sense to love me, though."

"Oh, yes it does. Love happens, and when it does, a sensible person admits it. Not to admit it would be very foolish indeed. That could get you into all sorts of trouble, deceiving yourself."

"And you'd never deceive yourself?"

"I hope not. I've always tried not to."

On that basis, and almost on that basis alone, she married him. He was due in New York on the following Monday, but on Friday afternoon they drove to the town of Peru, Indiana, where her uncle had a sizable farm. "My father's brother Bert. He's a widower," she said. "He raises standard-breds and races them at all the state fairs. He was never very fond of Josephine, but he liked me."

"Why are we picking him?"

"Because he's the only member of the family living that would understand my doing this."

"Why so?"

"When you see him you'll know."

A wooden arch painted white stood over the entrance to the Mississinewa Springs Farms, Bert J. Parsons, Prop. The driveway, lined with sycamores, was half macadam, on one side, half dirt road. A sign read: Autos Keep to Hard Surface—Drive Slow—No Horn Blowing. "Here the horse is king," said Nina. Some brood mares in foal looked up as Hubert Ward drove his rented Buick coupe to the main house, and in another white-fenced paddock some aged geldings stood undisturbed. At the top of the steep front-porch steps a man waited to greet the newcomers. "Uncle Bert," said Nina.

Bert Parsons was in his late fifties, early sixties. The veins in his nose and cheeks had come to the surface so that he seemed to be wearing a blue domino. He was wearing a slouch hat, an expensive suède windbreaker, whipcord jodhpurs and mud-caked jodhpur boots, and a pair of old-fashioned motoring gauntlets. From a cord around his neck hung a pair of goggles, and he had a half-smoked cigar in a corner of his mouth. As the car stopped he put the cigar in a concrete jardiniere and came down the steps.

"Hello, Nina, girl," he said. His voice was surprisingly gentle, his twang Indianan.

"Hello, Uncle Bert," she said. She kissed him. "This is another Bert. Hubert Ward."

"Well, it'd better be after what you told me over the phone. Howda do, Mr. Ward. You won't want your car, I expect. Leave it where it is and a man'll take it back in the garage." He shook hands with Hubert Ward. "Come on in, will you?"

Everywhere, in the hallway and in the rooms they saw, were pictures of harness horses, in and out of sulkies; an umbrella stand full of driving whips, and in the hall and the rooms glass-fronted cases of silver trophies and rosetted ribbons; silvered racing plates over the doorways; photographs of finishes in front of state-fair grandstands; and in the hallways and livingrooms, tall brass spittoons on large circular rubber mats. It could almost have been a country hotel. A rubber runner, rather than a carpet or rug, lay in the center hall, and the rooms to right and left had no appearance of being lived in; but Bert Parsons led his guests to the rear of the house and a room that was smaller than the others. Here the profusion of trophies and racing and horse mementos left literally no empty space on walls or mantelpiece, and this room was carpeted, had a fire already burning in the fireplace, a silver-leafed whiskey bottle and glasses on a taboret, a blind old Airedale that did not move when the newcomers entered. The leather chairs were worn smooth; a double-barrel Purdey gun and a box of shells rested on top of the desk; the carpet was stained by untrained dogs, spilt whiskey, gun oil, tobacco juice. "Only warm room downstairs right at the moment," said Bert Parsons. "Rest of the house'll warm up in about a half an hour. I don't have but very few fellows stay here overnight. If they come a distance, yes. But most of my visitors are from around here, and they'd just as soon go home nights and I'd just as soon have them, time they get a snootful of my liquor. Horse people are either teetotalers or heavy drinkers, there's no in-between. How about you two? This is pre-Prohibition bourbon whiskey, and I've got enough to last me the rest of *my* life, so don't hold back on that account." He handed Nina and Hubert Ward shot glasses of whiskey and poured one for himself. "Success to your marriage, happiness to the bride, congratulations to the groom. Three toasts in one, I guess you'd call that. Drink up . . . Nina, you know where to go if you feel the need."

"I'm comfortable," said Nina.

"Mr. Ward?"

"Not just now, thanks."

"Good," said Parsons. He now took off his hat and windbreaker, and the others took off their coats and hats. "Have a seat. I made all the arrangements, Nina. I have a fellow coming out from Peru with the papers for you to sign, and don't worry. I warned him against talking to any newspaper people. Six o'clock Reverend Zeebach said he'd be here, and he's like myself, a widower, so he won't be liable to tell his wife and let the cat out of the bag. There's nothing much to it, to tell you the truth. I know all these people around here, and they know me. I don't ask many favors, so when I want something I usually get it. Thought you might like to have a woman stand up for you, Nina, so I asked Mrs. Broadbill. You remember her from when you used to come here summers. She does the cooking for the men on the place and she's absolutely reliable."

"I remember her very well."

"Well, she was only too glad when I asked her. Tell you the truth, she cried a little. Now as to tonight and while you're here, I got Mrs. Broadbill to get things ready in the cottage and make it livable. I have men in and out here all day talking business, and in the cottage you'll have your privacy. The cottage, Mr. Ward, is a little house I built when I had a superintendent here, before I took over myself. It's small, but I have it fixed up pretty nice. A lot of famous people have spent the night or longer there. Or

I should say, owners of famous horses. The people aren't so famous."

"It's a darling place," said Nina.

"I always told Nina she could stay there any time she wanted to, but this is the first time she ever took advantage of the invitation."

"But we used to stay there when I was little."

"Yes. I didn't mean you'd never been there."

This man, smelling of whiskey and cigars and of the horse barn, was behaving with a strange delicacy, and Hubert Ward began to see why Nina had chosen him as well as his place for their elopement. He could refer explicitly to the coming night, to their desire for privacy, but without embarrassment to them or to himself. He was as impersonal as he might have been in discussing the mating of one of his mares with one of his stud horses, but it was a superficial impersonality; underneath it was real affection for Nina—and distrust of Hubert Ward. Again, as though Nina were a favorite mare, and Hubert Ward a stallion from a distant farm and without papers. Hubert Ward knew one thing: that this was no place where Nina would bring him for any pre-marital experimentation. Bert Parsons was a strait-laced old rounder.

"They'll be here any minute. Reverend Zeebach's driving out with the fellow from the license bureau. Yes, and here's Mrs. Broadbill herself."

Mrs. Broadbill, with a silent respectful nod to Bert Parsons, went directly to Nina and put her arms around her and kissed her.

"Little Nina," she said. "I'm so pleased for you."

"This is Hubert," said Nina.

"I'm pleased to meet you. You're getting a fine, fine girl. A fine girl. A fine woman, I should say."

"I know," said Hubert Ward.

"Well, just so you do," said Mrs. Broadbill, with an attempt at humor that did not come off. "The Reverend not here yet, Mr. Parsons?"

"Be here any minute now. Can I offer you a drink of whiskey?"

"You can offer it, knowing I won't drink it. Wine is what you ought to have for a wedding."

"I made Uncle Bert promise not to do anything like that. No fuss and feathers. All we want is the legal ceremony, don't we, Hubert?"

"I want whatever you want," said Hubert Ward.

"I had a big wedding, with Wayne," said Nina. "And I don't believe in going through all that the second time."

"Looking at it that way, I agree with you," said Mrs. Broadbill. "But what about your supper? I stocked the kitchen in the cottage, but—"

"I'll cook our supper. Really, we want this as simple as possible. And as quiet."

"Well, your Uncle Bert can take care of that if anybody can. Nobody's gonna go against his wishes and your wishes were always his wishes."

"Sit down, Mrs. Broadbill. You're getting all excited," said Bert Parsons. "This is just two people complying with the law, that's the way to look at it."

Mrs. Broadbill sat down. "It's no such thing, but if that's the way you want to look at it. It's our Nina getting

married, whether it's in some big church in Chicago or
your back office. But if that's the way you want to look at
it."

There was silence lasting seconds that threatened to
become oppressive, but the doorbell rang and Bert Parsons
went to answer it, returning with two men and wearing a
coat. Either of them could have been the clergyman; it
turned out the young one was. The court clerk, one Seaver,
was the most nervous person in the room, overawed by
Bert Parsons and by the movie star bridegroom. "I made
this out in the name of Richard H. Ward," he said. "What
Mr. Parsons told me to do."

"That's my real name."

"Well, I guess that'll disguise it. You both sign here,
and here, and here. Ma'am, you keep this, Reverend, this
is for you. That's about it, I guess. You want me to wait outside, Mr. Parsons?"

"Wait out in the hall."

"Oh, he can stay," said Nina. "That is, if he'd like to."

"Like very much to," said Seaver.

The Reverend Mr. Zeebach then conducted the ceremony, hardly more than five minutes of liturgical language
at the speed he read it by prearrangement with Bert Parsons. "You may kiss the bride," he said, and smiled, shook
hands with Hubert Ward and stuffed in his pocket the
envelope the groom passed to him. The bride was kissed
by her new husband, by her uncle, and by Mrs. Broadbill.
She shook hands with Zeebach and Seaver.

"Thank you, gentlemen," said Bert Parsons, to dismiss
the cleric and the clerk, and they left.

"Well," said Mrs. Broadbill. "All over so quick, you hardly realized. Do you feel all right about it being so quick, Nina?"

"Of course I do."

"A president of the United States was sworn in with no more fuss than that. Calvin Coolidge," said Bert Parsons.

"Well, he made a good president," said Mrs. Broadbill. "And you can take that for a good sign, Nina. And Mr. Ward. I guess I won't be needed any more, either."

"Nope," said Bert Parsons. "Lights on down in the cottage and all that?"

"Ready for occupancy."

"All right, then you can go," said Parsons.

"If you need me while you're here, I'm easy to find, Nina. I hope I'll see you before you go."

"Oh, you will, Mrs. Broadbill. Drop in tomorrow afternoon, maybe."

"No, I won't drop in, but if you phone me."

Parsons addressed the married couple. "Your baggage is all in the cottage, but it won't be unpacked. I guess you'll just want to walk down there by yourselves."

"Yes. And thank you for everything, Uncle Bert."

"I'd have done more, but this is all you wanted. This is a fine girl, Mr. Ward. They don't come any better than her."

"I haven't seen any better."

"I'm sure of that, all right. Well, bundle up, there's snow in the air. See you tomorrow, I guess." Parsons kissed his niece at the front door, and closed it when once she and Ward were together on the path to the cottage.

In the cottage kitchen they opened the door of the Frigidaire. "We have quite a choice. Mrs. Broadbill must be expecting us to stay at least a week. Well, my husband, would you like a steak? Chops? Chicken? Just say what you want."

"Whatever is easiest and takes the least time."

"Steak. How soon do you want it?"

"Well, I'd like to unpack and take a bath, wouldn't you?"

"While you're doing that I'll get supper ready, and I'll unpack and have my bath after supper."

He put his arms around her waist and she looked up at him and smiled. "Let's wait," she said.

"You're not nervous?"

"I don't think I'm as nervous as you are."

"You're absolutely right."

"You heard what Mrs. Broadbill said. You've got a fine *woman*. Did you notice she corrected herself, from girl to woman?"

"I did notice. But *I've* never been married before."

"Still, I don't think either one of us is a virgin," said Nina. "Let's have our baths and our supper, and then let nature take its course."

"All right."

"I'm not teasing you. You'll see."

"That's a very teasing remark."

"Yes, I guess it is. I didn't mean it to be. Go take your bath, get into your pajamas and dressing gown, and I promise you I won't put it off after supper. I confess, I am a little nervous. I want to get used to the idea of being with you. We've had very little time alone together."

"Okay."

"I love my ring. How were you able to get a wedding ring without causing comment?"

"Because I'm a great natural liar. I told Frank Terry—"

"Your *publicity* man?"

"Wait till you hear this. I told Terry that my mother had never had a really nice wedding ring, and I wanted to surprise her with one when I got to New York. 'And you know how it is, Frank,' I said. 'If I go to one of those New York stores and buy a wedding ring, everybody will jump to conclusions.' He bit. He swallowed it. I told him the kind of ring I wanted, gave him the cash, and there it is."

"I wonder about your mother. Shouldn't we call her?"

"We talked about that driving down from Chicago."

"I know, but don't you feel differently now? *I* do. Your getting the ring that way, Hubert—you could be so thoughtful. That would have been a very thoughtful thing to do for your mother. It shows that you are naturally a thoughtful person. And kind. You are."

"Well, I hope you say that ten years from now."

"It will be just as true then as it is now. *They* never had the chance to see that side of you. All they saw was a wild kid that was making trouble for them. And for himself."

"Don't expect things that aren't there, Nina."

"I don't. But don't you, either. We love each other with all the bad things showing, your naughtiness, and my puritanism. I'm not as good as I'm supposed to be, and you're not as wicked as you've told me you are. But wicked you fell in love with good me, and good me fell in love with wicked you. We mustn't try to change that— at least not too soon. After we've been married a while the too-good and the too-bad will mix . . ."

"What? What are you thinking?"

"They will mix. They'll mix to form our children. Go take your bath. You can see what's on my mind."

They had their supper in the kitchen, a cheerful room. "I have no dessert for you, so you have your cigarette and coffee and I'll do the dishes."

"I'll help you with the dishes."

"No, you'll only be in the way. You *won't* be in the way, but you'd hate it and I'm very quick at it. Talk to me while I'm doing them. Tell me more about Ken Downey, your director. Whenever you talk about him there's something in your voice that's never there any other time."

Hubert Ward talked about Ken Downey and she finished the dishes before he had completed an anecdote about the director. She sat with him until the end of the anecdote. "You see," she said, "when you talk about Downey you have to tell me much worse things than you ever told me about yourself. Have you ever thought of that?"

"Well, no, but nobody ever said Ken was Little Lord Fauntleroy. Several people have threatened to kill him. I mean kill. One man was crippled for life in one of his pictures, and he's had I don't know how many lawsuits. But he's a genius."

"A motion picture genius. You bandy that word about too freely. When I think of genius, I think of Leonardo da Vinci or Shakespeare. Beethoven. Brahms. They've stood the test of time. No movie has."

"I can't argue with you on that."

"I know," she said. She put her hand on his. "And you don't want to argue and neither do I. I'm going to take my bath now. I won't be very long. Sit in the livingroom and read the latest *Standard Bred Journal,* or whatever you can find. Or maybe something on the radio."

He waited in the livingroom, listening to the tub filling, then to the gurgling pipe sucking the water down when she finished her bath; but he did not hear her come in the room. She was in her bare feet and a nightgown and she was standing in front of him before he knew she was in the room. The nightgown was shaded dark at the points of her breasts and between her legs, and when he held out his hands to her she knelt in front of him, waiting for his first words, but he did not speak.

"Aren't you going to say anything?" she said.

"I wish I could," he said.

She slipped the top of the nightgown off her shoulders. "Still nothing?" she said.

He shook his head.

Now she stood up and stepped out of the nightgown and held her arms to her sides.

"No words," he said. "No words good enough."

She half smiled, contentedly. "No words are better than the things you said to other girls," she said.

"By saying nothing I said the right thing?"

"Not quite, but all right." She put out a hand to him. "Now you."

"Now me what?"

"Get rid of those things that are in the way. Called pajamas. Here, let me." She unbuttoned the coat, then pulled the drawstring. "And please take off those socks and those slippers. Don't hold out on me." They stood apart for a moment, but then they touched each other. "Oh, yes," she said. "So nice, and I *want* you so, and you want me, too. I wonder how I can tell that. I wonder how I can tell. You haven't *said* anything."

"But you can tell, can't you?"

"Yes. How can *you* tell?"

"I have ways," he said.

"Tell me about your ways, but not in here." She grasped his hand and they went back to the bedroom and she lay down. The playful mood covering her fear of awkwardness was now gone. "Now," she said.

"Right away?"

"Yes, inside me." She lay still and helped him with her hand and then, watching his face she waited, and feeling him she commenced to smile but almost immediately she wanted him more than she wanted to prolong pleasure and their minds lost control of their actions. "Darling, *dar*ling," she said.

"Yes. Lovely," he said.

She brushed her hair back off her forehead and her

head lay with one cheek on the pillow. Her eyes were nearly closed. "Was it lovely for you, darling?" she said.

"Oh, yes. Was it for you?"

"Oh, if you only knew."

"I do."

"Do you? Can it be as lovely for a man? I hope so. Oh, I do hope so. Men are so nice, to do this for women."

"It works both ways—when it works."

"Yes. Did I surprise you?"

"Yes."

"I did? How?"

"Everything you did surprised me."

"Do you know why I was so bold?"

"You mean coming into the livingroom? Yes, I think I know. You were timid."

"That's not all, though. I wanted to see you, so I thought if I let you see me first. Oh, I don't know. Maybe that's not true. Maybe I just wanted you to see me. You've looked at me a lot, but I've always been dressed before. Yes, I've always known when you were looking at me that way. You know, you can look me straight in the eye and still be staring at my bosom. Do you know that?"

"I guess that's true."

"But you've never even seen half of my bosom till tonight. Will you always stare at my bosom, Hubert? Please?"

"Your bosom, and elsewhere."

"My elsewhere requires your imagination."

"Not any more. My memory. My imagination before, but not any more. Just my memory."

"Or, you can always ask to see it and I'll let you."

"You will?"

"Sure."

"At a diplomatic reception in the White House?"

"Absolutely. We can always go behind a potted palm and I'll let you see it. Just for a second, of course. And if it's too dark, well, you can feel it."

"Just for a second, of course."

"Two or three seconds. Not any longer, though, I guess. Not at a diplomatic reception."

"You don't think that would be very diplomatic?"

"No. And I'm so receptive I might overdo it. With you. Not with anybody but you."

"You're damn right you won't."

"Are you going to be jealous?"

"Yes."

"I've always prided myself on not being jealous. But I was so jealous of that Simmons woman, and I'd only just met you. As a matter of honest fact, if I'd been completely truthful with myself that day, I watched you on that diving-board and the things I thought I won't even tell you now."

"Why? Why not?"

"I will, when they happen. Do you feel married?"

"No."

"Neither do I. Let's pretend we're not."

"All right."

"It's so ridiculous that I wouldn't do this last night, and yet I wouldn't have. I never would have, I don't think. But now that we are legally man and wife, I feel quite immoral. I suppose what I mean is that I feel very sexy, and

I've always been brought up to believe that being sexy was immoral. No Reverend Zwieback can change that so quickly."

"What about the lawyer you were going away with?"

"Do you know something awful? Suddenly he's become like a picture in a magazine. Not even an underwear ad. Mr. Good Citizen, never seen without his clothes on. Wears a suit to bed. To think I almost went away with him. And now I realize that if I had, I couldn't have married him, and all my moral principles would have been shattered. I'd have slept with him, then not married him, and maybe that would have happened quite a few times. You saved me from that, darling."

"Oh, I always knew I'd be a good influence somehow."

"Joke about it, but it's true."

"What about your husband—Wayne?"

She was silent.

"I withdraw the question," he said.

"It had to be asked in a conversation like this, sometime if not now. I'll answer the question. I loved him, loved and adored him. But in seven years with him I was never the way I've been with you tonight. I never looked at him on a diving-board and thought the things I thought about you. And incidentally, he was a much better diver than you. But if he'd stayed alive and you came along—I don't know. Maybe you would have wrecked that marriage. But you don't want to wreck it now, do you? It was good, and it never hurt you. It would have stayed good if you hadn't come along. And I need that marriage in bringing up my daughter."

"I want to ask you one more question, if I may."

"All right."

"Why did you only have one child?"

"The wedding night, when questions get asked," she said.

"They don't have to be answered now."

"I was prepared to answer the question, but not to-night. I thought you'd ask other kinds. How far did I let boys go."

"You're thinking back to your other wedding night," he said.

"Yes. He asked a lot more questions than you have. Every boy I ever kissed—there weren't many. Had any of them put his hand on me. Had I put my hand on any of them. Did I ever make a boy come. Did boys ever make me come. He wanted to know everything, and I told him."

"Did you resent his questions? It sounds that way."

"I guess I must have, but not very much. I was think-ing so much about going the limit for the first time. I didn't know how it was going to be, and I told him everything because I wanted to get on with it. It was odd, his asking all those questions. He was so inexperienced himself. We really had to learn everything together."

"And you finally did learn everything?"

"No. Far from everything, from him. The night before he left for Detroit it was practically the same as the first week we were married. But I adored him. Everybody did, but he was mine."

"How do you know there's more than what he showed you?"

"Young wives talk among themselves. Girls at school talked among themselves. And my own instincts to do other things, but he'd always stop me. You don't know much about him. He was very religious. He taught a class in Sunday School long after we were married. He was the kind that you would have called a Christer, but you never would have dared say it to his face."

"I'm not going to say anything against him, but I'm sure I wouldn't have liked him and he wouldn't have liked me."

"You'd have liked him if there were no girls around. Men gravitated toward him. He was a marvelous athlete."

"A man's man—only in Hollywood that means a fairy."

"He wasn't that."

"But I asked you before, why did you only have one child?"

"We didn't. We had two. We had a little boy, our second child. People outside the family think he was born dead, but he wasn't. He lived nearly a year. He was abnormal. He could never be anything else. There was no hope for him."

"I'm sorry."

"They even let me think he was born dead and they took him away, but then Wayne told me—oh, weeks later. And he didn't want me to have any more children."

"But your daughter is perfect."

"Yes. That was luck. And the little boy was bad luck. The doctors said we could produce normal children, but Wayne was afraid of what would happen to me if we didn't. His mother had an uncle that wasn't quite right, physically and I guess mentally. He had no testicles, and he was shaped like a woman. I never saw him, and neither did Wayne, but apparently this man, or half-man, lived in a little town in England, ran the town bakery. Led a normal life till he was pretty well along, and then he committed suicide."

"My father committed suicide."

"I know. But that was money."

"Yes, but sometimes I've wondered whether there wasn't something else in addition. I don't really know much about my father, and I wonder how well my mother really knew him."

"Does it disturb you?"

"Not very much. I don't let it."

"That's good. Don't let it. We all have somebody, every family. Uncle Bert, for instance. When we used to come here as children, we were always told not to kiss Uncle Bert. Then when I was ten or twelve we were told it was all right to kiss him. It doesn't take much guessing to figure out Uncle Bert's trouble."

"You mean syphilis?"

"Well, something like that. We were never *told* what it was. We were just told to shake hands with him, and we always stayed here in the cottage. He wasn't here all the time in those days. He was away a lot, racing at the fairs, and he had a house in Indianapolis where he lived most of the time till his wife died. Aunt Ella. We never saw much of her. She very seldom came to the farm, and she wasn't very *nice*. She had no family, and I got the distinct impression that Uncle Bert had married beneath him. Children know those things."

"So do adults. I got the distinct impression that your uncle thinks you've married beneath you."

"Well, that's because he always liked Wayne. Wayne drove some of his horses and took an interest. If Wayne had lived this place probably would have been left to me. But I don't want it. I love to come here to visit, but it's terribly hot in summer and mean cold in winter, and much too out of the way. And my daughter wouldn't have any friends here."

"I just thought of something. You ought to phone your sister, in Los Angeles. Tell her to start work on getting your daughter in some school out there."

"You are thoughtful. Thank you. What I'm going to do is write to her tomorrow, a long letter. I don't want to talk to her over the phone. She'd interrupt me with advice and so forth, and I don't want to be interrupted. I'm sure we can get the child in some good school. Dwight is pretty influential."

"Member of the California Club."

"You remember that. Yes. And all those things. He can probably do as much as Josephine."

"And I have to get a house."

"Can't we live in your apartment?"

He laughed. "I don't mind playing a game that we're

227

not married, but God only knows what you'd find in some of my bureau drawers."

"Just as long as it isn't Mrs. Simmons. She has quite a figure, that woman, but you *never* thought she was pretty, Hubert."

"I only saw the figure once. It's quite a figure."

"I'm not afraid of her, really I'm not. If you ever get tired of me, I don't think you'll go rushing back to her."

"No."

"You're supposed to say you'll never get tired of me. This is our wedding night. Shall I stop talking?"

"All right."

"And you just put your arms around me and we'll go to sleep for a few minutes?"

"Do you think we'll sleep?"

"No. But we might. And if we don't? Are you tired?"

"Pleasantly."

She lay with her head on his shoulder and her hand on his chest, then slowly she began to make circles on his chest and downward to his belly. "Do you mind if we put out the light?" she said.

"I'll do it," he said.

In the darkness he lost her for a moment, then found her, and she was where she wanted to be, where he hoped she would be.

Edmund Greenhill was standing to one side of his desk, a concession. He was not standing behind his desk, he did not sit at his desk and then rise as Hubert Ward entered the office. He did not come forth and greet Hubert Ward. But he was standing to one side of his desk. That far he would go. He put out his hand, and cocked his head to one side in a chiding attitude.

"Officially I'm sore as hell at you, Hubie. Sore as hell. But speaking personally I'm very happy for you. I hear you got a real lovely person. How you ever did it I don't know, you reprobate. Take a seat."

"Thanks."

Edmund Greenhill decided to sit on the davenport. "I understand you found a place to live and all?"

"Yes, way the hell out in the Brentwood section."

"Well, we're thinking of moving out that way. Maybe building. It's the coming section. I don't have anything against Beverly, but we got industry people on both sides of us. Laverne Rodney and her husband on the one side and some writer renting on the other side. If we got our price we'd like to build on Bristol. You anywhere near Bristol?"

"Quite near."

"You don't care for a cigar, as I recall."

"No thanks."

"You're sort of subdued, Hubie. Is that what married life did to you?"

"No, I'm just waiting for you to begin."

"Well, all right. We'll lay both our cards on the table. I have the right picture for you to follow *Destroyers* with, Hubie, but not what you're asking in the way of money. I give you my word, the studio won't pay it. I know you don't want to talk money with me, but I have to talk it with you. You have an agent that lost all sense of proportion, a Mr. Jack Golsen I believe he calls himself, although that isn't the name I knew him under when he was a lowly costume checker in Wardrobe on this very lot. Yes, that's what he started out as. From there to mimeographing scripts in the script department and then all of a sudden he blossomed forth as an agent. I give you the background of Mr. Jack Golsen to show you how much he *don't* know about pictures. This gentleman now presumes to know all about production figures, but if he ever saw a production chart I doubt it very much. He bases all his information on what he can read in *Harrison's Reports* and *Variety*. Maybe *you* don't know what he's asking for you, Hubie."

"Yes I do. Straight five thousand a week for three years."

"Did you ever hear of such a thing?"

"Why, sure I did. Do you want me to name some people that are getting more?"

"You don't have to. I know their names. I have some of them working for me. I know the salary of every son of a bitch acting in pictures today, or I can find it out by simply picking up that phone on my desk. You want me to prove it to you?"

"Yes. How much is Doris Arlington getting?"

"Doris? Doris isn't under contract to a studio. She'll work for twelve thousand dollars a week with a minimum four weeks' guarantee. Am I correct?"

"I don't know. I was just curious."

"Oh, I thought maybe you were testing me. Well, you could verify that."

"I don't want to verify it, Eddie, or talk any more about money. And I don't care whether Jack Golsen's real name was Hymie Fink or if he was a waiter in the commissary. I'm pretty sure that he'll get the most money any studio will pay, and I can't expect more than that."

"Oh. Then you lay *your* cards on the table, Hubie."

"What's the picture you have for me?"

"I have actually two pictures to follow *Destroyers* with."

"Is one of them an aviation picture? If so, nuts."

"One of them was an aviation picture, I'll grant you that, but if you don't want to follow one aviation picture with another aviation picture we can forget it. I'd rather see you in the other one anyway."

"And what is it?"

"It's a picture that we can book it into say the Rivoli and run it for a year on a reserved-seat policy, with a two-dollar top. We won't show it any place else in the world till we get at least a year's run out of it in New York and maybe London, and then we'll road-show it in the key cities for another six months minimum before it goes into the grind houses."

"But you didn't say what it is."

"No, and I won't say till you convince your Mr. Jack Golsen that he's pricing you right out of pictures."

"Come now, Eddie. That sounds like a threat."

"It isn't intended as such but maybe you ought to think about it from that angle. Even if I *was* given to understand your wife has independent means."

Hubert Ward rose. "So long, Eddie."

"Now wait a second, Hubie. Don't take it that—"

Hubert Ward closed the door behind him, and in the following weeks the industry buzzed with versions of how Eddie Greenhill had managed to lose the most valuable young male star in the business. It was especially humiliating because the industry was so sure that Eddie Greenhill had the inside track that no other studio had made serious efforts to talk business with Hubert Ward. Then when it was announced that Ward had signed with U. S. Films for three years at an undisclosed salary, New York told Eddie he might as well start looking for another job. He could settle his contract immediately for $100,000, or he could expect to be assigned to the company's financially successful but low-budget, unprestigious horse operas for the two years that remained of his contract. He settled. It is enough to say that Eddie Greenhill never bought or built in the Brentwood section and that from time to time in the late Thirties his name would appear in screen credits as author of original stories.

The first meeting of Nina Ward and Jack Golsen established the terms of the relationship that were to become permanent. It took place during the period of the negotiations between Golsen and U. S. Films. The time of day late on a Sunday morning. "I promise you I won't make it a habit," said Hubert Ward. "I'm all for keeping them away from here. But Golsen thinks Ziffrin is ready to sign. Monday, probably. And we want to get our stories straight."

"Why do you have to get your stories straight?"

"Because I could accidentally say something that Golsen wasn't ready to have me say. He'll be here tomorrow morning, eleven-thirty."

"What sort of creature is he? He sounds awful on the phone."

"He's pretty awful, but you won't have to more than say hello to him."

"Shall I offer him breakfast?"

"No, but he may need a cup of coffee. Saturday night he always goes on the town."

"He's not married?"

"No."

Hubert and Nina Ward entered the library together, and Jack Golsen turned to face them. With both hands he held out a long box from a florist. "To Mrs. Ward for disturbing your Sunday morning," he said.

"This is Jack Golsen," said Hubert Ward.

"I apologize for this intrusion," said Golsen. "But it honestly couldn't be helped, Mrs. Ward. Hello, Hubie. You I didn't bring anything except maybe some good news. Later."

"Shall I open it here? Now?" said Nina Ward.

"If that's your pleasure," said Golsen.

"Yellow roses. My favorites! Did Hubert tell you? He couldn't have, because he didn't know."

"No, I was only going by a description of you and a couple photographs that didn't do you justice."

"They're perfectly lovely. Thank you so much. I'll get something to put them in. Oh—would you like a cup of coffee?"

233

"If it's no trouble, I could sure use a strong cup of black coffee with one lump of sugar in it."

"Some scrambled eggs? Or fried? It won't take a minute."

"Please, Mrs. Ward. The very thought of food—in other words, no thanks. Just the coffee, please."

"It's strong and it's hot," said Nina Ward, and went to get it.

"I would say you're a very fortunate man, Hubie. She didn't have to open her mouth and I knew she was a class dame. And don't object to dame. In England they use dame as a title, the same as sir. Jesus Christ, I feel awful. I took this broad home to the apartment with me and she's still there. Some broad I seen her sitting on a bench waiting for a bus down on Wilshire. I was on my way to a party at some friends of mine on the other side of Wilshire, down past Western. Just some friends of mine. But I got stopped by a light and I had a quick gander at her and just for the hell of it I opened the door of the car and I said to her, 'Here I am,' and like she was expecting me she got in. She asked me where I was going and I said I was on my way to a party. About twenty-seven, twenty-eight years of age. Red hair, and thrown together like a brick shithouse I could see that. And she said, well would there be plenty of girls at the party because if not she didn't have anything better to do. 'What's your name?' I said. 'Mary Pickford,' she said, 'what the hell difference does it make?' So I knew right away this was my broad for the night. She said, 'You're a Jew, aren't you?' and I said, 'Yeah, and you get the hell outa the car,' and she said, 'Wait a minute. I like Jews,' and I said how many did she like, and she said well only one at a time. So that kind of made me laugh and I said why didn't we blow the party and spend a little money, Saturday night, everybody was spending money that had any. She's still there at the apartment. Or I guess she is. I don't know her name or where she lives or anything. But I'll tell you this much, I need that coffee." On seeing Nina with the tray he brought his story to a quick conclusion. "Ah, the mocha-java," he said. "Let me get some of this down and bring back my confidence."

"Take your time, it's good and hot," said Nina Ward.

"Yes, don't burn your tongue," said Hubert Ward.

"Looking around, I think this house used to belong to Jasper W. Tuttle, one actor that saved his money and invested it right. Actors will save their money, but investing it is another matter entirely. Your husband, he don't have anything but cash, regardless of what I tell him."

"I can understand cash, I can't understand the things you want me to invest in."

"Real estate you ought to be able to understand. You pay big rent for this house. That's real estate. Tuttle didn't build this house, you know. Who built it was old Geoffrey Masters. Sir Geoffrey we used to call him, long before the King gave him the right to be called Sir. He used to tell people it was a copy of his old home in Cornwall or some place, but I got him to level with me one time and the old phony admitted he never had any house in Cornwall. *Then.* But he sold the place to Jasper W. Tuttle and *then* he bought a house in England. I don't know if it was Cornwall. Tuttle sold it to the present owner. You know who the present owner is, don't you?"

"A lawyer named Fabrikant."

"Nah. Fabrikant's only a front. This house and the two houses on that side of you and from here to the corner on the other side, all owned by Doris Arlington."

"I'll be a son of a bitch."

"You let him talk like that in front of you, Mrs. Ward?"

"Oh, sure."

Golsen lit a cigarette. He kept waving the match long after it was out. "You mind if I tell you something, Mrs. Ward?"

"Please do."

"Don't you do the changing. Let him. This man is on the eve of a big career after futzing around for four years. Looking at it from strictly the agent's point of view, strictly mercenary, you're as good a thing as could have happened to him at exactly this time. Single, he could have gone haywire. Married to some broad, he could have gone haywire. But married to you, just from what little I know about you—but I know people—Hubert Ward is really going places. *Provided*. Provided he plays it right. Who he ought to pattern himself after is Ronnie Colman, for instance. Hubie is twenty-five years of age, four years in pictures, not an unknown, but from now on he's going to get *big* parts, *big* billing, *big* money. In other words he just graduated from high school, as far as pictures goes. We made nice money, but from here in—wow! And marrying you is the smartest thing he ever did—"

236

"I'll take a little credit for that," said Hubert Ward.

"Quiet, Hubie. Today using the brain is tough enough. To continue, Mrs. Ward. We're gonna surround this fellow with the aura of respectability. Why? Because in the long run it pays off. It's paying off for Ronnie, and I don't have to tell you about Garbo. We can't make this fellow into a man of mystery. It's too late for that, even at twenty-five. But the way I look at it, the country's ready for a leading man that's happily married, that don't chase around, that goes home from the studio and his wife is a non-pro. It's not only the country's ready. The industry's ready. I want this fellow to have it in his contract that he has to approve of publicity stills, and who he'll see for interviews and all that. Maybe we couldn't get that just now with one of the majors, but we can get it with U. S. Films and Ziffrin. You don't have any objection if we make him the symbol of respectability, your husband?"

Nina Ward looked at her husband and then at Golsen. "Do you always talk this way, Mr. Golsen?"

"Mrs. Ward, that don't offend me. That's the way I want you to be. I just as soon if you're a total ignoramus about people like me, and picture business. Tomorrow I have the crucial meeting with Ziffrin and them. On money we're not very far apart. On billing. Such details as those there. What I plan to do, I make a loud noise fighting about the money, and I wear them down and they wear me down till I give a little, and then I sneak in these other things about publicity stills and interviews. They won't fight me. No studio breaks their necks to get publicity for a star. Contrary to the general opinion, they hate to spend money on a star, and especially an independent like U. S. Films. They'll loosen up for a picture, because they have to, but it goes against the grain to spend good money on an actor or actress. So I look like I'm doing them a favor without knowing it, and that way I get it down in black and white that our boy here don't *have* to do stunts, have your house overrun with these photographers and interviewers. We practically dictate who he sees and who he don't see. And that means you're spared the ballyhoo stuff. So is your little daughter, and maybe you and Hubie will start increasing the population, who knows?"

Thus, on a Sunday morning, in a Tudor house in the Brentwood Heights section of Los Angeles, a star was fabricated by a man who at the moment was suffering from his excesses of the night before. The factors were neatly contradictory: the Lord's Day; the synthetic surroundings that had been originally placed there by a Cheapside boy who had once longed for the English countryside; the girl from the prairies who was about to be made famous by keeping her in obscurity; the subject himself, who had lived a quarter of a century without a thought of principle, and who was about to be converted by the movies into something his remote ancestors had been through conviction. Hubert Ward accompanied Jack Golsen to the door and came back to the livingroom, where Nina was looking at the Sunday paper. He slowly paced up and down in front of her.

"What is it?" she said.

"I was just thinking," he said. "Maybe I ought to write to my mother."

238

The photographs of Hubert Ward, in opera hat and tails, and Nina, in her mink, at the movie premières always had them together; walking, standing, sitting in the Packard town car that Ziffrin–U. S. Films gave Hubert Ward as a Christmas bonus. The captions always referred to Nina as the lovely socialite wife of the popular star. Hubert Ward had no contractual control over the newspaper photographers, but he needed none, since they rarely had a chance to take his picture where he did not want it taken. Nearly all his pictures in the files were Mr. and Mrs. Hubert Ward, chatting between chukkers at Midwick Country Club (Eric Pedley, Mr. Ward, Mrs. Ward, Elmer Boeseke); Mr. and Mrs. Hubert Ward sharing a box with Mr. and Mrs. Dwight Barley at the Pacific South West tennis tournament (front row, Mrs. Ward and her sister, Mrs. Barley; seated behind them, Dwight Barley and Mr. Ward); a gay group enjoying the Santa Barbara Fiesta (Mr. and Mrs. Thomas Joyce, Movie Star Hubert Ward and his socialite wife; Billy Fiske, noted bobsledder; Hugh Blue, noted yachtsman; Louis Rowan, young Pasadena polo star; Wright Ludington, noted art collector; Mrs. Louise Macy, of New York, former Pasadenan; Icky Outhwaite, popular society entertainer; Mr. and Mrs. Alfred Wright, of Pasadena); and Mr. and Mrs. Hubert Ward attending the Philharmonic concert at the Shrine Auditorium (the movie idol and his socialite wife discussing the program with Mrs. Dwight Barley, Mrs. Ward's sister).

There were photographic files devoted to Ward, Mrs. Hubert (Nina). The pictures were few in number and nearly all showed her with other women at tennis, at pool-

side, leaving the fashion shows at Bullock's-Wilshire and
I. Magnin's, and at society weddings (Mr. Ward was on
location in the High Sierras). There was one batch of
glossy prints that showed her leaving the Vendome restaurant and seated in the garden at her Brentwood Heights
residence with Mrs. Sanford Ward, New Jersey socialite
mother of the noted movie star . . .

She did not answer Hubert Ward's first letter. "But
don't give up," said Nina. "I'll write to her, or maybe it'd
be a good idea if I wrote to your sister first."

"I don't know where she lives, but I suppose I could
find out easily enough."

"Your uncle?"

"God no. There I draw the line, at that son of a bitch.
If he'd had his way I'd be at the bottom of the Amazon."

"The Amazons had big bottoms," said Nina.

"You know, Nina, I'm going to have to report you to
Jack Golsen."

"No, he wouldn't object to my risqué jokes. We're married, that's what he cares about."

"He didn't want you to change."

"Maybe I didn't change, very much. Maybe I didn't
change at all. I just never knew any boy that I could say
naughty things to, and they're not so naughty, really.
Amazons' bottoms. They had big bottoms and big thick
thighs. Crush a man to death, I should think. Maybe that's
what they did."

"As you were saying, speaking of my mother, who's
not an Amazon but maybe does want to crush me to
death."

"As I was saying, I'll write to her," said Nina.

Nina's letter got a response. Kitty Ward had been willing enough to accept her share of her son's fame, but before doing so she had to be able to show her brother that Richard had come to her, so to speak. Or so she believed. Franklin Hubert was bored with Kitty and her Sunday dinners and pride in her grandchildren and financial problems and lonely drinking and self-imposed exclusion from participation in the life of her son. New acquaintances would say to her, "I hadn't realized you were the mother of Hubert Ward," and as Richard became better known it became more difficult to refrain from accepting the homage due the mother of a film star. It became so difficult, in fact, that she did not take the trouble to maintain her early aloofness toward Richard the Broadway actor. "Oh, yes, he's my son," she would say, and her newest acquaintance would marvel at the quiet modesty of the proud mother.

"I can't say no to this letter," she said to her brother. "She sounds like a really nice girl."

"Then *don't* say no," said Franklin Hubert. "Blood is thicker than water. And it's time he did something about supporting you."

"You've been so wonderful, Frank."

"I haven't been wonderful. You're my sister."

"Yes, but not every brother would do as much as you've done." She refused to let him alter the self-portrait of a woman with a devoted brother and a penitent, famous son. "They want me to stay a month."

"Well, there's nothing keeping you here. Stay a month. Maybe you could even rent this house, if you like it out there."

"Oh, I could never leave all my friends now. But a few weeks in California. I've never been to California. I wonder if Nina's having a baby."

"I haven't the faintest idea. You'll be able to find that out when you get there."

"It might be just what he needs."

In her letter Nina had enclosed a cheque for two thousand dollars, "to cover traveling expenses and other things that might come up." Hubert Ward in his letter had only *offered* to send money. The clerk at the bank was very polite when Kitty Ward deposited the cheque; he could not completely hide his surprise at seeing the noted signature, but he made no special comment, and Kitty did not remember until later that the bank clerk might have some reason to show surprise. But by that time she had spent some of the money on a new outfit and the rail tickets.

Her son and his wife met her at the Pasadena station, Kitty's second experience of posing for newspaper photographers, but this one hardly to be compared to those dreadful moments at Sandy Ward's funeral. Actually the photographers' presence at the railroad station created a pleasant confusion that helped to get the three Wards over the first awkward minutes of greeting. "No more, please," said Hubert Ward. "Thanks, boys, but my mother's had a long trip. You understand."

An *un*pleasant little man from one of the Los Angeles

papers said, "Hubie, isn't this a sort of a reconciliation, you and your mother?"

Hubert Ward smiled and pretended not to understand the question. He leaned forward to the chauffeur. "Straight home, Harold," he said.

Nina did most of the talking on the ride down to Brentwood Heights, and Kitty Ward's contributions were largely comments on the *flora* of Southern California. At the house Hubert Ward said, "I have to leave you two, I'm shooting, but I'll see you this evening."

"Do you know, I *thought* he must be wearing make-up," said Kitty Ward, when he had left. "You know, I'm getting terribly near-sighted. It's age, I suppose. When am I going to see your little girl?"

"She gets home from school around four-thirty," said Nina.

"I brought a little present for her. Does she like dolls? I couldn't think of anything else."

"Loves them."

"I suppose she gets a lot of them, from movie fans."

"Well—not so many. She already had quite a few, though, before I knew Hubert."

"I must get used to you calling him Hubert, too."

"That's what the whole world calls him now. Or Hubie, but I don't like the nickname Hubie."

"No. It's a family name, you know. It was my maiden name. We go back, oh, long before the Revolutionary War, the Huberts. Of course you do, too, the Parsonses. That's an old New England name, isn't it?"

"Yes."

"And your first husband was Mr. Stephens. That's a good old name, too. A Reverend Parsons christened one of my grandchildren. I always thought that was a good coincidence, Parson Parsons. A friend of ours was named Sargent and he was a corporal in the Essex Troop. We were always hoping he'd be promoted to sergeant, but when the war came he was made a lieutenant. Your house is very English for California, isn't it? I expected something quite different—not that I don't like it."

"It isn't really our house. We're renting it," said Nina. "I didn't ask anyone for lunch, I thought you'd be tired. Tonight we're having my sister and her husband. They live in Beverly Hills. And Doris Arlington—"

"Doris *Arlington?* Wonderful. One of my favorites."

"She's coming, and a friend of hers, a Mr. Doyle Cordell."

"From the movies?"

"No, he's an oil man, I think. And Ruth St. Alban—"

"*Ruth* St. *Alban?* Coming *here?*"

"Yes. Why?"

"Well—you know—you get probably the wrong idea of a person from the parts they play."

"I should hope so. I'm glad Hubert isn't like some of the characters *he* plays."

"I never thought of that, but of course it's true. Hubert, as you call him, *was* a wild boy, and as his mother I'd be the first to admit it. But in just those few minutes I can see that he's changed a lot, and I think I know who I can thank for that. Are you happy, Nina?"

"Well of course."

"Then that's all I want to know. If you're happy, he's happy, and he wasn't very happy as a boy. A good deal of the trouble he got into was because he didn't seem to —I don't know, but he wasn't *happy*. But then you take my brother and I, Richard's uncle. We were happy as children, but I later on had to go through a lot, and my brother's not as happy as he should be in spite of all his success. You have to learn to take the good with the bad in life."

"How very true. Would you like a cocktail, Mrs. Ward?"

"Oh—are you having one?"

"No, but don't let that stop you."

"I don't think I will, thank you. We'll be having them before dinner and I can wait till then."

"This being the middle of the week, it's going to be an early party. I imagine Doris and Ruth will be going home around ten."

"That early?"

"Oh, yes. And Hubert has to be up at half-past five."

"Half-past five in the morning?"

"Yes."

Kitty Ward burst into hearty laughter. "Oh, that strikes me funny. Half-past five in the morning? Well, if the movies didn't do anything else they certainly changed one of his habits. We used to have to throw cold water on him to get him out of bed at *nine*. Wait till my brother hears that."

Kitty Ward and Nina were left alone together after the dinner guests departed and Hubert Ward had retired.

"I'd just love to sit up and talk, but I imagine you'd like to retire, too."

"I'll stay up a little while. I always have a cup of coffee with Hubert at breakfast, but I'm not tired. How did you like your first movie stars?"

"Doris is very witty, Doris Arlington. But she's so hard. I don't mean anything about her morals, but the things she says. And Ruth, Ruth St. Alban, she *is* like the parts she plays. The one I liked best tonight was your sister, Josephine. I'm older, of course, but she was really a kindred spirit tonight. I think she felt the same way as I did about the movie actresses, and underneath I'll bet you do too, Nina."

"No, I'm afraid I've gotten to like Doris. And Ruth is really rather pathetic."

"Pathetic? Why do you say that?"

"Well, I probably know so much more about her."

"Oh."

"Nothing very scandalous. But pathetic. And Doris seems hard because for a woman this is a very difficult business."

"I'll bet it wasn't very difficult for her. I was disappointed in Doris Arlington, I always thought I'd like her. I never did think much of Ruth St. Alban, and I'll bet your sister Josephine doesn't think very much of her right this minute. I hope Dwight isn't very susceptible, because Ruth St. Alban did everything but sit in his lap."

"Well, maybe he'd be better off if somebody did sit in his lap."

"Oh, you don't mean that, Nina. He and Josephine make an ideal couple."

"Oh, they are. But Dwight has no sense of humor, and if somebody like Ruth sat in his lap it might do him some good. Well, I'm afraid the time has come for me to—can I get you anything? I'm going to let you sleep in the morning. You ring whenever you want breakfast. I'll be out most of the morning, but I'll be back in time to take you to lunch. I thought I'd take you to the Vendome. That's a very dressy restaurant. Then after lunch we can drive around if you like."

"Fine. I have some friends in Pasadena I'd like to see while I'm here. Josephine knows them. But otherwise I'll do anything you say."

"We'll telephone them tomorrow. Goodnight, Mrs. Ward."

"Goodnight, Nina."

Hubert Ward was sitting up in bed, smoking a cigarette. "We can look forward to a month of that," he said.

"Oh, I'll keep her occupied. I'll take her sightseeing, some of the sights I haven't seen. And she likes Josephine."

"She's a total stranger to me."

"Well, you won't have to see much of her."

"But you will. I have a guilty conscience about that."

"Don't have. She's not going to be any trouble. Shall I make you forget all about her?"

"I wish you would."

"Have you got any love scenes to play tomorrow?"

"No."

"I wouldn't want to take away from your ardor."

"Oh, yes you would."

"No, I don't think that'd be fair. That's the way you earn your living, and if I make love to you the night before you *won't* be convincing. I don't mind if it's the other way, if making love for a picture makes you want to make love with me. But I don't think I ought to take away that look in your eye."

"It's there, is it?"

"Yes it is."

"Well, tomorrow I get wounded at the Battle of Bull Run. I think it's Bull Run. Maybe it's Gettysburg."

"Then it's all right if you look tired. I'll be right with you. Can't we tone down the lighting effects?"

"You're getting pretty damn professional about this."

"Well, I'd hate it if you called me an amateur."

"*That* you are *not*."

"Because I love my work. And I love you, too, unhappy little boy. I'll bet you were, as a matter of fact."

"The hell I was. Go on, get your clothes off, Nina."

"All right, lieutenant."

"I'm a captain. And a Southern gentleman."

"A Southern gentleman would never say, 'Get your clothes off, Nina.'"

"How do you know?"

"Well, as a matter of fact, I don't, so maybe you're right. Are you going to stab me, captain?"

"Honey, you bet I am."

"With what?"

"You know with what, and where."

"I'll be right with you, captain sir."

Nina filled Kitty's days with motor trips, shopping, and the social activities of women whose husbands were at work, chiefly women who were friends of Josephine Barley. They supplied Kitty Ward with a society background —"Very good family back East"—but she was so like them in her fondness for idle chatter and her pursuit of undemanding, uncompromising pleasures that they relaxed their vigilance against the snobbishness they always expected from an Easterner. For her part Kitty declared she had never met so many nice women in any one place, and it became a problem for Nina to remind Kitty that she was invited for a month. ("Goodness, your visit is half over and I haven't taken you to Santa Barbara. We'll do that next week.")

In the final week Kitty said to her daughter-in-law: "Nina, I want you to be perfectly honest with me. Is Hubert avoiding me? I've hardly talked to him alone since I've been here."

"Yes he is, in a way, and I think you can understand why," said Nina, who had been anticipating the question. "He wants this to be a pleasant visit, and not a time for going back over all those years."

"You're a very wise girl, Nina. But of course being a mother yourself, you knew I could sense that."

"Oh, of course you did. And hasn't it worked out better this way? I'm sure you must have been dreading the thought of rehashing all those years."

"I was, and it wouldn't surprise me if Hubert had got the idea from you."

"No, it was his idea, but I went along with it. Of

course he *has* changed, too. You've seen that. He's much more serious than he was. He takes everything more seriously. His work, for instance. He has a big responsibility, a lot of money is at stake when he does a picture. For instance, if he should fail to show up some day—the sniffles, or anything like that—really thousands of dollars would be lost, added to the cost of the picture. Thousands of dollars. That's why he's so careful what he eats, and goes to bed early. And they appreciate that at the studio."

"I hope they do."

"Oh, they do."

"When he finishes the picture what will you do?"

"We'll go somewhere together, away from everybody. We might charter someone's boat, or rent a log cabin in the mountains. Just be by ourselves for a month or so. Away from people and the telephone."

"And take your little girl with you?"

"Oh, no. I wouldn't take her out of school, and she loves being with Josephine."

"Maybe I shouldn't ask this, but are you and Hubert planning to have a family?"

"We certainly are. We want to have at least two children."

"Maybe when you come back from your stay in the mountains. I want you to promise me you'll let me know as soon as you're sure."

"I'm sure Hubert wouldn't be able to keep it to himself, even if I wanted to. He's very anxious to have children, almost as anxious as I am, and that's saying a lot."

"You're a wonderful mother, Nina. I think you ought

to have more children, you're so good with your own little girl, and she's a perfect angel of a child. She must have been a very great comfort to you."

"Yes, but don't forget Hubert helped to heal that wound."

They wanted to hear what they were saying to each other, so much so that either woman could have provided the other's next sentence. But no harm was done, except the slight damage to truth and candor; and since Kitty's visit was itself a small insult to truth—they had not invited her because they really wanted her—a few extra minor pretenses were in order. Kitty was packed off two days after her month was up. She had seen something of Southern California and the states along the Santa Fe right-of-way; she had met some top movie stars; made friends with women who would remember her if she returned to Los Angeles but would not think about her if she did not; she had become acquainted with a top movie star who was her own flesh and blood; she was much better off financially. On her last night Richard informed her that thenceforth she could count on an allowance of $10,-000 a year, which would be paid to her by his agent, Jack Golsen, in monthly installments. It had been a profitable trip. But on the train to Chicago she became unaccountably depressed. Nina was a perfect wife, far better than Richard had a right to hope for, and Kitty adored her. She even said as much to a woman with whom she had two meals in the dining-car. But Richard should not have married a perfect wife; he should have married a tart and stayed the way he really was, the way he always had been.

The movie star, aware of his responsibilities, mindful of the cost when the sniffles kept him from work, giving his mother ten thousand a year, rejecting the raffish element of Hollywood in favor of a sort of country club mixture—this was not Richard Ward. Richard Ward had vanished. Hubert Ward was a huge face on a billboard, and nothing like that had ever come out of her, and it was not what she had squeezed out of Sandy into herself.

In the earliest days the motion picture was manufactured in rooms called studios, not because the pioneers had delusions of art, but because the essential piece of equipment was the camera, and for nearly a century photographers had been calling their places of business studios. When the motion picture business moved to California and began to acquire acreage, the people in the business borrowed an old circus term and spoke of the studio as The Lot. As the industry prospered a new name was needed, but no one invented a good one; The Lot—the Warner Lot, the Paramount Lot—remained in acceptable usage in the trade, and The Studio became the designation that was adopted by the trade and the general public. No one wanted to refer to the studios as factories, but that is what they were. In the clothing business, from which so many of the non-performing personnel had come, there was some creative talent and a great deal of temperament—as in the manufacture of motion pictures—but no one objected to the word factory. In Hollywood, however, factory was a term of derision, and a man, usually a writer, who referred to a studio as a factory was likely to be the kind of person who used factory and salt-mines and studio interchangeably.*

Since he did not earn his living in a place called a factory but in a business that called itself a studio, Hubert Ward was permitted and even encouraged to call himself an artist. One studio, indeed, called itself United Artists, as another had called itself Famous Players. (There was no such nonsense in the name Warner Brothers. No one in the world ever paid a nickel to see a Warner brother, but there was no doubt about who was paying the artists they employed.) Joe Ziffrin was more than willing to have Hubert Ward consider himself an artist—remote, unavailable, self-confident—if Hubert Ward the artist would bear in mind that his art, to function at all, had to function in an atmosphere of dollars-and-cents profit. "There's more people see you in one picture than ever saw all of Shakespeare's actors in his whole lifetime," Joe Ziffrin told Hubert Ward.

"I have no idea how many people that would be," said Hubert Ward.

"Well, neither do I, but from the pictures of those theaters I bet they didn't seat over a hundred, if that. In *The Thin Grey Line* you'll be seen by millions, millions. That title is out, by the way. Somebody just remembered it sounds like a plug for a bus line. Also, I don't like the word *thin* in there, and never did. A good fifty gees down the drain we spent publicizing the old title, but a bad title can kill a good picture, no matter what they say. And we

---

* In later years the Irving Thalberg Building at Metro-Goldwyn-Mayer was known as The Iron Lung.

have a good picture, Hubie. You know what I consider a good sign?"

"What?"

"Marion Davies wants you to co-star."

"No thanks."

"Oh, we'll put her off, and the old man, but she only wants the top guys, and she never asked for you before. That's a good sign."

"Well, put them off as long as you can, I don't care how you do it."

"I'll do it by keeping you busy. I understand you and your missus are going away somewhere for a well-earned vacation, but take along a couple of outlines I got for your next picture. Just give them a cursory glance when you have a minute."

"Have I got any choice?"

"Legally, no, but you're pretty good at picking what's suitable. And you know why that is, Hubie?"

"Why?"

"Because you're developing a sense of box office. I'll never give anybody a term contract that includes the right to choose stories, but if I did give it to anybody, that person would be you."

"Thanks, Joe."

"And something else you got, absolutely remarkable in a fellow your age. You know when to stay out of the limelight. Some actors and particularly actresses want their name in every paper every day. But I can tell you from when I was a press agent, publicity that isn't tied in with a picture is only wearing out your welcome. Don't every time you eat in a restaurant think your name ought to be in Parsons's column. People get sick of seeing your name."

"Did I ever mention to you that my wife's maiden name was Parsons?"

"But she isn't any relation?"

"No relation, and we've never even told Lollie."

"It may come in handy sometime, but the way you're going you'll never need her. You would need her if you were looking for jobs, but you're all set, and if she does you a favor she expects one in return. I need her, but you don't."

"I hope I never do.'

"One of these days maybe you and the missus will condescend to come and have dinner at my house. Sylvia's most anxious to get acquainted with Nina, but I won't press it. That I can't legally make you do, and between you and I, the one that's goosing Sylvia into it is Mildred Simmons. You know, Hubie, I never heard a thing about you and Mildred all those years, but I think you were sticking it in there and fooling everybody."

"You're wrong, Joe."

"No. I may be wrong thinking you were laying her *all* the time, but I know you had a piece of it, because Mildred told Sylvia you did. And any time you want any more, it's there."

"I don't want any."

"Well, that's entirely up to you, but Mildred isn't giving up. You know who she's got now, don't you?"

"Don't know, and don't care."

"Well, it's the guy that gave you your start. Marty Ruskin. He's here talking a deal with Metro, producing."

"I saw that, yes."

"He's asking too much money, but if he comes down to earth I wouldn't be surprised to see him sign. He don't know a God damn thing about pictures, but Thalberg's getting ready to make him an offer. Marty was at the house the other night with Mildred, and don't think he doesn't bring up your name every chance he gets. There's a lot of people, Hubie, they're ready to cash in on your success."

"Good luck to the little fairy."

"Yeah? That I never knew. He's in the hay with Mildred."

"Double-gaited."

"That I can believe. He tried to tell me *you* had a bit of swish in you, and I wondered why the hell he'd say that, on *your* record. But now I begin to see daylight."

"I wouldn't call that trying to cash in on my success."

"Oh, I don't think he goes around saying it to everybody, but he can cash in and still put the knock on you. As far as that goes, Mildred blasts you, too, but Sylvia says you're a kind of a mania with Mildred. She hardly talks about anyone else. If it's any satisfaction, Marty Ruskin didn't take your place."

"It's no satisfaction."

"Marty said one funny thing, at my house. You know, he's one of those New York jerks that come out here and think they make an impression by knocking Hollywood."

"That's been tried before."

256

"By experts. But he got on the subject of—now I can't think of the word. What was Chesterton famous for?"

"I don't know."

"Paradox! Marty said the most amusing paradox is you. Now wait a minute till I get it right. He said the big laugh is Hollywood, everything about it. And everywhere you went there was a big laugh, like Hubert Ward suddenly becoming respectable. Hollywood is a place where Hubert Ward can pass for respectable. But the *big* laugh, he said, was going to be when they found out that you were more respectable as a bum than as—you don't mind if I say this?—than as a hypocrite."

"I don't mind anything Marty says, as long as he doesn't say it to me."

"He has it in for you, but now I know why. And he and Mildred between them really go to work on you. Well, it wasn't so long ago that they were all wondering what you got out of it, sitting and chatting with her. And now she's practically telling them. I told Sylvia to be careful of that dame. I never liked Charley much, but I'll bet she gave him a bad time. These last couple of years something was eating him, and it was her."

"Charley was a nice guy."

"Maybe he was and maybe he wasn't, but he was too good to her. No dame is ever going to do that to me. I'll screw anything. I knocked off a piece of tail here yesterday, right in this room. A girl works on the second floor and I never took particular notice to her before, but she happened to get in the elevator with me. 'All the way, Mr. Ziffrin?' she said and put her finger on the button, but she

257

meant it as a double meaning and I said yeah. I said I'd wait for her in my office and let her in through the hall door, so my secretary wouldn't see her. She was nothing special, not to look at, but she wanted to get laid and I'm the head of the studio. So we had a little screw. Listen, I don't have any illusions about myself, or about Sylvia either, for that matter. If she's getting it on the side, more power to her, because I could never be satisfied with one woman and she knows it. I don't care if they're a big star in pictures or some stenographer from the second floor, I'll take all I can get. It'd be different if I believed in love, but I don't. Who the hell would love an ugly little fellow like me? But I get plenty of tail. Some people complain about the way I eat. They say I don't have any manners. And they don't like how I dress. And I made plenty of enemies in business. So what? When I was a kid other kids used to run away from me, till I found out that money was power. So I used to steal money to take a girl to the picture show, and boy what went on there. You know what they call a shylock in New York City? That's a guy that lends you five bucks for six, a dollar a week interest. I was a shylock when I was sixteen years of age, loaning money to hack drivers. They didn't pay, I had a collector an Italian boy I'd give him five bucks to beat a guy up. He turned into Young Kid Marco, fought in Madison *Square* Garden a couple times. He got knocked off in some kind of a Black Hand war, but by then I owned my first theater on Avenue B. I took this studio away from Charley Simmons right under his nose, and I don't intend to stop here. Would Charley have showed me any mercy? No. Only he would have done it his way, and my way he called gangster ethics. So what? I been called worse names than that. If your grosses are up, don't ever mind what they call you. Hubie. And you got Jack Golsen to do your dirty work."

"Well, for the next couple of years the only dirty work he has is to pick up my cheque."

"And maybe by that time you can get rid of him. A couple years from now Sylvia has a brother that's coming up in the agency business, and maybe you'll want to go with him."

"Oh, I think I'll stick with Jack."

"No hurry. Just a suggestion for the future."

"Is that what you wanted to talk to me about, Joe?"

"Hell, no. You mean I pick up a little splitting commissions with my brother-in-law? No, I'm past that, Hubie. Five or six years ago I would have, but I'm too big for that now. Five or six years ago I was still looking for every dollar so I could buy stock in the company. I would of washed your car if it meant a dollar, almost. But the chicken-feed days are over, Hubie. I don't have to chisel any more. You know why I wanted to have this chat with you? You know why I wanted to sit here and relax, with probably six or eight guys sitting outside in my reception room, and my switchboard buzzing?"

"No. Tell me."

"Because you and I are going places together, and we ought to get acquainted. I got you under contract, I got five other top people under contract. I just signed the smartest woman in the business for my Eastern story editor that's going to line up the best properties and only the best. I got Ken Downey under an exclusive contract for five years, a personal contract with me, not with the company. *And,* if you can keep a secret, I got a wealthy man in New York, never put a nickel in any kind of show business before, that when the time comes, the psychological moment, he's ready with a blank cheque. How do you like that for a setup?"

"It looks very good."

"It looks very *good?* If I told you who the money man is I can hear you ask yourself how did this little heeb Joe Ziffrin get anywheres near So-and-so. Well, that's my secret, how I got to him, but I did."

"But I'm not that big, that—"

"No, you're not. But you're growing all the time, and right now I got you for pretty small money. Two years from now you'll only be twenty-seven-eight years of age, with many long years ahead of you. You play along with me now, and when the big things begin to happen, I'll take care of you. Just be satisfied for the present, Hubie. Play along with me. Make me look good now and by the time you're thirty years of age you won't be some washed-up ex-juvenile, you'll be one of the all-time big earners. Play it the way you *been* playing it lately. Stay out of trouble, stay out of the night clubs, and you'll be a second Ronnie Colman."

"I'd kind of like to be a first Hubert Ward."

"I don't care what you call it, as long as you know what I mean. Just let me remind you, though. Ronnie Colman is right now I guess the wealthiest actor in pictures, and if anybody wants to call me a second Louis B. Mayer,

I got no objections if the money goes with it. How much are you worth? You're worth around a hundred and sixty thousand dollars cash."

"I guess so. I'll take your word for it."

"*Take* my word for it. Right now your missus is worth more. Don't get sore. With me it's business, Hubie, I didn't pry into your affairs for curiosity. I gotta know what you're drawing to, what's your hole card. But I'll tell you this, Hubie. I got no objection to you being worth a million dollars on your thirtieth birthday, and two million by the time you're thirty-five. And a big fat three million when you're forty. Just as long as I'm making mine while you're making yours. And I can practically guarantee it. For a guy that was getting ninety a week on Broadway a short while ago, three million socked away at forty is pretty nice."

"I suppose you wouldn't tell me who your money man is in New York?" said Hubert Ward.

"I wouldn't tell that to Sylvia, my own wife. I won't tell you anything about my business transactions. Charley Simmons used to try to find out, but if I told him I wouldn't be sitting in his office today. And neither would you." He leaned forward over his desk. "Hubie, you and I are a couple of bastards together, so let's understand each other, huh?"

"All right."

"Everything we say to each other stays right in this office, okay?"

"Okay."

"And that includes if you ever get in any kind of a jam that I can get you out of, I'll do it."

"Why?"

"Because you don't want my job and I don't want yours, but the bigger we get, the more we're gonna need somebody we can go and talk to. You don't have any friends and I don't either, but I can talk to you and you can always talk to me. You know what ruined Charley Simmons?"

"What?"

"He couldn't face the fact that he was as much of a son of a bitch as you or me. The only son of a bitch he could talk to was his wife, and then he found out she was cheating on him. He didn't die of any broken neck. He was as good as dead as soon as Mildred told him about you."

"There wasn't much to tell."

"To Charley it was plenty. You know why, Hubie? Because she didn't *have* to tell him, the bitch. But when she told him, he knew she was doing it to ruin him. Oh, I know what people say about me. Vulgar and uncouth and all that, and slippery. But when it comes to people, I got a pretty good understanding."

"Are you always right?"

"The only one I was wrong about was myself. I thought I wanted to be a nice kid. But I didn't want to be a nice kid. That was listening to my parents. *They* wanted me to be a nice kid. I guess they took a look at me and decided 'This one we better be careful or he'll go to the electric chair, like Gyp the Blood.' He was a distant relative of my mother. You want to know the truth, I was headed in that direction. A few years older and maybe I'd of *been* Gyp the Blood. You killed a person."

"With a car, yes."

"Nobody in my family ever owned a car till I bought one. I was over twenty years of age before I ever knew anybody that owned a car. Now I got four of them, and I still don't know how to drive. Well, Hubie, I got a fellow out there I guess I kept him waiting long enough. But this was enjoyable, this little chat. Regards to the missus and have an enjoyable vacation, wherever you're going. Oh, the outlines. Take those outlines with you and just pore over them if you get a chance."

They had one dreadful flop together, but the other pictures Ziffrin made with Hubert Ward were financial successes. There was the Foreign Legion picture, directed by Ken Downey and co-starring Maxine Rodelle, the new French import; there were two light comedies co-starring Doris Arlington in one and Ruth St. Alban in the second; there was the romantic reunion of Maxine Rodelle and Hubert Ward in the daringly frank love story of life among the artists in Bohemian Paris, France. As each of these pictures went into production Joe Ziffrin said "It can't miss," and it did not miss. Female stars wanted to work with Hubert Ward; they had to share top billing with him now, but he was an ideal leading man in that he made the women seem attractive, desirable, and from a picture with Hubert Ward they invariably went on to better pictures. "He makes you look good," said Doris Arlington.

"He can't help it. Playing opposite Hubie Ward is as good as having your face lifted, and the smart girls are getting wise to that fact. I didn't realize it till Maxine showed me. That dame is way ahead of us Americans. She did that Foreign Legion opera with him, and she ran it over and over and over. Incidentally she can't stand Hubie. But she signed for that Paris picture and she got Ziffrin to run the Legion thing one afternoon, over and over. And she got together with Ken Downey beforehand and they have a scene in that picture that's the dirtiest thing I ever saw in a thirty-five-millimeter movie. But nobody can object to it."

"What scene is that?" said Doyle Cordell.

"In the attic, about halfway through the picture. She's going back to the guy that she left for Hubie, because he's supposed to be dying of T.B. She's saying goodbye to Hubie, and you know he's going to kiss her. But *where's* he going to kiss her? And if you remember that scene, he doesn't kiss her at all."

"I thought he did."

"You're a man. But he never does kiss her. That's left to the imagination of sixty million women. If Ken had let him kiss her smack on the mouth, it wouldn't have been dirty. But oh no. They fade out, and no kiss, and I defy any woman that's ever been laid not to fill in the next few minutes of that scene. That was entirely Maxine Rodelle's idea, which she handed over to Ken. And there isn't a damn thing the Hays Office can do about it. They wouldn't even know how to write a memorandum about it."

An anonymous critic on *Time* wrote irritably of "pouting Hubert Ward" and the participle was so right that it was taken up by other critics, but without noticeable effect at the box office. A writer employed by Samuel Goldwyn came up with the interesting statistic that in four successive pictures Hubert Ward had spoken the line: "Let's not think about it." As it happened, the writer had written the line in two of the earlier Hubert Ward pictures, and he declared that in writing for a Hubert Ward picture the line was unavoidable. At some point in any Hubert Ward romance the leading man and the leading woman would be placed in a situation that called for such a line, and it was given to Ward. The observation got back to Hubert Ward, and he demanded that Ziffrin buy a play by Clifford Odets. No Odets play was available, but an Odets imitator had a play for sale and Hubert Ward was placated. The picture was called *Prisoners of Starvation.* Hubert Ward played an idealistic young Jewish school-teacher who gets killed in the Spanish Civil War. Aside from some patronizingly approving reviews in the leftist press and a few statements of the plot by leftist reviewers in the capitalist newspapers the picture was a failure. It was cheaply made, and Ziffrin counted on foreign sales to minimize his loss, but overseas *Prisoners* was more savagely attacked than at home: Hubert Ward and Ziffrin and the obscure screen writers were exposed as counter-revolutionaries, boring from within, who had deliberately made a bad picture as a propaganda effort to ridicule the Loyalists. It was a confusing experience for Hubert Ward, who had only wanted to get away from "Let's not think about it." During the production period he was slightly surprised and pleased to be treated in friendly fashion by

Hollywood intellectuals who had hitherto ignored him; he was baffled and then annoyed by the sudden hostility of Dwight Barley and Barley's friends and the Los Angeles newspapers. He contributed small sums to the various Loyalist causes, in the belief that it was good publicity for the picture. But when the American leftists, taking their cue from the radical journals in Paris and London, reconsidered their attitude toward *Prisoners,* Hubert Ward and Ziffrin became the object of such vituperation as to make the Los Angeles papers' hostility seem a benediction. "I don't understand it," said Hubert Ward to his wife.

"Not hard to understand. Everybody thinks you're a Communist except the Communists," said Nina Ward.

"You don't think I'm a Communist."

"No, not really. But you never asked me what I thought about your doing that picture."

"Well, what *did* you think—now that it's all over?"

"It isn't all over. Some people are never going to forgive you."

"Dwight and Josephine, for instance?"

"Josephine more than Dwight. And your mother. And my uncle."

"That livery-stable man in Indiana, for God's sake."

"Who was very nice to us when we got married."

"Very nice to you, you mean."

"And to you. You didn't want any publicity, and he arranged so you didn't get any."

"Well, he never liked me anyway."

"That is true. He didn't."

"Do *you?*"

"What a stupid question."

"Well, *do* you?"

"Not always."

"Then it wasn't such a stupid question after all."

"Yes it was. I don't have to like everything you do."

"I could fix it so you'd have a lot more to dislike."

"Yes, you could. That's entirely up to you. Who with? Maxine Rodelle?"

"Now wait a minute, Nina. I haven't fooled around with Maxine or anyone else, and you know it."

"Do I know it?"

"If you don't, you should."

"I don't know what I know," she said.

They had a child now, a two-year-old son called Christopher after Christopher Columbus, Christopher Morley, Christopher Mathewson, or the saint whose gold, unblessed medallion was fixed to the glove compartment of Nina's Lincoln Continental.* The child was fat and blue-eyed and blond, and well loved by Nina and Hubert Ward and by his half sister. Nina noticed but did not comment on the fact that after the birth of her son the house in Brentwood Heights was protected with a series of burglar alarms that Hubert Ward had not suggested while there was only Nina's daughter in the household. Hubert Ward, who had never owned a revolver, now kept three Police Special .38's in his bedroom, his study, and in Nina's car. The child had an English nurse, a Miss Gribble, and Nina

---

* Neither the father nor the mother had heard of Christopher Ward's parodies.

bought a boxer which she called Henry, after Henry Armstrong.

About two months before the baby was born, and during the shooting of the Bohemians in Paris picture, Hubert Ward offered Maxine Rodelle a lift to the house she had rented in Beverly Hills. It was the first gesture of the kind he had made to her. "Will you care to stop for a drink?" she said.

"Of course," he said.

They were both tired and annoyed at Ken Downey, who had been using the technique of the insult to improve their performances. "That Ken, he is such a bastard," said Maxine. "You have worked with him more times than I. He does that very often?"

"Too often."

"Some day I walk off the set."

"He'll have the camera on you when you do, and he'll use the footage. He's a bastard all right. But he's good."

"Yes."

She was wearing black woolen slacks and a matching sweater, quite obviously without a brassiere, and drinking a split of champagne. Hubert Ward was drinking a Coca-Cola. "How is your wife?" she said.

"She's fine, thanks."

"When is the birth of the baby?"

"Seven or eight weeks, they figure."

"Your first baby?"

"As far as I know," he said, with a smile.

"Yes, as far as you know," she said. "I would like to have a baby sometime."

"All right. Shall we start one?"

"No thank you. You are a good husband, Hubie. No one expected you to be one. I was warned about you before I came to Hollywood."

"How nice."

"Yet you never made one single pass at me."

"Well, you've been pretty busy, Maxine."

"Is that why you never made one single pass at me?"

"No. In the old days I would have."

"That is better. A wolf, that is what I was told, but then this wolf never made one single pass at me."

"No, but don't tempt me. I'm in the mood."

"So am I."

"You are?" He got up and sat beside her.

"I don't like a man to be as rude as Ken. I wanted to cry but he wanted me to cry so I did not cry."

"You don't seem on the verge of tears now, but do you want to cry now?"

"No." She put down her glass. "Affection."

He kissed her and she joined in the kiss. She drew back her head and smiled. "They would pay to see this," she said. She pulled her sweater over her head and she kissed him again.

"Let's give them their money's worth," he said.

"But of course," she said. She pretended to be speaking to a camerman. "Pan to the bedroom." She got up and he followed her. She got out of slacks and girdle and sat

269

in the bed while he undressed. "How much would they pay for us now?"

"Quite a lot."

"I think they would pay a lot. We must give them their money's worth, Hubie. This they would pay a lot." She again spoke to the imaginary cameraman. "Close-up of this, please."

When it was over she said, "Thank you, Hubie."

"Thank *you*," he said.

"No, I will sleep better now. He was so rude to me, that Ken."

"Maybe I'd better thank *him*."

"Why? Oh. No, you go home to your enceinte wife and forget us. You promise?"

"I can't promise that, Maxine."

"No, you can't. But tomorrow I have my chauffeur take me home. And the next day and all days."

"In other words, this is a one-shot."

"One-shot? Yes, a one-shot. But nice. I like you better."

"I like *you* better."

She laughed. "A good lay makes friends, yes?"

"And a good bawling-out by that bastard Ken."

"Very true. Goodnight, Hubie. One kiss, and goodnight."

He tried to be neither more nor less attentive to Nina, but a few days later, for no immediate reason, she said, "Pretty soon you're going to have to stay away from me entirely, we're not going to be able to make love at all. What will you do?"

"The same as you. Do without."

"Can you? You never have."

"Sure I can."

"I knew a girl at home—this is an awful story. A girl was having a baby and she didn't want her husband to cheat on her, so she asked a friend to go to bed with her husband, and the friend said she would if my friend didn't hold it against her. Just sex."

"And what happened?"

"Well, they had sex and that was all there was to it, but then the other girl was having a baby and she asked my friend to do the same thing for *her* husband and my friend refused. Sort of made a whore out of the other girl, and they've never spoken since."

"Your friend was a bitch."

"My friend was me, Hubert. That's why it's such an awful story. The girl has never forgiven me, and I don't blame her. But I just couldn't sleep with her husband, on any grounds."

"But you were willing to let Stephens sleep with a friend of yours."

"Not willing. But I agreed, for health reasons."

"Next question. Was it your idea, or Stephens's?"

"His."

"He convinced you that it would have been bad for his health to give up sex?"

"Yes."

"Amazing. What was his argument? How did he convince you?"

"Listen, I didn't know anything about men, from personal experience. He had no trouble convincing me. I believed everything he told me about men. He said it was something about the prostate gland. It was so long ago I don't remember very well, all the details. But he explained that it was harmful to stop, once a man had got used to it."

"How could you have been so naïve? You're not about other things."

"I don't know, but I was. The whole thing about men mystifies me anyway. A woman—well, you can either put it in or you can't put it in. But a man has to get hard, and why does he get hard sometimes and sometimes can't. The doctor tried to explain it to me, but I guess I didn't listen carefully, or I was embarrassed or something."

"Still another question. The girl that Stephens slept with. Did you choose her, or did Stephens?"

"He did, or we both did. He suggested two or three names, and I picked one."

"The least attractive?"

"No, she wasn't. But I knew she'd had other affairs and I thought it would matter the least to her."

"And so you had her over for tea one afternoon and suggested she might do you the favor of sleeping with your husband."

"Almost like that. *I* went to *her* house. I was quite big, bigger than I am now."

"Go on. It's quite a scene."

"I said I was going to be frank and I wanted her to be, too. I said Wayne needed somebody to sleep with, and would she do it? I promised her I wouldn't be jealous and would keep it a secret, and that she'd be doing me a favor.

And she said she would as long as her husband didn't find out about it."

"Where did they get together, the girl and your husband?"

Nina was silent, then said, "In our house."

"With you waiting downstairs?"

"I usually went for a walk, but sometimes I waited downstairs."

"Oh, this went on for quite a while?"

"Over two months."

"Then you put a stop to it?"

"Yes. When I could resume relations with him."

"Resume relations. Weren't you jealous of the girl?"

"Horribly. But I tried to make myself believe I wasn't, that it was only sex."

"Like two animals? No fun? No affection?"

"I didn't let myself think about it too much."

"Did you go on being friends with the girl?"

"Curiously enough, I liked her a lot, and more than I ever had. But I never felt the same way about him. Especially when I found out that he'd made a fool of me."

"Didn't you feel that that gave you the right to have an affair with somebody?"

"I suppose I did."

"But you didn't have an affair with somebody else?"

"No."

"But you could have very easily, when your friend got pregnant and asked you to."

"I know. But with me it always had to be more than sex. I couldn't have got in bed with her husband. I could have got in bed, but I couldn't have done anything. I'd have frozen up. But the girl has never spoken to me again, and I don't blame her."

"Now, the big question. Why did you let Stephens get away with it?"

"Because for two reasons. I was afraid of him, and I was in love with him."

"How afraid? I didn't think you'd ever been afraid of anyone or anything."

"Not physically. Not that he would beat me or anything like that. A man wouldn't understand this. But I was afraid that he'd go have other women, and I'd lose him and my marriage. He wasn't a great lover or anything like that. I was much more of a woman than he was a man, sexually. In plain language, he didn't always satisfy me. But for some strange reason that was part of the hold he had on me. Sometimes he did satisfy me, and I'd be crazy about him. But when he didn't satisfy me, I blamed myself, although I *must* have known better."

"You wouldn't sleep with me before we were married."

"No."

"And when I first knew you you kept saying you wouldn't have anything messy. You don't call that messy, your husband and your friend?"

"I call it very messy. Don't you see how I hated it?"

"I suppose so."

"You suppose so? If you slept with another woman now I'd leave you. I wouldn't go through that again. And here the temptation is much worse, not to speak of the opportunities. All these actresses."

"Oh, nuts to that, Nina. It was one of your Lake Forest suburbanites that slept with your husband. And you, a Lake Forest suburbanite, that arranged it. Don't be so high and mighty about actresses."

"I was thinking more of opportunities, but I shouldn't have spoken that way about actresses."

"No, you shouldn't."

"I'm sorry."

Hubert Ward made a second effort in the direction of Maxine Rodelle but this one was unsuccessful. "Find someone else, Papa," she said. He found no one else because he looked for no one else, and he remained, with that single exception, faithful to Nina. It was annoying therefore that more than two years later she should single out Maxine Rodelle as a candidate for his attentions; particularly annoying, of course, because his relations with Maxine had been not quite completely innocent.

The minor disaster of Hubert Ward's single tenuous connection with Weltpolitik had no effect on his standing as a leading man. Ziffrin quickly put him in a South Sea island picture (shot at Catalina) with Maxine Rodelle beautifully miscast as a missionary's widow and a new-comer, Zella Flowers, as a half-caste child of nature. Maxine hated every minute of the competition with the Flowers bosom, and as a consequence the miscasting turned into an asset as she moved sternly through the picture, disapproving the infatuation of the copra planter (Hubert Ward) and the Polynesian maiden. The picture, in Ziffrin's words, made a mint of money in spite of a par-

275

tial boycott in the Southern states, where Miss Flowers was declared to be a mulatto. Her real name was Ellen Flannigan and she came from Buffalo, New York, but with a black wig, the right make-up, and her little Irish nose she looked plenty Polynesian. Ziffrin hesitated too long about putting her under contract and lost her to Metro, where she almost immediately became the mistress of Martin Ruskin, in his third year as a producer at the Culver City studio. Without the black wig Zella Flowers made the first of many appearances in the bread-and-butter series created and produced by Martin Ruskin, which told of romance and adventure in the life of a big city hospital. That old favorite of the legitimate theater, Philip W. Carstairs, was brought out of retirement to play the crotchety, lovable, non-denominational chaplain in the series, which were written by Ralph Harding, the Broadway playwright. The head nurse was played by Hildegarde Finney, another favorite of the legitimate theater.

As of anno Domini 1936 a fair statement of the fame of Hubert Ward would have been that his name and face were known in every community on earth that was served by electric current. It was probably true, and very nearly provable, that wherever there was the power to run a projection machine, his name and his likeness were familiar to men, women and children who would sit or stand to watch a Hubert Ward cinema. In many lands his true voice was less well known, since the voices of other men were substituted for Hubert Ward's, but in the hill towns of Northern India and in villages in Northern Ireland his appearance on the main thoroughfare would have stopped traffic for the same reason that the citizens of Hightstown, New Jersey, U.S.A., would have stared and gathered round him, eager to touch him, to have him scribble his name on a piece of paper. He was a big movie star. A *big* movie star. In the foreign lands they might—and usually did—change the titles of his pictures, but Hubert Ward's name stayed. He was often used by preachers as a handy symbol for sin; but he was also useful to the manufacturers of Chevrolets, Old Golds, Coca-Cola, and Colgate-Palm-olive-Peet products, whom he helped by recommending their wares. He had long since ceased to be known as the New York theater actor; in far-off places there were men and women who had seen Hubert Ward on screens under galvanized iron roofs, to whom the name New York meant nothing whatever. His photograph, cabinet-size and signed, rested on piano tops in the living quarters of royalty, and he now got mail addressed to Hubert Ward U.S.A. without delay. The larger mass of people were totally uncritical of his work as an actor; it was enough for them that he passed before their eyes once, twice, seven or eight times a year, embracing pretty women, engaged in combat with strong men, getting into and out of perilous situations; showing pleasure and fear and pain and sorrow. At least two women committed suicide with his photograph somewhere near them, and a young man in Danville, Illinois, had collected more than 9,000 newspaper and magazine clippings in which the name Hubert Ward was mentioned. A woman in Cleveland, Ohio, christened her twins Hubert Ward and Ward Hubert Malikowski. The

Hubert Ward Fan Clubs, Incorporated, no longer a studio-inspired stunt, published a monthly bulletin with a circulation of 200,000 copies distributed in the English-speaking countries, and annually the newly elected president of the Fan Clubs made a trip to Hollywood for a two-day visit with their idol and the presentation of a cheque in his honor to the Boy Scouts of America, the Motion Picture Relief Fund, or some equally worthy cause. A judge in Queens County, New York, refused to permit a German-Jewish refugee to change his name to Hubert Ward, on the ground that a new citizen ought to choose a worthier name than that of a movie actor.

The perquisites of his kind of fame were many; the potency of it was great so long as it was not put to any test. The perquisites consisted largely of luxuries and small courtesies. Hubert Ward would usually talk his way out of minor traffic offenses without displaying one of the numerous badges and shields signifying honorary membership in police departments and sheriffs' posses. He could cash a cheque anywhere in the world, and get a good table in a restaurant. When he traveled the railroads made him comfortable, and the telephone company would install an extension in his house in three hours. Such small favors as did not come to him on his own could be obtained through the studio. At the studio he was given princely treatment; beginning with his first appearance in the early morning, when the gate would be swung open for him so that he could proceed without halting, the studio made him feel important. His portrait in oils dominated the commissary, and he could leave his car unattended anywhere except in the space reserved for Joe Ziffrin. His dressing-room was actually a suite, redecorated annually and providing luxurious living quarters if he wished to spend the night on the lot. He was *Mister* Ward to men and women twice his age, and, in certain cases, many times his ability. He was a *big* movie star, getting the treatment reserved for big movie stars, and no outsider attempting to understand a movie star could ever merely imagine the effect of all the homage, servility, and obsequiousness that went with stardom. It had to be seen, and seen day after day, to be appreciated, and almost no one saw it who was not part of the industry. The outsider would hear about fantastic salaries, and could see the examples of conspicuous spending by the stars themselves—the houses, the motor cars, the jewelry, the furs—but it was the day-to-day, hour-by-hour, taken-for-granted, freely accorded palace treatment that affected these men and women, most of them of humble origin. A girl who at sixteen had run away with a trombonist in Sousa's band now had a private purse and an entourage befitting a queen; a young man who had been happy to get $10 on his twenty-first birthday and had been afraid of going to prison over a $37.50 cheque was now as famous as the Prince of Wales.

The women were more adaptable to their new circumstances than the men. Doris Arlington, for all her common sense and realistic attitudes, still typified the female stars' quick and continuing acceptance of their position. They were movie queens, and they lived up to their station and the accompanying responsibility to what they properly called their public. Privately, surreptitiously, they might make shrewd investments, but Garbo alone could eccentrically own an obsolescent Lincoln and successfully resist the demands on her privacy; and even Garbo in the beginning had posed in a track suit for publicity photographs. Doris Arlington, Constance Bennett, Joan Crawford, Kay Francis, Marlene Dietrich, Loretta Young, and Ruth St. Alban did what was expected of them, and Dolly Madison and Marie Antoinette had not done it better.

But the men were uncomfortable. There was always, with the men—including the most inflated egotisms among them—an embarrassed reluctance to take full part in the royal ceremonials at the premières, the industry banquets, the sporting events. The men were always a little awkward, always a bit apologetic, sometimes discernibly timorous, as though in fear of a rude remark or a rotten tomato. They were extremely aware of the fact that a top hat is a traditional target, that tailcoats were rare in Southern California, and that acting has never been regarded as the manliest way to earn a living. Consequently they had to force themselves to be cheerfully polite to the peculiar people who infested the ceremonials, and there was not a big star in the industry who could talk gracefully for three minutes without a script. They wanted to get away from the microphone in a hurry, and luckily they usually did. Unfortunately, they did not stay away completely or permanently; they were actors, and so long as other actors would be making appearances at the ceremonials, they all wanted to be there. It is above all a competitive occupation.

It was also a demanding occupation without quite being hard work. It was repetitive and monotonous, and therefore tiring; and on occasion there were discomforts and, on some fewer occasions, physical hazards. But somewhere between the work and the disproportionate rewards something was missing, and that absent factor was a feeling of accomplishment. No man in his right mind could continue to convince himself that his work in a picture was hard work as digging ditches is hard work, dangerous work as stringing transmission lines is dangerous work, or useful work as surgery, teaching, or farming is useful work. And even the advanced cases of egotism could not uphold their acting abilities against the seldom expressed but constantly implied superiority of men who had trouped with Merivale and Standing and Sothern and Cohan. The fame and the money were earned only to the extent that in the general inflation of notoriety and profit a man was entitled to his share, but neither the acting nor the rewards provided the satisfaction of accomplishment, and the male stars sought escape from the unrealities in various ways. For some the means of escape was women; for others, booze; for a few, gambling. And some escaped by escaping to sport, to non-professional companionship, to periods of privacy at places removed from the movie colony. There were some who could shoot, and they shot; some who could honestly sail a sloop, and they sailed. They were the lucky ones, who would sit in their dressing-rooms between takes and dream and talk of the guns they had ordered from Purdey and the animals they would destroy; the boats they had ordered from Olin Stephens and the waters they would sail in. There were a few who got invited to the

parties on Long Island, and campaigned for their Racquet
Club hatbands. There were others who fled to foreign tol-
erance to escape from their heterosexual masquerade. And
there were the pitiful ones who took trips on which they
were accompanied by a studio press agent and who got
out at every five-minute stop to attract movie fans.

Hubert Ward had escaped into respectability a short
time before becoming a big star, and respectability remained his personal escape instead of women, alcohol,
gambling, guns, sailing, homosexuality, social-climbing,
or the intellectual pursuits that attracted almost no one of
his standing. The novelty of respectability after his
picaresque early life remained sufficiently attractive to
have held him for possibly four or five years, but Nina had
knowingly married a rogue, and one morning at twenty
minutes to eleven, one night at half-past eight, and then
at various times of various days she discovered and re-
discovered that the domesticated rogue was boring her.

It was not the way things were supposed to work out,
according to men and women who had known Hubert
Ward. All the predictions held that Hubert Ward within a
year of his marriage would be sleeping with his co-stars or
anyone else who caught his fancy and was agreeable. Nina
herself had been vigilant against some such development.
But except for the lapse with Maxine Rodelle, Hubert
Ward had been faithful to his wife, and in his fidelity he
had failed her. Nina's vigilance was a stimulating habit,
and when the necessity for it apparently had vanished,
Hubert ceased to be stimulating. Likewise their life in
Southern California. Nina had believed that she was afraid

of what the motion picture industry could do to a marriage, and she was at first pleased that their life was as little different as possible in the circumstances from life in Lake Forest. But the day came when their life was, in effect, Lake Forest, Los Angeles County, California, and Dwight and Josephine Barley and their friends, assisted by Hubert Ward, had banished picture people. Nina's pleasure in this accomplishment lasted only as long as her movie star husband was exciting.

"Let's have a party and have the whole movie crowd," she said one evening.

"Good God, what for?"

"Do you object? I thought you'd be pleased. We owe thousands of invitations."

"Thousands of invitations we declined."

"That's just it. Before you married me you'd have gone, and every once in a while a little remark here and there—I get the feeling that they resent me."

"Let them."

"No, I don't like to be a villainess," she said. "Fancy dress! Come as your favorite villainess, or villain. How about it?"

"Well, what the hell—all right."

They took over the Victor Hugo restaurant and hired Phil Ohman's orchestra. Fifteen outstanding movie actresses came as Mata Hari without duplicating costumes; eight men came as John Wilkes Booth, and one of them had a fist fight with one of the three men who came as Adolf Hitler. Two women came as Shirley Temple. A Pasadena friend of the Dwight Barleys arrived in a wheelchair, impersonating Franklin D. Roosevelt, and Nero was popular among the stout guests, outnumbering Benito Mussolini eight to five. Catherine de Médicis, Cleopatra, Catherine of Russia, Sappho, Lydia Pinkham (impersonated by Jack Rodney, the hair stylist), Queen Elizabeth, Marie Antoinette, and Amelia Bloomer (impersonated by Karll Langlie, the set dresser) were represented as villainesses. The villain-villainess theme was somewhat distorted by actors and actresses coming as heroes and heroines, owing to the rather limited supply of readily recognizable symbols of wickedness. Hubert Ward dressed as Satan; Nina, in tights and fig leaves, as Eve After the Fall, the first villainess of all. They had a dinner party for forty at their house, and the first guests were already dancing when they arrived at the restaurant shortly before eleven o'clock. It was almost the last Hubert Ward saw of his wife until the party broke up at five. "I don't know if anybody else had a good time, but *I* did," she said. "Did you?"

"Nice of you to ask."

"In other words, you didn't. You danced a lot."

"Oh, you noticed that? Who was the character dressed as Benedict Arnold, or I guess he was supposed to be Benedict Arnold."

"Very smart of you. People kept asking him if he was supposed to be George Washington. That was Michael Tremaine."

"Who's he?"

"You ought to know. He's a writer at Metro."

"How would I know a writer at Metro? They have a

hundred writers at Metro, most of them nobody ever heard of."

"You must have heard of this one. He writes plays. He wrote *Love and Anna Collier*. Wasn't that a big hit?"

"It was a big hit. I never read it. Who did he come with?"

"Joan and Franchot. They asked to bring him."

"No wife?"

"Not here. She's staying back East."

"Well, you kept him from getting homesick for one evening."

"Very good dancer. Well, I'm glad we gave the party. It was well timed. People *were* criticizing me. It doesn't pay to be a snob. They couldn't hurt me, but they could take it out on you. Ziffrin said it was a very good idea to have the party just at this time."

"Why?"

"Because a lot of people had never met me, and they sort of resented me. We don't have to have them swarming all over our house, but industry good will—anyway, that's what Ziffrin said."

"Ziffrin is full of shit. If it was such a good idea I'll send him the bill. This thing is going to run close to twenty thousand bucks."

"Don't you take it off your income tax?"

"That isn't the same as handing me twenty thousand bucks."

"Well, *I* had a good time, and I'll pay half if you want me to."

"You must have had a good time. When are we seeing Mr. Tremaine again?"

"How did you know that?"

"When are we?"

"He's coming out to play tennis next Sunday. I thought we could have a few people in for lunch, and those that wanted to play tennis, could."

"Nina, what gives?"

"What gives what?"

"This brawl tonight, and next Sunday people for lunch."

"Don't you ever get tired of the same old faces? I do. You see other people at the studio, but I might just as well be in Lake Forest."

"You'd never wear that costume in Lake Forest."

"But I'm not in Lake Forest. Ziffrin said I could have a screen test."

"Aren't you proud?"

"Oh, he wasn't serious."

"Maybe not about the screen test, but a screen test costs a thousand dollars."

"Are you implying that Joe Ziffrin wouldn't give a thousand dollars to sleep with me? If you are, you're wrong. And if you think Joe Ziffrin was the only one that propositioned me tonight you have another think coming."

"I see. That's what you consider a good time."

"Any girl does, and heaven knows, Hubert, it's a long time since I've had a compliment from you."

"Cost me twenty thousand dollars to find out that

286

you're getting bored with me. Expensive education. Good-night."

"Goodnight."

Michael Tremaine was a tall man with bushy greying hair, who chop-stroked every ball, forehand and backhand, and laughed contemptuously when he scored points. "I play to win," he said. "The hell with form."

"But you've got the meanest chop, you put the worst cut on the ball," said Nina.

"What are you squawking about? You beat me."

"But I'm exhausted after two sets."

"The hell you are. Let's play some doubles. Hubie?"

"No thanks, I'm not playing today."

"Come on, for Christ's sake. Work up a sweat, it'll do you good."

"No thanks. I really don't like to play against a chop stroke."

"Why not? It's all tennis."

"That's just it, I don't think it is."

"Tell you what I'll do. I'll play you for a hundred dollars, and I don't know how good you are."

"Hubert would beat you, Mike."

"Maybe he would, but the offer's still good."

"I honestly don't think I want a hundred dollars that much."

"All right, make it worth your while. I'll play you for a *thousand* dollars."

"Why are you so anxious to play me? I'm not going to play you, so stop making those ridiculous offers."

Tremaine reached in the pocket of his tennis shorts

and drew out a money clip. It was stuffed out of shape with too many banknotes. He counted off ten bills. "One thousand dollars. It's not a ridiculous offer."

"Oh, of course you have the money. I'm sure everybody knows that. What I wanted to know was, why do you want to play me? If I wanted to play you I'd play you for nothing."

"Oh, it's personal."

"I guess it must be, yes. I've seen you play, and Nina's right. I think I could take away your thousand dollars without a hell of a lot of trouble, chop stroke or no chop stroke. But *why* do you want to play *me?*"

"Oh, give up, both of you. Hubert, you make me so damn mad," said Nina.

"Why do I make you mad?"

"Let's not go into it," she said. "Come on, Mike, we'll get two others and play doubles."

"I'm going to take a nap. By the way, Tremaine, you don't have to carry your money in your pants pocket. It's safe here." Hubert Ward walked away, said a few words to the other guests, and retired to his room. He turned on the radio and lay on his bed, and after a while he fell asleep. The California sun had disappeared when he was awakened by Nina's presence in his room. "Are you looking for something?" he said.

"Yes. A coat for Mike. Can I borrow your old polo coat?"

"No, I'm fond of that coat. Where are you going?"

"We're all going down to Malibu for supper. Shall I tell him you refused to lend him a coat?"

"I don't give a God damn what you tell him. Take another coat, for Christ's sake. That Burberry, the blue tweed. I don't like it, I never did. When will you be back?"

"I don't know. Nine-thirty. Ten, probably. We're going to that place that used to be Thelma Todd's."

"I didn't ask you where you were going—"

"Yes you did."

"Yes, so I did. But I don't really care. I just wanted to know what to tell the children."

"I've said goodnight to the children. I don't know why you're being so disagreeable, but I haven't time to talk about it now."

"Let me know when you do have time, and you can fit me into your busy schedule."

"I'll think about it." She put the blue tweed coat over her arm and departed, and in a few minutes he heard the cars leaving the property. He put on a suit and went to the nursery to say goodnight to his son, and he stopped and kissed Nina's daughter (whom he had legally adopted) in her room. He took the Continental and drove up to Sunset Boulevard and turned toward Beverly Hills for no other reason than an instinctive desire to go in the opposite direction from Nina and the others. The traffic was heavy, but he had nowhere to go, and in a little less than an hour he was in his suite at the studio. The silence was oppressive, and he had not felt so alone since the final days on the Cape, with the prospect of a jobless New York ahead of him.

The silence was formidable. There was a radio in the suite, but he did not wish to break the silence with the radio. He looked several times at the telephones, but no one would be calling him from outside the studio. No one but the watchman at the studio gate knew where he was. No one in the world but that one man in his sentry-box, reading the early edition of the Los Angeles *Examiner*, and too well trained in the eccentricities of movie stars to risk disturbing Hubert Ward. "I'm sure he expects a dame to show up," said Hubert Ward, breaking the silence.

He was a prisoner. He could not go alone to the Vine Street Brown Derby without having to answer questions. He could not call anyone without raising questions. It was Sunday night, and he could not even make a play for any of the studio women in the Ziffrin manner. He could not show up at Maxine Rodelle's or Ruth St. Alban's or Doris Arlington's. He looked at his watch and at the clocks in the suite; it was twenty past eight and all the people he knew were having Sunday night supper. The little girls he had once known were all five years older than they had been when he last called them—married, dead, working as waitresses, featured players, living with their lovers, busy, busy, busy. *Golsen!* Jack Golsen.

He telephoned Golsen at his apartment, but there was no answer. He was disappointed, then just as well pleased. Golsen would have a girl and a table at the Trocadero for ten o'clock, and he would make an emergency, a crisis, of a telephone call from Hubert Ward at this odd hour on a Sunday. Golsen would get rid of his girl, come to the studio, start guessing and master-minding—and from preaching he would proceed to procuring. Golsen was no solution, but one valuable thought had occurred while he had Golsen in mind: this was not an emergency, but Hubert Ward knew it to be a crisis. Twenty-six past eight.

He thought of calling KNX, the radio station. "Girls of Southern California," he would say. "This is Hubert Ward. I am all alone in my suite at the U. S. Films studio. Come and get it." He wandered about, gazing at the photographs he knew so well of himself in scenes from all his pictures. Some but not all of the photographs included women; friends, mistresses, mistresses who had become friends, but there was not one he could call now, for conversation, for consolation, or for sex. He was not quite ready to commit himself to adultery; if he did, Nina would know it the moment they confronted each other. And there was no one in Hollywood, no one in the entire world, in whom he could confide his tentative contemplation of infidelity. The suite was crowded with reassuring evidences of his fame, and it was the fame that had become so precious that it compelled him to sit alone with it and nothing else in a silent studio on a Sunday night, while the free and anonymous ones could be with each other. Ten minutes of nine.

He went out and started his car. "Forgot something, Jerry," he said to the watchman.

"Coming back, Mr. Ward?"

"I don't know, I'm not sure," he said. He drove up to Sunset and headed homeward.

She came home shortly before eleven. She hung his coat in the foyer closet. "Mike asked me to thank you for the coat," she said. "Did you go out for supper?"

"I went down to the studio. No, I didn't have any supper."

"What did you get all dressed for?"

"I was going to spend the night at the studio, but after I was there a while I changed my mind."

"Haven't you had anything to eat?"

"Yes. I had some corn flakes and a sliced banana, in the kitchen."

"I had the worst steak I ever ate, bar none. One thing about coming from the Middle West, it spoils you for the rest of the country when it comes to steaks. Don't you want something more to eat?"

"No thanks."

"Well, then I'm off to bed. Did you leave word what time you want to be called?"

"Six o'clock."

"I won't see you that early. Is the Thermos in the kitchen with your coffee?"

"Coffee, and the orange juice is squeezed. Before you leave, what about Tremaine?"

"What about him?"

"Well, are you seeing him again?"

"Hubert, I haven't seen Tremaine, the way you imply. I haven't been alone with him. He wants me to have lunch with him tomorrow, but I can't. However, I am having lunch with him and two other people on Friday, and he's coming here to play tennis next Sunday."

"No he isn't."

"Yes he is. Don't make an issue of Mike Tremaine, or you may be sorry."

"I may be sorry if I don't. I don't want the son of a bitch in my house."

"I never said a word when you had friends of yours I didn't particularly like. But if I can't have my friends here, I'll just have to meet them elsewhere. Take your choice."

"Tremaine is no friend of yours. You've seen him twice —as far as I know."

"I'm not going to have an affair with Mike Tremaine."

"How do you know?"

"Because I don't want to. You've gone away for weeks at a time, on location, and had breakfast, lunch and dinner with other women and I haven't complained. So I repeat, don't make an issue of Mike Tremaine."

"I have made an issue of him."

"All right. I'll disinvite him for next Sunday. It's your house. But in that case I'll tell him I've changed my mind about tomorrow."

"You're going to have lunch with him tomorrow *and* Friday?"

"Yes."

"Okay, Nina. You haven't come to bed with me since we had that God damn party, and now you're slapping me in the face with this noisy, cheap showoff. I gather you know what you're doing."

"I know what I'm doing, and I know a veiled threat when I hear one, too."

"Well, I'll take the veil off it. Tremaine is a married man, and you're having lunch with him three times in one week—"

"Twice."

"Three times. Plus dinner tonight. You've never done that before. If you're not having an affair with him you're giving it a damn good chance to develop into one."

"If it does, I'll tell you."

"Thanks, you're so honorable it kills me."

The first public notice of trouble was in a New York paper, in the form of a question by the columnist Ed Sullivan: "The Hubert Wards acting silly?"

"What about this, Hube? Is there any truth in it?" said Joe Ziffrin.

"Just Nina taking an interest in play-writing," said Hubert Ward.

"I didn't know you'd be so frank about it," said Ziffrin.

"Why the hell not?"

"Yeah, why the hell not, as long as you stay out of court."

"We're nowhere near that stage."

"I flatter myself I'm an expert on women, but what does Nina see in this Tremaine?"

"Well, for that matter, what did she see in me?"

"That's easy. You got the answer to that in fifty million women going to your pictures. But no woman I know of would ever pay money to see Tremaine, in or out of pictures. I guess he's so different from you. Well, Hube, a certain party named Zella Flowers been asking me about you. She saw this thing in Ed's column."

"I hear she's Marty Ruskin's girl."

"No girl is Marty Ruskin's girl for long. And anyway, what if she was? You wouldn't be marrying her. Maybe

Marty would, but you wouldn't. They keep asking in the papers, when is Marty Ruskin marching up the aisle with Zella Flowers. Questions like that are responsible for a hell of a lot of marriages in this business. The dame wants a husband, and a guy like Marty figures what the hell, a luscious young broad for a couple years. Maybe a kid or two. And in Marty's case, to convince people he give up being a fag. You never had a thing with Doris Arlington, did you? That always surprised me. You two would of been a natural, somewhere along the line."

"A lot of people thought that, I guess. But when I was on the town I wasn't big enough."

"Big enough where? I know, I just couldn't resist the gag. I don't care what you do, Hube. Zella Flowers. Doris. But now nobody's gonna blame you, whereas till recently they would have."

"All right. Come and have dinner Tuesday," said Doris Arlington.

He went to her house, having had his secretary telephone Nina that he would not be home for dinner. Doris was wearing black velvet slacks and an embroidered blouse, and she sat with her legs arranged tailor fashion in what may have been deliberately discouraging to physical intimacy. She came immediately to the point. "You know I have a fellow," she said.

"Doyle Cordell? Is he still it?"

"Just so you know that, Hubie. But if you want somebody to talk to, you're my friend and Nina never was. I like Nina all right, but she could never be a friend of mine.

Ruth is the only woman friend I have, and I don't trust her too much either. So what's on your mind? First I'll ask you a question. Is Nina going to bed with this Tremaine?"

"I'm not sure."

"You have some doubts about it. If you want my opinion, I don't think she is. That's not saying she won't, but I have a hunch she isn't yet. You want what I think in a nutshell, Nina is attracted to Tremaine because he's about as different from you as anyone could be. *Now.* But you were different, too, when you first knew Nina. Now you're getting more and more like that brother-in-law, Barley, and Tremaine is as different from you now as you were from Barley five or six years ago, whenever it was."

Nothing else that was said during the evening stayed with him through the next day.

A couple of weeks passed, and Hubert Ward was lying on the sofa in his suite at the studio during the lunch break. His telephone buzzed. "Will you see Mr. Martin Ruskin?" said Lillian, his secretary.

"Will I see him? Is he *here?*"

"In the reception room."

"All right, bring him in."

Hubert Ward remained on the sofa. "I'm sure you'll forgive me for not getting up," he said. "What the hell do *you* want?"

Ruskin had aged, not so much in the inevitable ways of natural aging—hair, skin, teeth—as in the sad evidences of the confirmed voluptuary, especially in the clouded eyes and the thick, undisciplined lips. "You know damn well what I want. I want you to stop bothering Zella. I'm going to marry Zella—or I was."

"Zella who?"

"I expected some cheap wisecrack from you, Hubie. Richard Hubert Ward. But I don't have time for your wise-cracks."

"You seem to have all the time in the world, Marty. Driving all the way from Culver City during lunch hour."

"You were with her the night before last. You had her over here Monday afternoon. Sunday you were at her apartment all afternoon. Three times you been with her this past week."

"I thought Bill Powell was the Thin Man on your lot. Do you do this shadowing yourself or did you hire a dick?"

"You see this?" said Ruskin.

Hubert Ward raised his head. "I see it. Put it away or it might go off." In Ruskin's hand lay a Colt .25 automatic pistol.

"I carry it with me. The next time I see you with Zella I'm going to use it. You lousy son of a bitch, I took enough from you, you dirty stinking bastard. You ruined my life."

"I ruined your life? I haven't even seen you for damn near ten years. Use your head. Put that thing away and pull yourself together."

"This is loaded, I tell you."

"I know it's loaded, and you've got the God damned safety off. I've handled guns more than you have, Marty. Put the gun on the table. Go on, Marty. Put it on the table."

"No."

"Marty, put the gun on the *table* and let me unload it. I'll give it back to you. You don't want to shoot me, you don't want to shoot anybody. But that thing can go off and you will shoot me or shoot yourself. Put the gun down on the table and then we can talk."

Ruskin laid the gun on a coffee table.

"Now sit down," said Hubert Ward. He did not rise from the sofa. "Do you want a drink? What do you want? Scotch? Rye?"

"I don't want anything from you. Nothing." Ruskin backed into a chair, sat down and put his head in his hands, and Hubert Ward quickly got up and removed the clip and ejected the remaining cartridge. "I'll send this to you at Metro. Do you want a drink?"

"No."

"Then go on home and get some sleep. You look as if you hadn't slept for a week."

"A week? It's over a week. Give me back my gun."

"No. I'll send it to you tomorrow," said Hubert Ward. "Marty, if this got around you'd be cooked."

"I don't care."

"Don't be a fool. You've got a damn good job, you're making plenty of dough." Ruskin was not listening, but Hubert Ward continued. "You can go on making plenty of dough. They like you at Metro and you can stay there forever."

Ruskin suddenly got up and walked out. Hubert Ward put the pistol and ammunition in a desk drawer, and telephoned Zella Flowers at the Metro studio.

298

"Your friend was here. He just left," said Hubert Ward.

"Marty? Did you have any trouble?"

"Zella, I don't want to frighten you, but he came here with a gun. I conned him out of it. I've got it here. But he can get another one easily enough."

"He told me he was going to kill you, but I thought he was bluffing. What do you think I ought to do?"

"I don't know. He said he *was* going to *marry* you."

"He talked about it, but *I* don't want to marry *him*."

"Then I don't think you'd better see him any more."

"That's not going to be so easy. I work for him."

"Yes. That makes it tough."

"And I'm under contract here."

"Yes. Well, then maybe you'd better not see *me* for a while."

"Just like that?"

"For a while. And let's not kid ourselves. Do you want to get shot over me?"

"It was you he was going to shoot, not me. But if you're afraid—what the hell?"

"I'm afraid. I'm always afraid when a man has a gun. You ought to be, too, especially a guy like Ruskin. You know he's a fag."

"He told me he went that way sometimes. But he says he loves me."

"He probably does, Zella. But the point is, he's a bit cracked in the head, I think. What they call emotionally unstable."

"Who isn't?"

"True. But right now we're talking about Ruskin. Ruskin and you. You have to decide, I'm only telling you what happened five minutes ago."

"Decide what?"

"Well, he knows exactly when I've seen you lately, either by having you followed or following you himself."

"The little son of a bitch."

"Yes. The question is, Zella, do we want to take a chance on getting shot or shot at—and the publicity would be just as bad if we got shot at. And the other thing is, you work for Ruskin."

"This sounds to me like you were asking me to give myself the brush-off. That's a switch, I will say that much. Hubie?"

"What?"

"It was fun, sweetie." She hung up, and he never heard her speak again. He was to hear her voice again, on sound tracks of the few films she had made. But she died that night, and Marty Ruskin along with her, in her apartment on South Rodeo Drive. The bullets came from a .32 Smith & Wesson revolver, and though no note was found, the police declared it to be a case of homicide and suicide, unmistakably a lovers' quarrel.

The Ruskin-Flowers story was so lacking in mystery that it vanished from the papers in a few days, and Hubert Ward was not mentioned at all except in the list of Zella's films. The theory was advanced that the reason for the shootings was religious differences between Ruskin and Zella, which prevented their marriage. But religion was a touchy subject that at that time did not sell papers, and Ruskin was not identified as a Jew or Zella as a Roman Catholic. Ruskin, moreover, from the standpoint of news value was a dull, uninteresting man, who had never produced an "A" picture or been associated with any of Metro's top stars. The story lasted as long as it did only because it provided opportunities to publish photographs of Zella in Polynesian prints and bathing suits. The Los Angeles photographers who covered Ruskin's memorial service had to be satisfied with producers, bit players, character actors and a few writers. Zella's body was shipped back to Buffalo, New York, where her requiem Mass got only local coverage. Metro sent out an announcement of the next picture in the hospital series, but did not mention Ruskin or Zella Flowers. In the word that was to become familiar a few years later, they were expendable; in the then still current slang of the industry, their tragedy laid an egg. They had never made it big, Ruskin as a producer, or Zella as an actress. Hollywood was willing to forget them, and promptly did so.

But Hubert Ward did not.

"You all right about this, Hube?" said Joe Ziffrin, in the first days of the notoriety.

"I guess I'm safe, if that's what you mean. The cops haven't been around, and I guess they won't be now."

"I didn't only mean it from that angle. What did Ruskin want the day he was here?"

"You knew he was here?"

"Sure I knew. I have to make sure I know it if a producer from another lot visits one of my top stars. He wanted to talk about Zella?"

"He threatened me with a .25. I talked him out of it. I have the God damn gun in my desk drawer."

"Let me have it and I'll get rid of it for you. I'll drop it in the Channel on the way over to Catalina. You depressed about Zella?"

"How did you know that?"

"Well, what the hell. You're that human, and she was a good little doll. Four-five years she would of got fat and probably ended up a hooker, but she could certainly—well, she's dead so let's leave her respectable."

"Oh, you, too?"

"Hubie. A thing like that I wouldn't pass up. Sure. But she was a good Joe. Maybe I'm kidding myself, but when she got fat I would of always given her a couple days' work, if there was a spot for her. Some you're glad to see the last of, but her I kind of liked. And you did too."

"I guess I did. Yes, I did. I really did." He told Ziffrin of his final telephone conversation with Zella Flowers.

"That's what I mean, she was a good Joe. What about Ruskin, Hubie?"

"He gave me the creeps, he always did. I pegged him as fag the first time I ever saw him. He was like some teachers I knew in school. And he was on the make for me, I wouldn't deny that. But the other day I couldn't help but feel sorry for him. He was convinced that somehow or other I was responsible for all his bad luck. I was persecuting him. It was ten years since I'd seen the son of a bitch, but he blamed me for all his troubles. About Zella, he had reason to be sore at me. But what other bad luck did he have that I was responsible for?"

"He had a fixation about you. It didn't make any difference whether you saw him or not, Hube. How many days a year could he pick up a paper and not see your name somewhere? That's a fixation he had. He hated you, talked about you all the time, but he was in love with you."

"Yeah."

"What are you thinking?"

"A long time ago," said Hubert Ward, and told of the *parti à trois* with Ruskin and the girl whose name he could not now recall.

"Oh, *well*," said Ziffrin. "You insulted his manhood, his womanhood, his faghood, his everything else. No wonder he hated you. And he never made any real dough out of you, don't overlook that. I heard that story, only he told it different. The way he told it, he laid the dame, but that I found hard to believe. That I wouldn't buy, but I didn't say anything. You know Marty was a friend of my wife Sylvia, and that gang she pals around with. The Communist intellectuals. They never had any use for you. You can be lucky they don't know what I know. I mean about you and Zella, or Marty pulling a gun on you. They'd throw a bucket of shit at you right now if they could."

"You believed I was a fag. When did you stop believing it?"

"I didn't say that. But I used to hear Marty as much as say you were his boy friend, and you wouldn't be the first actor that some ugly little guy like Marty helped along in his career. I could name you a dozen."

"I could name *you* a dozen."

"Sure you could. Get a couple English actors letting their hair down sometime and you'll think everybody's queer. That London must be a fags' paradise, to hear them talk. Personally I never had a man go for me, not since I grew up. In the tenement where I lived an old guy used to give us kids pennies to let him play with our pecker, but he was just a dirty old man and the mothers finally got wise to him and a bunch of them one night tied him up and cut off his beard. He moved away, or the next thing they were going to pour scalding hot water over him. With women, though, I always seem to catch a lot of them at the right moment. And not all dogs, either. I probably get more tail in a year than any you handsome fellows. Marty used to say it right in front of Sylvia. 'The big laugh in this town is an ugly bastard like Joe Ziffrin or I getting more tail than these pretty boys like Hubert Ward.' Everything was the big laugh with Marty. But how many times did anybody ever see Marty laugh at anything? And who's the big laugh on now, the poor son of a bitch?"

We have come now to the end of this chronicle. It is not, of course, the end of the story of Hubert Ward, which has not yet ended. He is around, and there is enough left of the big reputation to keep his vanity warm and his hopes alive. Thirty years of top billing in the show-business world makes a man hard to forget, and the public do not want to forget. A movie star's fame is mysteriously enduring; he is remembered and recognized well past his prime; his reputation is like the mysterious longevity of popular songs. A 1962 gathering of men and women in their thirties will unanimously remember the tune and most of the words of "Smiles," which was fourteen years old before the oldest man in the audience was born. A 1962 gathering of men and women in their twenties will instantly recognize the name Hubert Ward, although most of them have never seen a Hubert Ward movie in a theater. They know who he is, and so long as they continue to know who he is he has his vanity and his hopes. ("You know who sat across from me on the plane? Hubert Ward. Honestly." "You know who I saw getting gas on the Parkway? Hubert Ward, in a Jaguar." "Guess who put Ma's suitcase up on the rack. Hubert Ward, the movie star. That big heavy suitcase." "You know who I think that is, dancing with the Stribling girl? I think that's Hubert Ward's son by his first wife. I'm almost positive. Anyway, he looks enough like him.")

Vanity? It needs no explanation. Hopes? The hopes of any actor. Top top billing in an all-star cast, a part as long as Hamlet, notices that can be framed, a play that will close to standees whenever the actor chooses to close the play, followed by a movie production with another but different all-star cast, with Hubert Ward the only actor carrying over from the stage play. It will not happen, because Hubert Ward will not let it happen. He will always do something to defeat his own hopes.

It is his form of self-destruction, equal in intensity to his instinct for self-protection. He was a rogue who had his middle period of respectability, that lasted only so long as Nina made respectability comfortable for him, that ended when Nina wearied of him. But his instinct for self-destruction compelled him to abandon the habits of respectability in spite of its rewards. His refusal to believe that Nina was not having an affair with Michael Tremaine brought about an affair that was not satisfactory to Nina or to Tremaine, but made it impossible for her to deny that technically Tremaine had been her lover. Hubert Ward's marriage to the English actress Patricia Stanford was an act of defiance that even she recognized as such, and she made him pay dearly in money and in public affronts to his vanity, and in the loss of his friendship with Doris Arlington. ("I'd of sooner married you myself than see you married to that Limehouse slut. For a wedding present I'll send you a roll of toilet paper.") He was given odd jobs and a major's commission in the Air Force, a piece of luck that kept him in England for two years and suspended the personality attacks that could have caused him permanent damage inside the movie industry. He came home with silver leaves and a slightly dubious Air Medal, and was put right to work to cash in on his military service. His marriage in 1951 to Mary Jo Kitzmiller, widow of both Roy Ed Kitzmiller of Houston and Joe T. Biggs of San Antonio, can be regarded as successful because, in Mary Jo's words, "Hubie and I don't figure to cramp one another's style, if you know what I mean and I'm sure you *dew*." It would be supererogatory to say that this marriage has very little to do with respectability. It would be accurate to say that Hubert Ward has logged many more hours in Mary Jo's private aircraft than in bombers in 1943-44. The Hubert Wards have not missed a Kentucky Derby since Count Turf's year and to date their most serious quarrel has been over Hubert Ward's inability to wangle an invitation to Grace Kelly's wedding.

Mary Jo fully understands Hubert's reluctance to spend much time in Houston; she feels the same way about San Antonio, where Joe T. Biggs's five brothers live.

Consequently the Hubert Wards maintain a house in Palm Beach that they call home, and apartments at the Waldorf, the Paris Ritz, the Bel-Air in Los Angeles, and a cottage in Saratoga Springs. At all these residences the *Hollywood Reporter* and weekly *Variety* are delivered by airmail if necessary throughout the year, so that Hubert Ward is never more than a day or two late with the news of show business. Mary Jo's formula for avoiding unhappiness over money matters was stated on the day they took out their marriage license: "I'll let you keep all you have, and you let me keep all I have." On the one occasion of his proposing that she might want to invest some money in a motion picture production she said, "You can ask Judge Blaylock, but I don't think he'll go for it." Sam Blaylock, her Houston lawyer, expressed his opposition in such courteous terms that Hubert Ward said it was a pleasure to hear him say no, if that was what he was saying. "Then I'll *say* no, if you'd rather," said Blaylock.

Even in the jet age it takes time to get from place to place, and Hubert Ward's year is segmented by travel and the brief stopovers in California, Texas, Florida, Kentucky, New York, and France. He has long since learned the names of the permanent servants in their various establishments maintained by Mary Jo, and half a dozen times a year he accepts their welcomes and farewells as genuinely cordial, which in some cases they are. He is Hubert Ward the movie star, and no son of a bitch can take that away from him.

Ha ha ha ha ha.

About the Author

John O'Hara (1905–1970) was the bestselling author of over four hundred stories and fourteen novels, including *Appointment in Samarra, Butterfield 8, Pal Joey,* and *Ten North Frederick*, which won the National Book Award.